Love Must Not Be Forgotten

Love Must Not Be Forgotten

BY ZHANG JIE

Introduction by Gladys Yang

CHINA BOOKS & Periodicals, Inc.
San Francisco

Panda Books
Beijing, China

Second Printing, March 1987

Library of Congress Catalog Card Number: 86-70557
ISBN 0-8351-1699-9 (casebound)
ISBN 0-8351-1698-0 (paperback)

Printed in the United States of America by CHINA BOOKS & Periodicals, Inc.

in cooperation with Panda Books, Beijing, China

To the Reader

With the publication of *Love Must Not Be Forgotten*, China Books & Periodicals, Inc., proudly introduces a new series—New Chinese Fiction. Our purpose is to make known to the American public some recent works by China's best authors. Chinese literature has recently undergone many of the same dramatic changes that have enervated Chinese society. The creativity and energy that were held in abeyance during twenty years of isolation and cultural upheaval has now been stimulated by China's new spirit of openness. There is official affirmation of creative freedom and a heartfelt desire on the part of today's writers that Chinese literature make its contribution to the world. This "literature of the new era" is still young and developing, yet its universally accessible techniques and themes, and its rich portrayal of the mind and landscape of today's China indicate that it will surely find a wide, responsive audience in the West.

Contents

Preface

"I once thought I was like a darting dragonfly, with no goals in life and no substantial pursuits. Only through literature did I discover myself. Successful or not, I am still very persevering . . . Some people spend a whole lifetime and still do not find or understand themselves. Others, of course, have a much easier time of it. For me, it took all of forty years." So writes Zhang Jie in an essay about writing, an essay titled *My Boat**.

She was born in 1937. During the anti-Japanese war her parents separated and her mother, a teacher, brought her up in a village in Liaoning Province. She had a passion for music and literature, but was persuaded to study economics as being of more use to New China. Upon graduating from the People's University she worked for some years in an industrial bureau, then in a film studio where she got a chance to write two film scripts, *The Search* and *We Are Still Young*. She is now a full-time writer, one of China's most popular authors.

Zhang Jie did not start to write until after the fall of the "Gang of Four" and end of the Cultural Revolution. She was then forty years old. In 1978, her story *The Music of the Forests* won a prize as one of the best short stories of that year. Since then she has written many stories, essays, novellas and a novel, *Leaden Wings*, which recently won China's prestigious Mao Dun Literary Prize. She is a

* See Biographical Note.

ix

member of the Chinese Writers' Association and now works for the Beijing branch of the China Federation of Literary and Art Circles. She has visited West Germany and some other European countries, and participated in the seminar of Chinese and American writers held in Beijing in October, 1984.

Her earlier themes were mainly the problems of youth and love. She had divorced her husband because he maltreated her, and in a society still influenced by traditional ideas that was considered a stigma. She thus bitterly experienced the discrimination against women about which she writes so pungently.

Zhang Jie's later themes cover a wide range. Whether writing satirically or in a romantic vein she tackles current social problems with deep insight, lashing out at male supremacy, hypocrisy, corruption, bureaucracy, nepotism and other malpractices holding up China's advance. Some Westerners on the look-out for dissidents find it strange that she exposes the seamy side of China so ruthlessly, yet defends the socialist system as that best suited to China. Zhang Jie herself sees no contradiction here. Her responsibility as a writer, she feels, is to educate her readers and inspire them to eradicate social evils. As she puts it in *The Ark*, writing of a woman her own age: "She possessed neither the unshakeable optimism of previous generations, nor the blind pessimism of the younger generation. Her generation was the most confident, the most clear-minded and the most able to face up to reality."

From her teens on Zhang Jie took part in many political movements. A firm believer in socialism, she joined the Chinese Communist Party at an early age. But during the Cultural Revolution she was fiercely criticized and had to write a self-criticism in which she cited her own weak sense of class struggle and her individualism. Collegues attributed this "weakness" to the influence of the western novels she loved to read, novels of the 18th and 19th centuries. Now Zhang Jie recalls with some pride that she behaved decently in the Cultural Revolution, never betraying or slandering other people, because she loved the humanism in classical literature.

She finds it stimulating to be under fire. I have watched her several times being interviewed: she welcomes provocative questions and swiftly rebuts them or skillfully evades them.

Zhang Jie deserves credit as a pioneer who highlighted women's problems before authorities fully recognized them or took official action. As a consequence some of her stories have been most controversial. The first story in this collection, *Love Must Not Be Forgotten*, caused quite a furor when it was published in 1979. It justified love outside marriage, albeit of the most platonic kind, implying that the only moral marriages were those based on love. It also suggested that a girl should remain single unless she could find a man she loved and respected. Because of this, critics accused Zhang Jie of undermining social morality—most Chinese take it for granted that everyone must marry. She received anonymous letters attacking her. But she also received letters approving her stand and her courage.

The Ark proved no less controversial. This novella describes three women who are divorced or live apart from their husbands, and how hard it is for them to find suitable work and retain their self-respect in a male-dominated society. Some readers applauded Zhang Jie's fearlessness and acclaimed this as China's first feminist novel, though she denies that she is a feminist—she writes on all manner of themes. Certain detractors denounced her for encouraging women to let their resentment against men embitter them, so that they behave in an unwomanly way and are not really happy. Others claimed that she distorted socialism by painting too black a picture of women's difficulties. Yet others took an opposite line, objecting that most of the characters in this story were recognizable as living individuals. In this connection Zhang Jie wrote in *My Boat*: "Characters in literary works are perhaps composites of many people in real life, but they are still fictitious, something created by the author through logical reasoning."

The other stories in this collection gave rise to less public discussion than *The Ark* and *Love Must Not Be Forgotten*. All are sensitively written with feeling and insight. Their detailed descriptions of everyday life and the thoughts and hopes of widely differing characters should shed light on Chinese reality for foreign readers. For although China has opened up for some years now, to many westerners the Chinese are still an inscrutable people.

Zhang Jie presents them as credible human beings. During her recent visit to Europe she was reported on in all the main West German papers, and the title of one feature article was: "A Faraway Country Gradually Moves Nearer." This delighted Zhang Jie, who believes that most of the world's troubles arise from misunderstanding—from lack of communication—and modern Chinese writers are best fitted to introduce their country abroad.

Her important novel *Leaden Wings*, not included in this collection, has as its central theme the modernization of industry. The publication of this book aroused further controversy. Exposing various abuses and man-made obstacles to modernization, it came under fire for "attacking socialism." But many readers welcomed it as painting a truthful picture of modern Chinese society. Her fan mail included the assurance, "If ever you're in trouble, come to me."

Zhang Jie is physically frail, mentally tough. She has heart trouble and easily grows tired. One evening she called when we were having a party at which some young people were dancing. She exclaimed, "I can't stay, I might have a heart attack."

Another visit was equally typical. Zhang Jie appeared, the light of battle in her eye and a tape-recorder in her handbag. She had been confronting someone who had passed on to her the accusations that *Leaden Wings* was "anti-Party, anti-socialism." Taping the interview, Zhang Jie refuted these charges, declaring, "I wrote that book precisely because I'm for socialism and China's modernization." Then, on her way to our flat, she passed the free market outside our gate and felt it her duty as a Party member to intervene so as to stop a peddler from charging exorbitant prices.

Because Zhang Jie is thoroughly militant, with a strong sense of social responsibility, she will no doubt continue to tackle sensitive issues with disregard for her own welfare. While affirming her complete faith in socialism she will go on exposing its present shortcomings, thus courting criticism from her more conservative readers. In *My Boat* she envisages herself putting out to sea and braving angry waves.

. . . I renovate my boat, patch it up and repaint it, so
that it will last a little longer. I set sail again. People,

houses, trees on shore become smaller and smaller and I am reluctant to leave them. But my boat cannot stay beached for ever. What use is a boat without the sea?

In the distance I see waves rolling towards me. Rolling continuously. I know that one day I will be smashed to bits by those waves, but this is the fate of all boats—what other sort of end could they meet?

Gladys Yang, Beijing, September, 1985

Love Must Not Be Forgotten

I am thirty, the same age as our People's Republic. For a republic thirty is still young. But a girl of thirty is virtually on the shelf.

Actually, I have a bonafide suitor. Have you seen the Greek sculptor Myron's Discobolus? Qiao Lin is the image of that discus thrower. Even the padded clothes he wears in winter fail to hide his fine physique. Bronzed, with clear-cut features, a broad forehead and large eyes, his appearance alone attracts most girls to him.

But I can't make up my mind to marry him. I'm not clear what attracts me to him, or him to me. I know people are gossiping behind my back, "Who does she think she is, to be so choosy?" To them, I'm a nobody playing hard to get. They take offense at such preposterous behavior.

Of course, I shouldn't be captious. In a society where commercial production still exists, marriage like most other transactions is still a form of barter.

I have known Qiao Lin for nearly two years, yet still cannot fathom whether he keeps so quiet from aversion to talking or from having nothing to say. When, by way of a small intelligence test, I demand his opinion of this or that, he says "good" or "bad" like a child in kindergarten.

Once I asked, "Qiao Lin, why do you love me?" He thought the question over seriously for what seemed an age. I could see from his normally smooth but now wrinkled forehead that the little grey cells in his handsome head were hard at work cogitating. I felt ashamed to have put him on the spot.

Finally he raised his clear childlike eyes to tell me, "Because you're good!"

Loneliness flooded my heart. "Thank you, Qiao Lin!" I couldn't help wondering, if we were to marry, whether we could discharge our duties to each other as husband and wife. Maybe, because law and morality would have bound us together. But how tragic simply to comply with law and morality! Was there no stronger bond to link us?

When such thoughts cross my mind I have the strange sensation that instead of being a girl contemplating marriage I am an elderly social scientist.

Perhaps I worry too much. We can live like most married couples, bringing up children together, strictly true to each other according to the law. . . . Although living in the seventies of the twentieth century, people still consider marriage the way they did millennia ago, as a means of continuing the race, a form of barter or a business transaction in which love and marriage can be separated. Since this is the common practice, why shouldn't we follow suit?

But I still can't make up my mind. As a child, I remember, I often cried all night for no rhyme or reason, unable to sleep and disturbing the whole household. My old nurse, a shrewd though uneducated woman, said an ill wind had blown through my ear. I think this judgment showed prescience, because I still have that old weakness. I upset myself over things which really present no problem, upsetting other people at the same time. One's nature is hard to change.

I think of my mother too. If she were alive, what would she say about my attitude to Qiao Lin and my uncertainty about marrying him? My thoughts constantly turn to her, not because she was such a strict mother that her ghost is still watching over me since her death. No, she was not just my mother but my closest friend. I loved her so much that the thought of her leaving me makes my heart ache.

She never lectured me, just told me quietly in her deep, unwomanly voice about her successes and failures, so that I could learn from her experience. She had evidently not had many successes—her life was full of failures.

During her last days she followed me with her fine, expressive eyes, as if wondering how I would manage on my own and as if she had some important advice for me but hesitated to give it. She must have been worried by my naiveté and sloppy ways. She suddenly blurted out, "Shanshan, if you aren't sure what you want, don't rush into marriage—better live on your own!"

Other people might think this strange advice from a mother to her daughter, but to me it embodied her bitter experience. I don't think she underestimated me or my knowledge of life. She loved me and didn't want me to be unhappy.

"I don't want to marry, mother!" I said, not out of bashfulness or a show of coyness. I can't think why a girl should pretend to be coy. She had long since taught me about things not generally mentioned to girls.

"If you meet the right man, then marry him. Only if he's right for you!"

"I'm afraid no such man exists!"

"That's not true. But it's hard. The world is so vast, I'm afraid you may never meet him." Whether married or not was not what concerned her, but the quality of the marriage.

"Haven't you managed fine without a husband?"

"Who says so?"

"I think you've done fine."

"I had no choice. . . ." She broke off, lost in thought, her face wistful. Her wistful lined face reminded me of a withered flower I had pressed in a book.

"Why did you have no choice?"

"You ask too many questions," she parried, not ashamed to confide in me but afraid that I might reach the wrong conclusion. Besides, everyone treasures a secret to carry to the grave. Feeling a bit put out, I demanded bluntly, "Didn't you love my dad?"

"No, I never loved him."

"Did he love you?"

"No, he didn't."

"Then why get married?"

She paused, searching for the right words to explain this mystery, then answered bitterly, "When you're young you don't always know what you're looking for, what you need, and people may talk you into getting married. As you grow older and more experienced you find out your true needs. By then, though, you've done many foolish things for which you could kick yourself. You'd give anything to be able to make a fresh start and live more wisely. Those content with their lot will always be happy, they say, but I shall never enjoy that happiness." She added self-mockingly, "A wretched idealist, that's all I am."

Did I take after her? Did we both have genes which attracted ill winds?

"Why don't you marry again?"

"I'm afraid I'm still not sure what I really want." She was obviously unwilling to tell me the truth.

I cannot remember my father. He and Mother split up when I was very small. I just recall her telling me sheepishly that he was a fine handsome fellow. I could see she was ashamed of having judged by appearances and made a futile choice. She told me, "When I can't sleep at night, I force myself to sober up by recalling all those stupid blunders I made. Of course it's so distasteful that I often hide my face in the sheet for shame, as if there were eyes watching me in the dark. But distasteful as it is, I take some pleasure in this form of atonement."

I was really sorry that she hadn't remarried. She was such a fascinating character, if she'd married a man she loved, what a happy household ours would surely have been. Though not beautiful, she had the simple charm of an ink landscape. She was a fine writer too. Another author who knew her well used to say teasingly, "Just reading your works is enough to make anyone love you!"

She would retort, "If he knew that the object of his affection was a white-haired old crone, that would frighten him away." At her age, she must have known what she really wanted, so this was obviously an evasion. I say this because she had quirks which puzzled me.

For instance, whenever she left Beijing on a trip, she always took with her one of the twenty-seven volumes of Chekov's stories published between 1950 and 1955. She also warned me, "Don't touch these books. If you want to read Chekov, read that set I bought you." There was no need to caution me. Having a set of my own why should I touch hers? Besides, she'd told me this over and over again. Still she was on her guard. She seemed bewitched by those books.

So we had two sets of Chekov's stories at home. Not just because we loved Chekov, but to parry other people like me who loved Chekov. Whenever anyone asked to borrow a volume, she would lend one of mine. Once, in her absence, a close friend took a volume from her set. When she found out she was frantic, and at once took a volume of mine to exchange for it.

Ever since I can remember, those books were on her bookcase. Although I admire Chekov as a great writer, I was puzzled by the way she never tired of reading him. Why, for over twenty years, had she had to read him every single day? Sometimes, when tired of writing, she poured herself a cup of strong tea and sat down in front of the bookcase, staring raptly at that set of books. If I went into her room then it flustered her, and she either spilt her tea or blushed like a girl discovered with her lover.

I wondered: Has she fallen in love with Chekov? She might have if he'd still been alive.

When her mind was wandering just before her death, her last words to me were: "That set . . ." She hadn't the strength to give it its complete title. But I knew what she meant. "And my diary . . . 'Love Must Not Be Forgotten.' . . . Cremate them with me."

I carried out her last instruction regarding the works of Chekov, but couldn't bring myself to destroy her diary. I thought, if it could be published, it would surely prove the most moving thing she had written. But naturally publication was out of the question.

At first I imagined the entries were raw material she had jotted down. They read neither like stories, essays, a diary or letters. But after reading the whole I formed a hazy impression, helped out by my imperfect memory. Thinking it over, I finally realized that this was no lifeless manuscript I was holding, but an anguished, loving heart. For over twenty years one man had occupied her heart, but he was not for her. She used these diaries as a substitute for him, a means of pouring out her feelings to him, day after day, year after year.

No wonder she had never considered any eligible proposals, had turned a deaf ear to idle talk whether well-meant or malicious.

Her heart was already full, to the exclusion of anybody else. "No lake can compare with the ocean, no cloud with those on Mount Wu." Remembering those lines I often reflected sadly that few people in real life could love like this. No one would love me like this.

I learned that toward the end of the thirties, when this man was doing underground work for the Party in Shanghai, an old worker had given his life to cover him, leaving behind a helpless wife and daughter. Out of a sense of duty, of gratitude to the dead and deep class feeling, he had unhesitatingly married the daughter. When he saw the endless troubles of couples who had married for "love," he may have thought, "Thank Heaven, though I didn't marry for love, v ᵻ get on well, able to help each other." For years, as man and wife they lived through hard times.

He must have been my mother's colleague. Had I ever met him? He couldn't have visited our home. Who was he?

In the spring of 1962, Mother took me to a concert. We went on foot, the theater being quite near. On the way a black limousine pulled up silently by the pavement. Out stepped an elderly man with white hair in a black serge tunic-suit. What a striking shock of white hair! Strict, scrupulous, distinguished, transparently honest —that was my impression of him. The cold glint of his flashing eyes reminded me of lightning or swordplay. Only ardent love for a woman really deserving his love could fill cold eyes like those with tenderness.

He walked up to Mother and said, "How are you, Comrade Zhong Yu? It's been a long time."

"How are you!" Mother's hand holding mine suddenly turned icy cold and trembled a little.

They stood face to face without looking at each other, each appearing upset, even stern. Mother fixed her eyes on the trees by the roadside, not yet in leaf. He looked at me. "Such a big girl already. Good, fine—you take after your mother."

Instead of shaking hands with Mother he shook hands with me. His hand was as icy as hers and trembling a little. As if transmitting an electric current, I felt a sudden shock. Snatching my hand away I cried, "There's nothing good about that!"

"Why not?" he asked with the surprised expression grown-ups always have when children speak out frankly.

I glanced at Mother's face. I did take after her, to my disappointment. "Because she's not beautiful!"

He laughed, then said teasingly, "Too bad that there should be a child who doesn't find her own mother beautiful. Do you remember in '53, when your mother was transferred to Beijing, she came to our ministry to report for duty? She left you outside on the veranda, but like a monkey you climbed all the stairs, peeped through the cracks in doors, and caught your finger in the door of my office. You sobbed so bitterly that I carried you off to find her."

"I don't remember that." I was annoyed at his harking back to a time when I was still in open-seat pants.

"Ah, we old people have better memories." He turned abruptly and remarked to Mother, "I've read that last story of yours. Frankly speaking, there's something not quite right about it. You shouldn't have condemned the heroine. . . . There's nothing wrong with falling in love, as long as you don't spoil someone else's life. . . . In fact, the hero might have loved her too. Only for the sake of a third person's happiness, they had to renounce their love. . . ."

A policeman came over to where the car was parked and ordered the driver to move on. When the driver made some excuse, the old man looked around. After a hasty "Goodbye" he strode back to the car and told the policeman, "Sorry. It's not his fault, it's mine. . . ."

I found it amusing watching this old cadre listening respectfully to the policeman's strictures. When I turned to Mother with a mischievous smile, she looked as upset as a first-form primary schoolchild standing forlornly in front of the stern headmistress. Anyone would have thought she was the one being lectured by the policeman. The car drove off, leaving a puff of smoke. Very soon even this smoke vanished with the wind, as if nothing at all had happened. But the incident stuck in my mind.

Analyzing it now, I realize he must have been the man whose strength of character won Mother's heart. That strength came from his firm political convictions, his narrow escapes from death in the revolution, his active brain, his drive at work, his well-cultivated mind. Besides, strange to say, he and Mother both liked the oboe. Yes, she must have worshipped him. She once told me that unless she worshipped a man, she couldn't love him even for one day.

But I could not tell whether he loved her or not. If not, why was there this entry in her diary?

"This is far too fine a present. But how did you know that Chekov's my favorite writer?"

"You said so."

"I don't remember that."

"I remember. I heard you mention it when you were chatting with someone."

So he was the one who had given her the *Selected Stories of Chekov*. For her that was tantamount to a love letter. Maybe this man, who didn't believe in love, realized by the time his hair was white that in his heart was something which could be called love. By the time he no longer had the right to love, he made the tragic discovery of this love for which he would have given his life. Or did it go deeper even than that?

This is all I remember about him.

How wretched Mother must have been, deprived of the man to whom she was devoted! To catch a glimpse of his car or the back of his head through its rear window, she carefully figured out which roads he would take to work and back. Whenever he made a speech, she sat at the back of the hall watching his face rendered hazy by cigarette smoke and poor lighting. Her eyes would brim with tears, but she swallowed them back. If a fit of coughing made him break off, she wondered anxiously why no one persuaded him to give up smoking. She was afraid he would get bronchitis again. Why was he so near yet so far?

He, to catch a glimpse of her, looked out of the car window every day straining his eyes to watch the streams of cyclists, afraid that she might have an accident. On the rare evenings on which he had no meetings, he would walk by a roundabout way to our neighborhood, to pass our compound gate. However busy, he would always make time to look in papers and journals for her work. His duty had always been clear to him, even in the most difficult times. But now confronted by this love he became a weakling, quite helpless. At his age it was laughable. Why should life play this trick on him?

Yet when they happened to meet at work, each tried to avoid the other, hurrying off with a nod. Even so, this would make Mother blind and deaf to everything around her. If she met a colleague named Wang she would call him Guo and mutter something unintelligible.

It was a cruel ordeal for her. She wrote:

> We agreed to forget each other. But I deceived you, I have never forgotten. I don't think you've forgotten either. We're just deceiving each other, hiding our misery. I haven't deceived you deliberately, though; I did my best to carry out our agreement. I often stay far away from Beijing, hoping time and distance will help me to forget you. But when I return, as the train pulls into the station, my head reels. I stand on the platform looking round intently, as if someone were waiting for me. Of course there is no one. I realize then that I have forgotten nothing. Everything is unchanged. My love is like a tree the roots of which strike deeper year after year—I have no way to uproot it.
>
> At the end of every day, I feel as if I've forgotten something important. I may wake with a start from my dreams wondering what has happened. But nothing has happened. Nothing. Then it comes home to me that you are missing! So everything seems lacking, incomplete, and there is nothing to fill up the blank. We are nearing the ends of our lives, why should we be carried away by emotion like children? Why should life submit people to such ordeals, then unfold before you your lifelong dream? Because I started off blindly I took the wrong turning, and now there are insuperable obstacles between me and my dream.

Yes, Mother never let me go to the station to meet her when she came back from a trip, preferring to stand alone on the platform and imagine that he had met her. Poor mother with her greying hair was as infatuated as a girl.

Not much space in the diary was devoted to their romance. Most entries dealt with trivia: why one of her articles had not come off; her fear that she had no real talent; the excellent play she missed by mistaking the time on the ticket; the drenching she got by going out for a stroll without her umbrella. In spirit they were together day and night, like a devoted married couple. In fact, they spent no more than twenty-four hours together in all. Yet in that time they experienced deeper happiness than some people in a whole lifetime. Shakespeare makes Juliet say, "I cannot sum up half my sum of wealth." And probably that is how Mother felt.

He must have been killed in the Cultural Revolution. Perhaps because of the conditions then, that section of the diary is ambiguous and obscure. Mother had been so fiercely attacked for her writing, it amazed me that she went on keeping a diary. From some veiled allusions I gathered that he had questioned the theories advanced by that "theoretician" then at the height of favor, and had told someone, "This is sheer Rightist talk." It was clear from the tear-stained pages of Mother's diary that he had been harshly denounced; but the steadfast old man never knuckled under to the authorities. His last words were, "When I go to meet Marx, I shall go on fighting my case!"

That must have been in the winter of 1969, because that was when Mother's hair turned white overnight, though she was not yet fifty. And she put on a black arm-band. Her position then was extremely difficult. She was criticized for wearing this old-style mourning, and ordered to say for whom she was in mourning.

"For whom are you wearing that, Mother?" I asked anxiously.

"For my lover." Not to frighten me she explained, "Someone you never knew."

"Shall I put one on too?" She patted my cheeks, as she had when I was a child. It was years since she had shown me such affection. I often felt that as she aged, especially during these last years of persecution, all tenderness had left her, or was concealed in her heart, so that she seemed like a man.

She smiled sadly and said, "No, you needn't wear one." Her eyes were as dry as if she had no more tears to shed. I longed to comfort her or do something to please her. But she said, "Off you go."

I felt an inexplicable dread, as if dear Mother had already half left me. I blurted out, "Mother!"

Quick to sense my desolation, she said gently, "Don't be afraid. Off you go. Leave me alone for a little."

I was right. She wrote:

> You have gone. Half my soul seems to have taken flight with you.
>
> I had no means of knowing what had become of you, much less of seeing you for the last time. I had no right to

ask either, not being your wife or friend. . . . So we are torn apart. If only I could have borne that inhuman treatment for you, so that you could have lived on! You should have lived to see your name cleared and take up your work again, for the sake of those who loved you. I knew you could not be a counter-revolutionary. You were one of the finest men killed. That's why I love you— I am not afraid now to avow it.

Snow is whirling down. Heavens, even God is such a hypocrite, he is using this whiteness to cover up your blood and the scandal of your murder.

I have never set store by my life. But now I keep wondering whether anything I say or do would make you contract your shaggy eyebrows in a frown. I must live a worthwhile life like you, and do some honest work for our country. Things can't go on like this—those criminals will get what's coming to them.

I used to walk alone along that small asphalt road, the only place where we once walked together, hearing my footsteps in the silent night. . . . I always paced to and fro and lingered there, but never as wretchedly as now. Then, though you were not beside me, I knew you were still in this world and felt that you were keeping me company. Now I can hardly believe that you have gone.

At the end of the road I would retrace my steps, then walk along it again. Rounding the fence I always looked back, as if you were still standing there waving goodbye. We smiled faintly, like casual acquaintances, to conceal our undying love. That ordinary evening in early spring a chilly wind was blowing as we walked silently away from each other. You were wheezing a little because of your chronic bronchitis. That upset me. I wanted to beg you to slow down, but somehow I couldn't. We both walked very fast, as if some important business were waiting for us. How we prized that single stroll we had together, but we were afraid we might lose control of ourselves and burst out with "I love you"—those three words which had tormented us for years. Probably no one else could believe that we never once even clasped hands!

No, Mother, I believe it. I am the only one able to see into your locked heart.

Ah, that little asphalt road, so haunted by bitter memories. We shouldn't overlook the most insignificant spots on earth. For who knows how much secret grief and joy they may hide. No wonder that when tired of writing, she would pace slowly along that little road behind our window. Sometimes at dawn after a sleepless night, sometimes on a moonless, windy evening. Even in winter during howling gales which hurled sand and pebbles against the window pane. . . . I thought this was one of her eccentricities, not knowing that she had gone to meet him in spirit.

She liked to stand by the window, too, staring at the small asphalt road. Once I thought from her expression that one of our closest friends must be coming to call. I hurried to the window. It was a late autumn evening. The cold wind was stripping dead leaves from the trees and blowing them down the small empty road.

She went on pouring out her heart to him in her diary as she had when he was alive. Right up to the day when the pen slipped from her fingers. Her last message was:

> I am a materialist, yet I wish there were a Heaven. For then, I know, I would find you there waiting for me. I am going there to join you, to be together for eternity. We need never be parted again or keep at a distance for fear of spoiling someone else's life. Wait for me, dearest, I am coming—

I do not know how, on her death bed, Mother could still love so ardently with all her heart. To me it seemed not love but a form of madness, a passion stronger than death. If undying love really exists, she reached its extreme. She obviously died happy, because she had known true love. She had no regrets.

Now these old people's ashes have mingled with the elements. But I know that no matter what form they may take, they still love each other. Though not bound together by earthly laws or morality, though they never once clasped hands, each possessed the other completely. Nothing could part them. Centuries to come, if one white cloud trails another, two grasses grow side by side, one wave splashes another, a breeze follows another . . . believe me, that will be them.

Each time I read that diary "Love Must Not Be Forgotten" I cannot hold back my tears. I often weep bitterly, as if I myself experienced their ill-fated love. If not a tragedy it was too laughable. No matter how beautiful or moving I find it, I have no wish to follow suit!

Thomas Hardy wrote that "the call seldom produces the comer, the man to love rarely coincides with the hour for loving." I cannot judge them by conventional moral standards. What I deplore is that they did not wait for a "missing counterpart" to call them. If everyone could wait, instead of rushing into marriage, how many tragedies could be averted!

When we reach communism, will there still be cases of marriage without love? Perhaps . . . since the world is so vast, two kindred spirits may never be able to answer each other's call. But how tragic! Could it be that by then we will have devised ways to escape such tragedies? But this is all conjecture.

Maybe after all we are accountable for these tragedies. Who knows? Should we take the responsibility for the old ideas handed down from the past? Because, if you choose not to marry, your behavior is considered a direct challenge to these ideas. You will be called neurotic, accused of having guilty secrets or having made political mistakes. You may be regarded as an eccentric who looks down on ordinary people, not respecting age-old customs— a heretic. In short they will trump up endless vulgar and futile charges to ruin your reputation. Then you have to succumb to those ideas and marry regardless. But once you put the chains of an indifferent marriage around your neck, you will suffer for it for the rest of your life.

I long to shout: "Mind your own business! Let us wait patiently for our counterparts. Even waiting in vain is better than loveless marriage. To live single is not such a fearful disaster. I believe it may be a sign of a step forward in culture, education and the quality of life."

Translated by Gladys Yang

Emerald

Dusk, like some enormous opaque sponge, slowly absorbed the last glimmerings of daylight. Gradually the hubbub of the town died away, till the place seemed like a pot of cold porridge. Inside, it was already too dark to see anything except the mosquito incense glowing in one corner like a faint red signal.

The evening breeze was ruffling the pale chintz curtains and rattling the window panes. Even on windless days they rattled when people walked past, for this was an old house with drab musty walls and cracks between the floor-boards, which Mrs. Lu, the housekeeper, polished till they shone. It was easy to bump into the knobbly mahogany furniture, and the windows were like those in the church, high, narrow and arched.

From the upstairs windows Lu Beihe could see an old large-leaved walnut tree, a crabapple tree and two old Japanese pines which never seemed to grow. In the twenty-odd years since she had moved in here they had remained the same height. They looked older, though. Trees age just like human beings.

In summer the walnut and crabapple trees filtered the blazing sunlight and screened the household from prying eyes. These trees lost their leaves in winter, but then who would want to stand in the cold wind spying on other people?

The grey brick walls of their compound were overgrown with

creepers, which had encroached on their windows so that they looked like old wells surrounded by thick moss, where few people came to draw water—just as few visitors now called on Zuo's family. Before Beihe's marriage to Zuo Wei, however, his family had apparently had more callers. In her dealings with other people Beihe stuck to certain ingrained principles like that of keeping a certain distance from people, which she had picked up early, growing up in a family which had come down in the world.

And so she loved the gloom of this old house, which had been the property of Zuo Wei's father. It had come through unscathed during the ten years of turmoil of the Cultural Revolution, because he was so well-known not only in China but abroad. Thus he had been protected.

She and her husband could have applied for a flat of their own, but she was unwilling to do this. It wasn't a question of the expense, more that it would force them to waste energy coping with troublesome problems.

Since supper Beihe had been sitting motionless, alone, mulling over a problem. Zuo Wei had gone to the station to see off their son. Even if he'd been home she wouldn't have told him what was on her mind. He never had any definite views of his own anyway. Beihe smiled. She stood up and switched on the standard lamp by the sofa. It shed a small patch of light through its green shade, and she moved away from it to another sofa.

When would her son grow up and be able to manage this household for her? He didn't take after her in the least. He was a true Zuo, yet not even up to Zuo Wei in his young days. Unlike most other women she didn't allow her love for them to blind her to their faults.

She picked up a palm-leaf fan and fanned herself slowly as she thought of her husband and son with mixed feelings. Perhaps young people today were quite different from them in their young days. Now they acted on impulse, seldom considering the effect on other people, or the political consequences. They seemed to live only for today, with no thought of tomorrow.

Xiangdong was so immature politically, he hadn't even applied to join the Youth League. His mother had urged him many times to do this, nearly gone down on her knees to plead with him.

He always said, "OK Mom, I'll write an application."

"Show it to me when you've written it."

"All right."

A month went by, in which he did nothing. If she prodded him he would probably lose his temper. She felt tempted to write an application for him. But he would still have to hand it in himself—she couldn't stand in for him or make a pledge under the Youth League flag. If he didn't want to join the League that was up to him. But what would others think? Her colleagues in the research institute, for instance. Would they say she was a poor deputy Party secretary and deputy institute head, unable to bring up her own son properly?

And if he didn't join the Youth League or Party, that would affect his work assignment in the future and his chances of studying abroad. The boy didn't worry his head about such things. And she could hardly state them explicitly. If she did he would leap up and shout, "So that's why you want me to join!" He'd lose all respect for her.

This summer he was going with some classmates on a pleasure trip to Yunnan, and Zuo Wei had bought him a sleeper ticket. All his classmates were travelling hard seat. Why should he alone have a sleeper? It wasn't that she begrudged the money. Money was no problem for the Zuo family. But this was no way to spend it. It was tantamount to announcing that they were bourgeois intellectuals or from decadent bourgeois families—she had never been allowed to forget her own class origin. And who could guarantee that there wouldn't be another political movement? It was said that there would be no repetition of the Cultural Revolution, but plenty of ultra-Leftists would like to repeat it under a different name.

Anyone with any political sense should follow her example, cooking tremella, ginseng or swallow's nest at home unknown to the outside world. That was money well spent. The housekeeper she had chosen was thoroughly reliable. She paid her more than most, but all these years Mrs. Lu had never breathed a word about their household's doings, not even during the Cultural Revolution."

Because she was so tight-lipped, Zuo Wei's mother often compared her to a brick wall. What was wrong with a brick wall? She didn't hobnob with other housekeepers, carrying her master's baby to sit in the shade of a tree or in the sun at the foot of a wall, gossiping about her employer's habits and shortcomings. If you didn't tell her something, she asked no questions and turned a deaf ear to what was said in her presence. If visitors came when the family were out, she wouldn't say where they had gone. Not even if they were frequent visitors for whom she had served tea or cooked meals countless times. She would treat them as strangers. When visitors complained about this, Beihe simply smiled.

Mrs. Lu wasn't a housekeeper, she was a treasure. Unlike her predecessor who had gabbed on about everything and wouldn't mind her own business. Soon after her marriage Beihe had found an excuse to get Zuo Wei to dismiss her. The woman had grabbed Beihe's hand on leaving and wept, making Beihe feel so uncomfortable that she saw her to the long-distance bus depot.

Beihe and Zuo Wei had only this one son. Zuo Wei, too, had been an only child. Their son Xiangdong had not been born until they had been married for many years. Before that her mother-in-law had looked accusingly at her flat stomach, making her wish to conceive.

Beihe saw the vexation in old Mrs. Zuo's eyes. Was the old lady sorry that Zuo Wei hadn't married Zeng Linger instead? If so, why had she used Linger's love for Zuo Wei to get her to wear a "Rightist's" cap in his place? Why had she let her be sent to the border region, while he had stayed behind? Now the Zuo family behaved as if Linger had never existed. The hypocrites!

They treasured Xiangdong. But that didn't mean they should spoil him. They should have taught him how to hold his own politically, that was what really counted. Her in-laws and husband bought the boy a sleeper ticket whenever he went on a trip, without worrying that he didn't know how many vice-premiers China had, or the names of the members of the State Council. Their priorities were all wrong.

She sighed, her eyes settling on a large photograph on the wall. She shifted the lampshade to let the light shine on it. It was their wedding picture.

She stared at the picture, recalling what many people had said, that she and her husband were very alike. In what way? No one had made that clear. He had a long straight nose, arched eyebrows, flashing eyes. With his lean face and clean-cut features he looked a strong character. And she had twinkling eyes like a smiling Buddha, which hid what she was really thinking. Her round nose and round face gave her an affable look.

In temperament too they were very different.

In college Zuo Wei had been a social activist. As chairman of the student committee of their department, he organized spring outings, autumn sports, entertainments, and parties with the Soviet students. He had spoken at the municipal meeting to commemorate the May 4th Movement of 1919. . . . In short, he appeared at all important functions. He dressed smartly in good clothes, without overdoing it. But although so handsome and gifted, academically he was mediocre. Perhaps his social activities took up too much of his time.

She remembered how a certain film studio planned to make a film about college life. They scouted for actors in several colleges, and finally the director asked Zuo Wei to play the main part. Most youngsters would have jumped at the chance, but he turned it down. Asked why, he just smiled and said nothing. Only Beihe knew that his family would not approve—not that he told this to her or anyone.

They hadn't been on close terms at that time. If they spoke to each other briefly it was about work. Though so dashing and debonair, Zuo Wei didn't mix much with girls. Probably Zeng Linger was the only girl he had ever loved—if it could be called love. This wasn't a matter of principle, but simply because he was incapable of love. Some people seem to be born without the capacity to love. In fact, when finally he married Beihe it was with the same feeling as picking up a girl on the street.

She herself had always been just an average student. In high school she was secretary of the Youth League branch, in college the Party secretary for her year. In those days student Party members were so rare that there could be only one Party branch for each year. Now she was deputy head of her institute and deputy secretary of its Party branch. She would probably remain a Party secretary all her life. For years other people had shot up or plummeted down, as if on a whirling merry-go-round. Only she had never shone particularly, had never been disgraced either.

Oddly enough, no matter how carefully anyone watched her, she gave no hint of having come from a once well-to-do family. Since the fifties the fashions for women's hair, clothes and shoes had changed many times, yet she always wore her hair bobbed, with a plain black hair-slide. Her blouses were always pale blue, pale grey or white, with a turndown collar and two big breast pockets. She wore dark blue or dark grey trousers and black leather shoes. While at college she had reinforced the soles of her shoes with rubber.

In Party meetings she kept as quiet as she could, sitting in the back row or on a corner seat. From under half-lowered eyelids she silently watched everything going on around her. If asked to sit in a more prominent position, she declined with a modest smile. "I'm fine here. Hurry up and start the meeting." She kept reminding herself that she was merely number two. If by any chance number one was away, she would make someone else preside.

Whenever anyone came to make a report to her, she listened intently, her eyes on the speaker's face, never strolling about with her mind on something else. From time to time she might nod, or exclaim with sympathy or astonishment, "Really?" Finally she would grip the visitor's hands, see them to the gate, and stand there watching till they were out of sight. If asked any favor, as long as it wasn't too involved, she did it as well and as quickly as possible.

But people always said they were alike. What resemblance was there between the two of them? If asked in what way, they couldn't exactly say.

Strange, in what way were they similar?

Hearing steps on the stairs she knew that Zuo Wei was back. "Did he get off all right?"

"Yes." Zuo Wei took off his grey short-sleeved shirt and draped it over the back of a chair, then switched on the fan and overhead light. At once the room became bright. "Why didn't you go down to watch TV?" he asked. "There's a football match this evening."

Beihe hung the shirt he had dropped on a clothes-stand in one corner. "Your mother's heart has been playing up again, I didn't want to disturb her." She omitted to say that she'd wanted to be quiet to think something over.

Zuo Wei was a filial son. His birth had been a difficult one—a Caesarian. Nowadays that wasn't considered a major operation, but at that time medical treatment was so poor that his mother's health had been affected. Whenever she had aches and pains, Zuo Wei felt uneasy, as if he were to blame. So no matter what disputes they might be having, if she complained of feeling unwell he said no more. Beihe could understand this.

Zuo Wei glanced at her now with a smile. His smile was still as captivating as ever. It melted her heart, as it had when she was a girl. She fetched his slippers from the bedroom for him. "How hot you look," she remarked. "I'll go down and fetch you a bottle of beer." As she passed him he caught hold of her hand. "Let me go," she said. "You're just back. You need a rest. I'll go." She slowly withdrew her hand.

The light was still on downstairs in the southern room, so maybe the old lady hadn't yet gone to sleep. Beihe tapped on the door.

"Come in." Her mother-in-law's voice managed to be indolent and imperious at the same time.

Beihe carefully opened the door, and saw the old lady lolling against the bedstead, her eyes closed. "Are you feeling better, Mother?" she asked softly.

"Oh, you know how it is. Has Donger gone? Old Mrs. Zuo never called her grandson Xiangdong.

"Yes, would you like one of your pills?"

These were pills Beihe had bought the previous year on a fact-finding trip to Japan. They were said to be effective for angina pectoris. Having spent all her foreign currency on these, she hadn't bought anything for Xiangdong, who had stamped his foot and fumed, "You might at least have bought me a pocket-size tape recorder.No one else would have wasted the chance to bring something in duty-free."

"You've got a big tape recorder, haven't you?"

"I can't take that with me on outings."

She had thrown her unreasonable son a stern glance.

I don't want them," the old lady answered icily. "Haven't you read the papers? Those Japanese pills use pig's gall bladder instead of bear gall."

Beihe's heart sank. But she said, "Yes, they shouldn't use substitutes like that in medicine. Don't take any more. If there's anything you want, ask Mrs. Lu to fetch it." She moved the bell on the cupboard by the bed closer to the old lady's hand. "I came down to get Zuo Wei a drink. Is there anything you'd like?"

"No."

"Where's Dad?"

"Reading in his study. Never mind him. Let him go get his own drinks."

"All right, have a good rest."

The old lady closed her eyes again with an imperceptible nod. Beihe withdrew, softly closing the door behind her, and took a deep breath as if there had been too little oxygen in the room.

All the Zuo family were short-tempered.

The old lady disliked her. Not that she ever spoke to her sharply or glared. Still Beihe sensed her deep-rooted antagonism and being her daughter-in-law was difficult. Nonetheless, despite the old lady's aversion to her, Zuo Wei had married her. His mother would soon be seventy-three. It was commonly said that the seventy-third and eighty-fourth years were pitfalls for old people. Was there anything in that, she wondered.

Mrs. Lu came out of her little room and looked inquiringly at Beihe. Her prominent cheekbones made her face seem top-heavy.

"It's nothing, Mrs. Lu. You go to bed, I can manage." Beihe opened the glass door of the cabinet and took out a cut-glass blue tumbler. Mrs. Lu disappeared as silently as a shadow. Beihe took a bottle of beer and some ice-cubes for her husband from the fridge.

She knew that certain people thought her and Zuo Wei ill-matched and marvelled that they got on so well—to all appearances. The reason was very simple: Even erratic animals, if stroked, would close their eyes and keep still. Men were the same. She had caught Zuo Wei on the rebound, not because she was attractive, but because at that special time he needed her. He had made a show of being head over heels in love with her, and she of being moved by this. Ever since then they had kept up the pretense, till they came to believe in it or had grown accustomed to it. That was the truth of the matter.

Beihe put the bottle, ice-cubes and glass on a tray, which she slowly carried upstairs. She was wondering how to explain to Zuo Wei what she had been considering that evening. Should she say nothing about it? That wouldn't do. He would find out eventually. And suppose he lost his temper and refused to co-operate? Then all her careful planning would go by the board. What was the best way to broach this without making him lose face?

That afternoon, at the meeting in E city to plan the trial man-ufacture of a new supermicro-computer, it had been decided—thanks largely to Beihe—to invite Zeng Linger to join the micro-code group. Word had already gone round that Zuo Wei was to head this group. Although this hadn't yet been officially an-nounced, and although certain procedures had to be gone through, it seemed a foregone conclusion.

Beihe understood her husband better than anyone else, includ-ing Zuo Wei himself. He had self-confidence, but without her support and manipulation what could he have achieved? On no account, though, could she let him sense this. In college she had seen his weaknesses but not realized just how incompetent he was. She had no regrets, however, because she loved him.

Love! She had sufficient good sense and strength to resist all temptations and safeguard herself. But she couldn't help loving Zuo Wei. No doubt everybody had some similar weakness.

She was both anxious and pleased about his heading this group. Anxious because he might expose his incompetence, pleased because this would be a respectable ending for his career. He should be able to muddle through with this job till his retirement. She knew that he wasn't considered up to it. People had hinted that without a wife in her position he would never have got anywhere.

She must hold onto this chance, must give Zuo Wei this last opportunity to shine. With this in mind she had rather un-scrupulously insisted on Linger joining the microcode group. Linger had been the best student of her year in college, and mathematics was her favorite subject, so she was the right person for the microcode group. If she were to join it, she could do all the actual work while Zuo Wei remained a figure-head.

But would she be willing to take on the job if she knew it meant co-operating with him? That would put her in an embarrassing position, especially since there had been some opposition to recruiting her. If she made some excuse, they might well find someone else.

At the meeting someone had said, "There's no doubt about Comrade Zeng Linger's ability. As for her character, well, she had her Rightist label removed in 1979; but her way of life. . . . In recruiting intellectuals, both their ability and moral character have to be taken into consideration. . . . I mean, we don't want to rush into things without discretion."

A silence had fallen. Who was willing to speak up for Zeng Linger? Beihe was the only person there who knew her. But even she had only second-hand knowledge of Linger's behavior since her graduation.

Linger had worked quietly as a scientist for over twenty years in a small border town. If she hadn't published a paper on multiple operation in computers which had been well received and aroused attention abroad, then even experts in the field would never have heard of Zeng Linger, a former Rightist who had led a loose life. And who could understand how hard it had been for her in her position, with such primitive working conditions, to stick to her research and make a breakthrough? To people who hadn't been there, that small border town was just a dot on the map. Who was interested in finding out about such an isolated place, or what life there was like? The same applied to Linger.

Normally, in a situation like this, Beihe would have kept quiet. And after a silence, with no one opposing the motion and no one supporting it, the matter would have been dropped. But if someone spoke up in favor, it might be passed.

Beihe said, "I agree. We need technicians who have both ability and political integrity. But it is years now since Comrade Zeng Linger slipped up. More than twenty years, isn't it? She was still young then and had just been labelled a Rightist. In those strange far-away surroundings, cut off from her family and friends, she may have succumbed to her feelings and let someone take advantage of her. . . . But that was the only time. No one is perfect. And later she turned over a new leaf. To speed up our modernization, we should mobilize all the positive factors we can."

Beihe spoke with considerable feeling, which was not in character. In all fairness, she hadn't said this solely for Zuo Wei's sake.

No matter what Linger had done since she and Zuo Wei parted, the Zuo family owed her something. And so did Beihe.

So the matter was decided.

* * *

Insects were still chirping in the grass after dark. The curtains hadn't been drawn tight, and moonlight coming through the gap moved silently through the room. It fell first on the stool, then on Zuo Wei's bed, and now on Beihe's bed, shining on her face so that she couldn't sleep.

She didn't get up to draw the curtains closer, knowing that her husband was still awake. He had turned over surreptitiously thirteen times. And she didn't want him to know that she, too, was awake as if she were keeping tabs on him. Judging by his stealthy movements, he didn't want *her* to know either that he was awake or to guess what he was thinking. Otherwise he wouldn't have minded waking her.

When he heard Linger's name he seemed unaffected and took Beihe's announcement very calmly. But wasn't there something funny about all this?

And Beihe herself always kept a poker-face, even when in bed.

Zeng Linger. . . . Zuo Wei had long since forgotten their affair. Had put it completely behind him. Now he and Linger were to meet again. Was the world such a small place after all?

"Own up! Who else was in the plot?"

"Come clean and you'll get off more lightly!"

Hundreds of people were yelling at a shadowy figure on the platform. It was like a scene from the Cultural Revolution. Beihe woke up with a start, uncertain whether this had been a memory or a dream. In those earlier days Linger had been an innocent, smiling as she stood on the platform, the target of criticism. Luckily that was before the Cultural Revolution, or she would have been beaten to death for her attitude.

Linger had fixed her eyes raptly on Zuo Wei, who was sitting in one corner hanging his head. Come clean? Confess? She could think of nothing but him, the man she loved. She would gladly sacrifice everything for him: her political future, her career, her freedom and the respect of other people.

"Out with it! Who wrote that big-character poster?"

"I did."

In fact, as Beihe knew, Zuo Wei had written it and Linger had copied it out, good calligrapher that she was. Beihe had happened to go into the classroom to fetch a book while she was copying it. The pen-name he had used had enabled Linger to take the blame in his place.

"That's a lie! Zeng Linger's hiding something."

"Come clean!"

But Linger had said no more, had turned a deaf ear to their roars of denunciation. Turned a blind eye to the fists being shaken at her, the cameras trained on her.

Later Beihe had got a photograph of Linger at that meeting from an editor of the college magazine. After one look at it she had turned it over, unwilling to look again. Apart from pictures of martyrs she remembered from church in her childhood, she had never seen any portrait with such a saintly expression.

That meeting had been a tremendous emotional shock because all three involved had been there: the eye-witness, the scapegoat and the real writer of the poster. Beihe was afraid Zuo Wei would be so moved that he'd run up to the platform, push Linger aside and own up to the truth. Then not only would he be finished, Beihe too might be involved. Luckily he kept his head, just sitting there with downcast eyes, not doing anything foolish, which wouldn't have helped matters anyway.

How cruel he had been. Linger stood on the platform like a delicate flower buffeted by a storm, doing her best to shield Zuo Wei from the wind and rain. How contemptible he had been.

His mother had sought out Beihe, who was secretary of their Party branch. "He's my only son," she said. "He's just headstrong, you know, and careless of how he talks."

Beihe had to keep quiet. The college's Party committee had given her a quota of Rightists. Well, that was easier to fill than reading a book or working out a problem. She loved Zuo Wei, had loved him for five years, waiting for a chance to catch him; but then Linger had grabbed him.

Had she hinted that Mrs. Zuo should tackle Linger? She couldn't remember what she had said at the time. Had the old lady spoken to Linger? Beihe didn't know, and probably neither did Zuo Wei. Only his mother and Linger could have answered that question. But the whole business was shelved when Linger became a Rightist.

Had Beihe the courage to go to E city? At first she hadn't meant to attend this meeting since she had work to do at the institute. But she had to go, to persuade Linger to join in this project. When she saw her what should she say? Had Linger changed? She must have, after her experiences. If she were still as ingenuous as before, then things would be much simpler.

Beihe suddenly recalled the sports rally in their first year at college. One event for the girls was sit-ups. When the others had done two hundred one by one, they gave up, but Linger went on from nine to eleven o'clock, refusing to stop, even though she was the sure winner already. The college principal went over to the mat and said, "That's enough, don't do any more!" But she didn't seem to have heard and went right on. The principal, the sports master and the college doctor hovered round her anxiously. She gave up only after four hundred sit-ups, then lay motionless on the mat, her eyes staring, her lips purple.

One of the male students commented that her stomach must be like a steel plate.

That was how she came by the nickname "Steel Plate".

Zuo Wei kept asking himself if he still owed her anything, if he had done all he could. Having answered these questions he ought to go to sleep, but his mind was in a turmoil.

She was said to have fallen a long time ago. Soon after going to that little town she had given birth to a son, a son without a father. He had heard this news with mixed feelings. How could she have forgotten him so quickly? She had belonged to him. At the same time he felt liberated—if she had gone to the bad that absolved him from his guilt. But often after he had made love to Beihe and still felt the warmth of her body, or after he had played with Xiangdong and could still hear the boy's chuckles, Zuo Wei would suddenly feel disconcerted. Beihe and Xiangdong were baffled by his abrupt changes of mood. They would ask him, "What's wrong?"

What was wrong? That was a secret. If he wanted to continue living in comfort, respected by all, he must never disclose that secret. In his imagination, Linger's son kept rising up before him then disappearing, like the ghost of Hamlet's father.

A fantastic notion struck him: Could he be *my* child? But generally he took comfort from the reflection: Impossible, we spent only one night together. If he were mine, Linger would surely have told me. She didn't because she was ashamed to admit that I wasn't the father. He didn't owe Linger anything. . . .

Just after she had been labeled a Rightist, Zuo Wei had gone to his department head to ask for a letter vouching for him, so that he could go and register his marriage to her.

"Don't be swayed by emotion, Zuo Wei," the department head had warned him. "Now's the time to draw a clear line of demarcation between yourself and Zeng Linger. You should break with her completely. Yet here you are thinking of marrying her. Have you considered the consequences of that? You'd be expelled from the Youth League and sent with her to the border, far from your parents, where maybe you'd have to stay for the rest of your life."

"You don't have to tell me that." Zuo Wei blocked his ears. He knew it all. But Linger had saved his life, he had to repay her. "Please write me a letter of introduction. Please!"

Oddly enough, once he had that letter in his pocket, the letter which was to bind him closely to Linger, to prove his courage and integrity, Zuo Wei faltered with an aching void in his heart. He had thought this would deepen his love for her. But instead his former love had vanished without a trace the moment he had the letter. He kept reminding himself that Linger had saved his life, he owed everything to her; but he no longer loved her. This realization staggered him. He broke out in a cold sweat.

He sat thinking things over in the pine wood behind the campus, trying to convince himself that this was a fleeting fancy, an aberration. Hundreds of people suffered from strange delusions, so why shouldn't he? The sun set. It was dark in the wood. The grave of some unknown ancient seemed like a large beast sleeping there peacefully, while its occupant had long since turned to dust. A huge grave mound, an empty coffin and the sighing of pines in the wind were all that remained.

Zuo Wei realized that this was no fleeting fancy. His love was dead, had died a violent death. Now he could only try to salve his conscience. Finally calming down, he decided that his behavior might have been worse. Other people in his place would have broken with her completely.

He went home and when Linger arrived and unfolded the letter of introduction, she stroked the paper with her slender fingers, as in the past she had stroked his eyebrows and lips. For some reason, when he took her in his arms, she felt this was a dream. She kept touching him as if to prove that he really existed and loved her.

For the same reason she bent her head in silence to stroke the letter over and over again. Then big tears fell onto the paper. Zuo Wei hastily took it from her and dried the tears with his hand-kerchief. "Look out, you're smudging it."

"Sorry. I can't help it. I'm—I'm too happy. I don't know how to thank you. . . ." That should have been a perfect day. Yet, face to face, they had nothing to say to each other.

Zuo Wei bustled about and rattled away, afraid to confront her in silence. He brought out the fabric he had purchased for her. "What do you think of this material? Best make a dress out of it. With a low neckline to show off your graceful neck. Better still, wear a jade pendant on a black velvet ribbon. Do you realize what a lovely neck you have? When you hold up your chin, that beautiful straight line down to your throat makes you look like a princess."

Why was he jabbering away like this? "Did you choose this pretty material for me yourself?" she asked.

"Of course, went to several shops before I found it."

"Thank you. But I'm no princess. I'm a fisherman's daughter."

Zuo Wei's heart sank. He roused himself to bring her from the cupboard a pair of cream-coloured shoes with low heels. "Try these, I didn't buy shoes with high heels because you're already too tall. Think how a man must feel if he has to stand on tiptoe to kiss his wife!" He laughed uproariously.

Linger made no move. Just sat there motionless.

Zuo Wei picked up a shoe and went to squat at her feet. "You know," he said, "plenty of men, even after years of marriage, don't know what size shoes their wives take. But I know. Don't you think I'm an ideal husband?"

Linger stopped him from taking off her shoes. She pleaded softly, "Kiss me. . . ."

He hesitated for a second, a second only. Perhaps because his mind was still on the shoes. Then he stood up and bent over her. Linger's eyes looking up into his seemed rather frightened. He avoided them, not wanting to guess what she was afraid of, then hastily kissed her on the mouth. She had halitosis. Eating and sleeping badly had evidently undermined her health.

"Shall I make you a cup of coffee?" he offered.

"No, don't leave me!" she cried sharply, as if this were a final parting.

He sat again and crouched at her feet. "What's wrong?"

"Do you still love me?" She kept her eyes fixed on him.

"Don't be silly. Haven't I brought the letter to get our marriage certificates? We'll soon be married." Perhaps because crouchingthere was uncomfortable, he stood up and sat down beside her.

"Marriage isn't the same as love," she said. This was a weakness of hers, this habit of quibbling. In a girl it might be lovable, but in a wife it would be intolerable.

In the past she had never asked him, "Do you love me?" Not even when she was chasing him so hard. As if sure that one day he would love her. Yet now, when he was doing his best to show concern for her and fill the awkward silences between them, she insisted on asking this question.

Zuo Wei grinned, but his eyes were not smiling. "If I don't say, it means I love you. If I didn't love you I'd tell you. Understand? That's a joke made by an American called Johnson."

"But it doesn't suit me. I want to hear the answer of a Chinese called Zuo Wei," she said with a broad yet grim smile. "I'd like to crack a joke too, really I would, but I can't. If I could that would be good." A long silence followed.

Zuo Wei finally lost patience and flared up, smashing several glasses onto the floor in an hysterical outburst. "What's made you so suspicious? You didn't used to be like this."

"We didn't used to be like this," replied Linger, stooping to pick up the broken glass. "Let's not lose our tempers. Listen, in the future life may be even harder than this. Then we may be sorry— oh!" She had cut her finger on a splinter of glass.

"Did you do that on purpose?" Zuo Wei ran over to suck her bleeding finger. She watched him, smiling yet with tears in her eyes.

"I wish I could cut another finger," she said.

"You idiot!" he bellowed.

She rested her head on his shoulder and they sat motionless on the floor till dusk.

Linger's soft voice was swallowed up at once in the darkness. "This evening I'm not leaving."

That night Linger became a woman.

Zuo Wei watched in astonishment the next morning as she calmly put up her hair, walked confidently across the room and straightened her clothes in silence. Her calculated movements made him tense. It seemed incredible that this cold, aloof Linger was the Linger of last night. After making love had they really wept in each other's arms like children? Had she really gazed raptly at him as if to suck out his soul?

"Give me that letter," Linger had ordered him hoarsely. "Good, let's go and sit on the balcony." This was another order.

It was still early. As yet no cicadas were shrilling in the trees, the tops of which the sun was just dyeing red. An old milkman was riding past on a pedicab filled with rattling milk bottles. Dewdrops still glistened on the flowers, grass and the foliage of trees. In the distance a steam whistle sounded. The street cleaners were finishing their work. . . .

"I hope you'll remember this morning." She hadn't asked him to remember the night before. Then giving him a strange look, she got up and moved to the other end of the balcony where she swiftly tore up the letter of introduction. As Zuo Wei rushed over to snatch it, she leaned over the balustrade and stretched out her hand. At once the slight wind carried off the scraps of paper. They whirled through the air like snowflakes, some falling to the ground, some on to the trees, some sailing off on the breeze. . . .

"Look, they'll soon melt away like snowflakes." There was a fixed smile on her face. From not having slept all night, she had black circles under her eyes and her face was deathly white. "We've already married, you've paid me back; now we can part with easy consciences."

Zuo Wei wanted to break into sobs or burst out laughing. He was overwhelmed by a sense of deliverance, which he could never confide to anyone. So this was why they had wept in each other's arms last night. Linger must have known then that this was their final parting.

After that, right up to the day she left, Linger refused to see him. Zuo Wei posted himself under the old locust tree outside her dormitory. From there he could watch her window and must be visible to her too. He wanted her to know he was waiting for her

Even more, however, he hoped she would stick to her decision. He felt as if he were on a high peak looking down on bottomless chasms on both sides. If he lost his footing he would fall to his death. He went without food and sleep till he was emaciated, with sunken eyes that flashed fiercely. In his heart, though, he knew that this could not compare with the sacrifice that Linger had made for him.

And so she left. Not leaving a note or a single word of reproach. Naturally no one would go to see her off. As the train pulled out, had she looked at the platform? Had she wept? Did she forgive him?

He had no way of knowing.

He had searched his drawers for some small memento of hers. Even a rubber band she had worn on one plait, a photograph or a note. But he found nothing.

He remembered receiving notes from her, but after reading them he had thrown them away. In those beginning days he had thought they would always be together. Besides, her notes were not like love letters. Since she never called him "dearest," what was the point of keeping them? She found terms like "dearest" sickening. She had had a strange way of showing her love—by letting him watch her solve mathematical problems quickly and accurately. No one else in the world would use this method of courtship.

Whenever he discovered hair-slides, notebooks or handkerchiefs of hers, he returned them to her promptly. Since he had *her*, why keep such things? He wasn't like foreigners who kept a lock of their loved one's hair by their hearts. To him hair-clippings were dirty and rather revolting. And so Linger had vanished from his life. As imperceptibly as the passage of time.

Now she had reappeared. Beihe had just told him briefly that Linger would be working on microcodes in his group and she hoped he would put the work first, and not let personal considerations interfere with their working relationship. She wanted them to co-operate well to expedite the modernization program. But Zuo Wei knew she was keeping something back.

Even after living together for twenty-odd years, he didn't fully understand Beihe. It always paid him to take her advice, however, since she was more clear-headed. When she told him about

Linger's coming they hadn't looked at each other. He realized that once again they were acting as accomplices, preparing to take advantage of the same person they had exploited before. Was this very despicable? He wouldn't probe too deeply into the question. Besides, it was Beihe's decision, had nothing to do with him. He hid his face in his pillow.

He suddenly remembered a question from a quiz when he was a boy: Which is heavier, a pound of iron or a pound of cotton?

He couldn't help reverting to his old problem: Who could tell him who was the father of Linger's child?

* * *

Linger felt rather dizzy after a sleepless night. The reason, a rather laughable one, was because today she would be on the train. She had often heard others complain of insomnia caused by anxiety. She understood, having spent sleepless nights like that too.

But now her nights were peaceful. Peaceful as the blue-black sky far removed from the clamor of the dusty world. After Taotao drowned she had gone through hell and drunk the waters of Lethe, then forgotten all the past.

If asked what she looked forward to, it was the train which passed regularly each night. She could wake punctually and lie quietly in her small adobe hut close to the railway, waiting with pleasurable anticipation for the rumble of the express as it approached, shaking the earth, then receded. In imagination she followed it long after the echoes of its whistle had died away. What did that train really mean to her? She couldn't exactly say. But she slept especially soundly till dawn after it had passed, like a child who has been nursed and changed by its mother.

Tonight at last she'd caught this express. Like a black arrow it thundered through the black night, cleaving it in two. It seemed from the clash of metal as if the tracks and the wheels were deadly foes, trying desperately to grind each other to powder. All this thrilled Linger.

By contrast her carriage was quiet and softly lit, to let the passengers sleep peacefully. She lay with eyes open on her berth, motionless, enjoying the rocking of the train, so rhythmic and gentle. How could she go to sleep? It was such a treat!

In the middle berth opposite, a young bride was laughing softly and murmuring indistinctly in her sleep. Linger felt guilty for eavesdropping on someone else's secrets. The young woman and her husband were going to E city for their honeymoon.

The man on the top berth was snoring non-stop. His thunderous snores ran up and down the scale. The little boy in the lowest berth must have mistaken them for a tiger's roar. He woke with a start exclaiming, "Mama, I'm scared of the tiger!"

His young mother, making an effort to wake up, patted him carelessly on the back and muttered, "There's nothing to be afraid of. Go to sleep, be a good boy." That hadn't been Linger's way. When Taotao was small, he had only to kick in his sleep and instantly she was wide-awake.

Still she couldn't sleep. This was her first train trip in over twenty years. She felt as if returning after many years to her old home which had been renovated, so that it seemed both familiar yet strange to her.

From time to time she fingered the smooth partition covered with cream-coloured laminated plastic. When she first came to the border the partitions had been made of wooden planks. In the daytime when not used the middle berth had to be lowered, otherwise the people below couldn't sit up straight. The little tables under the windows were movable. If you bumped against the folding legs of one, it would collapse, upsetting everything on it.

That was how her blue cut-glass tumbler had been smashed. It had so upset her at the time, big beads of sweat had stood out on her forehead. She had gritted her teeth and clenched her fists, digging her nails into the palms of her hands. Tears had streamed down her face. That tumbler had been the only thing of Zuo Wei's that she'd kept. Why had he given her something so easily broken? She should never have kept it out to use on the train. Had she been like a girl newly in love, eager to display her first gift from her lover? No, of course not. But she was nervous, having made no preparations for the difficulties now confronting her. Keeping the tumbler with her was like having Zuo Wei at her side to give her courage.

At that time she had no idea that she was pregnant. When she found out, she was beside herself with joy and felt as if she had discovered a goldmine. Overnight she, a beggar, had become a millionaire. Every night, having dragged herself wearily to bed, she softly laid her hands on her swelling stomach and prayed silently to a God she didn't believe in to give her a son just like Zuo Wei. How could she have blamed fate for being cruel? Hadn't it given Zuo Wei back to her?

Her heart was at rest. No longer afraid to look back for fear of seeing all the worst in Zuo Wei, she forgave him for abandoning her and felt nothing but gratitude and deeper love for him. Even her looks improved. Her eyes sparkled, her cheeks were rosy. She had a son to keep her company. This helped her through her trials and humiliations, the certainty that this unborn son understood her.

"You must own up to your mistakes and examine their political, ideological, historical and social roots. Who was the man involved? Where? Was this the first time or are you promiscuous? What was your motive, your aim?" People came one after another to put pressure on her to confess. Her hands shielding her womb, she simply shook her head.

"We've explained the policy to you. If you refuse to confess your punishment will be harsher, your sentence longer. You're guilty on two counts now: a Rightist and a bad character. Landlords, rich peasants, counter-revolutionaries, bad characters and Rightists, you belong to two of those five categories." Still Linger said nothing, simply nodding her head.

She felt Taotao move in her womb. What are you up to? She asked her son. Want to come out to protect your mother and father? Don't worry, I'll never betray him, never. Foolish child, you still don't understand. Mother's not a blade of grass, she's a tree. She'll spread her boughs to shelter you and your father. I want him to make good.

So many people were stabbing her in the back. Whether at meetings, listening to reports or in the canteen, no one would sit beside her or talk to her. Once, after she had taken a seat at a meeting, she went to the lavatory. A woman arriving late, not knowing that it was Linger's seat, sat down beside it. When Linger came back the woman leapt up with a shriek, flapping her handkerchief in front of her nose and brushing off her clothes, till everyone stood up to see what was happening.

Even the cooks let slip no chance to humiliate her. One cook chucked her under the chin. This was more than she could take, and she threw a bowl of soup in his face. The cook beat her over the head with his soup ladle, then bashed her in the stomach. People gathered round to watch the fun, not a single person interceding for her, because they felt she deserved this.

She bent double, protecting her stomach with both hands, putting up with the beating in silence. She wouldn't plead to be let off, wouldn't run away. As he lashed out the cook swore, "Stinking bitch! See how she's shielding the bastard in her belly! A tramp pretending to be a decent woman."

Later the Party secretary lectured her, "Don't forget that you're here to be reformed. You must behave yourself." Her son turned over and kicked uneasily. Are you cross? she asked. Why are you crying? Don't be afraid, child. Let them curse. Mother will keep faith. Don't worry, time will show them. So long as no one stabs your father in the back, whatever I have to put up with is well worth it.

She was doing heavy labor in those days, carting coal, vegetables or other supplies to their office. She needed food to keep up her strength, and for Taotao. The commissary cooks never gave her full helpings of rice or vegetables. When there were freshly steamed buns or rice on the table, they gave her rancid leftovers. And they jeered at her in chorus. She had no money to buy food outside, with only her monthly allowance of eighteen yuan. Hunger often made her dizzy.

She had no experience of childbirth. Not until her labor pains started did she set off to the hospital. There were no taxis then, and it was midnight when even pedicabs were not to be had. Their unit had a car, but she didn't ask for it. They wouldn't have let her use it anyway. Doubled up with pain she staggered and crawled all the way to the hospital, leaving a moist trail behind her.

A nurse filled out the entry form for her since she had gone straight to the delivery room. Name, age, place of birth, work unit, address, telephone. . . .'What's your husband's name?''

Linger was silent.

"Your husband's name?" the nurse repeated more loudly, but Linger didn't move or speak.

"Zeng Linger, I need to know your husband's name," the nurse reiterated slowly and sharply. Finally she snapped the case history shut, as if slapping Linger's face.

She had forgotten to bring her toilet things. Since no one came to see her there was no one who could bring them. The day after Taotao was born, she asked a nurse to buy her a set in the hospital shop. "Go yourself, I've no time," the nurse answered frostily.

The corridor was cold and drafty, though outside it was spring.

The grim-faced gynecologist ordered a nurse to take a specimen of her blood. "What for?" Linger asked. The nurse glanced at her superciliously. "To test for syphilis."

"How can you treat patients like this?" demanded Linger indignantly.

"Your unit asked us to."

So someone from her unit had come. No wonder the doctors and nurses were treating her so badly. You couldn't blame them. How else should they treat a Rightist and bad character?

The three other patients in her ward made a point of teasing their husbands when they came. "Have a good look, is this your son?" One mother thrust her baby into her husband's arms.

"With those jutting-out ears there can't be any mistake," he answered fondly.

Another woman scolded, "I told you I don't want chicken soup, but you've gone and bought a chicken." She pushed the soup away, threw down her chopsticks and turned her back on her husband.

"All right, don't be so cross. Tell me what you want and I'll get it."

"I want to eat your heart!"

"I'll boil it for you tomorrow."

His wife glared, then burst out laughing and sipped some soup.

The third, nursing her baby, leant against her husband's shoulder.

"Look, he recognizes you. See, he's staring at you."

"So he is. Good boy, say Dada."

"How foolish of you. How can a baby speak? You must be out of your mind."

Linger turned her face to the wall in embarrassment. In their husband's eyes these mothers had done something splendid.

Every morning these women sniffed in disgust, then threw

open the door and windows, exclaiming, "How this place stinks!"
As if Linger were rotting away with syphilis. But holding Taotao in
her arms she was oblivious of this. Taotao was her bastion of iron,
even though he was a puny, undernourished baby. Her milk was
thin since she was given no nourishing food. Wrinkling his wiz-
ened face, he sucked so hard at her breast that he hurt her. His
feeble wails of hunger made her heart ache.

Often she stared at the green mailbox, tempted to write to Zuo
Wei to tell him that he had a son; that Taotao hadn't enough to eat,
and there was nothing she could do about it. Her heart was torn
between her love for Zuo Wei and her love for her son. In the end
she didn't write, though she wondered if she was letting Taotao
down.

Once, though, when Taotao fell ill, she was desperate. She
rushed like a crazy woman to the telegraph office to make a long-
distance call. When it came through she was too distraught to
speak. She heard Zuo Wei's voice, now clear, now faint: "Hello . . .
hello. . . ." She felt she would faint or go out of her mind, she so
longed to fly to him. In the phone booth she slid to the ground,
pressing the receiver hard against her ear. She had gritted her
teeth to stop herself from calling out. She longed for Zuo Wei to say
"Hullo" again, but he abruptly hung up.

Her tongue numb, her arm limp, she walked home as if in a
trance, to rest her head by Taotao's pillow. All that night she knelt
by his bed. When the sun rose in the morning his fever had gone
down. She murmured to him, "See, we came through all right
without telling him, didn't we? When you're grown-up you'll
know that it's best to rely on yourself, not on anyone else."

But Taotao didn't grow up. When he was fifteen, swimming with
his friends in a pond, he dived in and never surfaced. When they
fished him out there was mud in his nose and mouth. For three
years Linger was haunted by the memory.

Why had she had chances to save Taotao's father, but no chance
to save Taotao? She had been a fisherman's daughter all for nothing. Taotao had never even seen the sea, had lost his life in a pond.
It had been stupid of her to think that only the sea could swallow
up men's lives.

The newly-weds sitting opposite were bickering over a package of cookies. It was a pretty package with a dark green and yellow design, quite different from the brown wrapping paper of her young days. She felt as if she had lived in a mountain cave for years and had now come out to find that life had improved.

The bride took the last cookie out of the packet, and flourished it in front of her husband. "This is the last, I'm having it."

"No, give it to me." He made a grab at it.

She pouted. "All right, you have it."

"I was teasing, of course it's yours."

"Let's play the finger-guessing game, and the winner will get it, right?" He won. But still gave her the cookie.

Linger watched them enviously. How good it was to see people head over heels in love. She and Zuo Wei had never sparred like that. Perhaps she was incapable of teasing. Was that a serious defect in a woman?

She couldn't understand women who passively enjoyed their husbands' love without giving anything of themselves. But havingonly been in love once, her experience was limited. She considered that love should be unstinted giving, with no thought of recompense. Since first setting eyes on Zuo Wei she had felt like a snowflake melting away in the sunshine. Wasn't that a snow-flake's destiny?

The wind coming through the window ruffled a Japanese maga-zine on the table. It was colourfully illustrated. "May I look at this?" she asked.

"Please do," answered the bride.

It was light reading, suitable for a journey. Advertisements, world features, travel notes, jokes, anecdotes about celebrities, and short, lively articles. Linger leafed through it till she came to a section on horoscopes preceded by a piece on birthday gems. According to this, since the sixteenth century different precious stones had been associated with the twelve months of the year. The appropriate gem was often made into a ring or necklace for a birthday present. The different gems for the twelve months were listed.

Next she looked up her own horoscope. She read "Emerald." Ardent. She smiled to herself, then abruptly lowered her head.

Putting down the magazine she looked out of the window at a far-stretching wasteland, with no villages in sight. Some clumps of weeds had withered, others were sprouting. The sparse purple flowers of thorn bushes added a touch of color to the scene. The drooping branches of a gnarled tree reminded her of a kindly grandmother shielding her little grandson. So even this barren soil was teeming with life.

In the ditch beside the truck the saplings were shaking in the wind, all bent in the same direction. Their leaves too were facing in the same direction like tiny green flags unfurling. A solitary horse sprang into view in the distance. It was plodding slowly along as if fated never to reach the far-off horizon.

"Ma, I want to wee-wee." The little boy who'd been frightened by the snoring last night, was clutching at his split pants. His young mother carried him off to the lavatory.

In 1960 Linger had bought a white enamel wash-basin, which Taotao had used as his potty. He had to try out each purchase for himself carefully, especially since she so seldom bought anything. Any money she could spare she spent on food for him, during the three hard years when cakes cost six yuan a pound. She couldn't afford to buy more than one at a time. Each time he finished it, sighing with satisfaction and licking his fingers, she felt a pang.

Taotao had been precocious, not easy to cope with. She'd never been able to fool him. His schoolmates often bullied him because he had no father and the teachers discriminated against him too. Nothing could be kept a secret in that small town. But he never complained to Linger. Once he came back from school looking as if he'd been in a fight. His nose was streaked with blood, one of his pockets was torn and the front of his jacket was wet as if he had washed off the blood on it.

"Have you been fighting, Taotao?" she asked in dismay.

"No." He avoided her eyes. When she asked again he clamped his mouth shut and said nothing. She didn't like to put more pressure on him. That evening he went to bed behind the curtain and lay so still that she thought he was asleep. But then he got up and came to sit by her desk. "Can you stop working for a minute, mother?" He looked so lovable in his baggy pyjamas made over from an old blue dress of hers, he reminded her of Zuo Wei.

"Of course I can." Linger put down her pen and stroked his soft hair. He moved away and asked, as solemnly as a grown-up, "Do I have a father?"

Linger withdrew her hand. She'd known the time would come when she'd have to answer this question, but hadn't expected it to be so soon. That made it more difficult, since Taotao was too young to fully understand. "Yes, you have a father."

Taotao's face brightened. "What's he like?"

"Very lovable."

Taotao looked sceptical. "Then why doesn't he come to see us?"

"He's too far away. Too far ever to come."

"Mother!" he exclaimed.

"What is it?"

"When I grow up, however far away you are I'll go to see you."

"Thank you, Son."

"Mother?"

"Well?"

"Are you crying?"

"No."

"Let me see your eyes."

Linger made herself turn to face him. "My foolish child, mother never cries. All right, back to bed now, quickly. I still have work to do."

Taotao's first composition subject happened to be "My Father." Linger remembered every word of it.

My Father

My father is my mother, my mother is my father. Because she does more than other people's fathers. There's nothing she can't do.

In winter she digs a shallow pit for vegetables. She pulls carts of coal back from way out in the country, craning her neck and humping her back like the little donkeys in the production brigade. I run after the cart and push it. Pushing and pushing, and not letting on when I'm tired. But Mother knows everything. Once she lifted me on to the cart and asked, "How's that?" I said, "Fine!" Because I'd never ridden on a cart. Never been on a bus either. Mother says when I'm big enough, she'll see me off by train to go to a university far away. I don't want to go far away. I want to help mother push carts.

You've forgotten, child, you helped dig it too. You weren't the height of the shovel. You struggled with that big shovel, not stopping even to wipe your runny nose. I felt sad to think you'd soon be a big boy, not needing me to wipe your nose for you.

> Mother makes perfect slingshots. Not the wire kind that can't shoot far or make the stone rebound to hurt your hand. She makes them with the forked branches of small trees. She told me magpies' nests are pointed below, crows' nests are rounded, and sparrows don't have nests—they squeeze into some crack or under the eaves to sleep.

But the first slingshot I made was a flop. Have you forgotten how soon it broke? Or didn't you want to talk about my failure? And the one I made later of date wood was taken away by your schoolmaster.

> She can make handsome clothes. For Children's Day she made me a sailor suit.

You upset me by saying that, Taotao. I so seldom made you new clothes. And that sailor suit, made out of some old clothes of mine, didn't fit you properly.

> She helps me with all the lessons I can't do. And her explanations are easy to understand. She works out problems in math every day till late in the evening. When I wake up in the night to pee she's still hard at work at her desk.

> I wish she wouldn't spend so much time on math problems, because they stop her from telling me more stories or playing games with me.

Oh, love, I'm truly sorry. I had to work in the daytime and had only the evenings for research. As a baby you cried so much, it stopped me from concentrating, so I gave you a pacifier to suck. After I read that this might give you a stomach ache I made a cloth wrapper, like a Cantonese woman's, to carry you on my back. Then you didn't cry and I could concentrate. But you often wet my back. If I changed your clothes and played with you for a bit, you opened your toothless mouth and gurgled with such delight that it took great determination to go back to work.

> Mother is brave. No matter what troubles come along, she never cries. . . .

No, Mother cried. Late at night, my precious, when you were sound asleep.

The teacher had written "Excellent" in large red characters across the top of this composition, and brought it to show Linger. This was her first visit to their home, and Linger was so pleased and flustered that she forgot the pork simmering on the stove. When the teacher left she discovered that it was burnt. That was a big blow—over two pounds of pork, enough to last Taotao for several meals.

The teacher, tears in her eyes, had said, "You've put up with hardships and humiliation and now you're having your reward. Taotao's such a promising child I expect him to be a great writer when he grows up."

Hardships? Linger wasn't finding life hard. Taotao's need for her had made her forget her troubles. But suddenly he had gone.

Gone.

She had reproached herself, "I knew men could drown in the sea, but never imagined anyone could drown in a little pond. I should-n't have let him swim there, I was too careless. . . ."

Hearing her, women wept, men fell silent. Because of this tragedy they forgave her past and pitied her. But, without Taotao, this meant nothing to her.

* * *

She needed to test her strength. So after putting her luggage in her room, Linger hurried downstairs two steps at a time. It pleased her to find that at least she was still quick and nimble, could judge distances correctly. Going up two steps at a time was easy, but going down wasn't so simple.

In the lobby of the hotel she met the honeymoon couple. "Would you like to go for a swim?" the bride asked her.

"Not now. It would be more fun in the evening."

"That's what *he* says; I'll have to go on my own."

"Sorry." Linger was in a hurry to get away.

"Will you come with us this evening then?" asked the young man.

"Gladly, what's your room number?"

"207."

"I'm in 321. Give me a ring, will you? See you this evening."

"So long."

It was strange. After a lapse of a quarter of a century the two-storey telegraph office still stood in its old place, a faithful medium for communications. Linger stroked the green mailbox in front of it, then picked a tiny yellow flower by the roadside and stuck it on the small aluminum notice of the collection times. It was here that Zuo Wei had once posted an impassioned letter telling his parents how Linger had saved his life.

Once more she asked herself: Had she only rescued him because he was Zuo Wei? Wouldn't she have done the same for anyone else? Yes, she would. That was how her father had brought her up.

Maybe Zuo Wei's error of judgment dated from then, and he had mistaken his gratitude for love. For in any emergency she always went to his rescue. He had been under no obligation to love her and she had never demanded such compensation, simply wanting to do all she could for the man she adored. She had hoped her love would evoke a response from him, not that she expected he would repay her by a show of love. After all these years here she was making another post-mortem. It no longer pained her, but of course it was too late.

She went to the only shop in E selling local products, and bought herself a straw hat with a green ribbon. One summer when they had camped here, she had bought a smart man's hat like this for Zuo Wei, but he stubbornly refused to wear it because of the green ribbon. She hadn't minded.

In the handicrafts shop a ring caught her attention. A slim engraved ring inset with a small pearl, priced at 150 yuan. It reminded Linger of the magazine she had read on the train. No one had ever given her jewelery made with her birthstone. Her parents were both dead now, and probably no one else knew the date of her birthday.

On the spur of the moment she decided to buy herself a ring with her birthstone. "Have you got any emerald rings?" she asked the old shop assistant.

"I'm sorry, we haven't. Emeralds are very rare. You might get one in an antique shop in Beijing or Shanghai," he replied courteously.

"Then please let me see that pearl ring." Linger slipped it on to the third finger of her left hand, the finger for a wedding-ring. It fitted perfectly. "All right, I'll take this."

She had money now, her salary was over a hundred yuan a month. She could have bought Taotao any number of cakes. But when she'd needed money she hadn't had a cent. Smiling, she rubbed the ring and left the shop. Wearing the ring gave her the strange sensation of having just married someone. Not Zuo Wei of course.

The chandler's shop still stood by the crossroads. But the old chandler had been replaced by a girl, now immersed in a large book. In the showcase candles of all types were displayed. Linger looked them over carefully and was struck by a pair of big red ones. That year she and Zuo Wei had seen an identical pair of candles here. She had decided to buy a pair like this for their wedding. When Zuo Wei teased her for being so "countrified," she insisted that their room would look much better by candlelight. It was too bad that all her life she'd missed out on these red candles.

"Excuse me, comrade, how much is this pair of candles?"

"Eighteen yuan," said the shopgirl.

"Please let me have a pair."

Linger carefully put the candles, wrapped in paper, into her handbag, sure that the newlyweds would like this present. On her way out she imagined their happiness when they had lit them, almost as if her own youthful dream of happiness had come true.

She felt hungry. The breakfast on the train had been inedible. She didn't need to ask the way to the restaurant serving western food. Like the telegraph office and the other shops it was still in its old place.

Zuo Wei had invited her to a meal here once. Since it had been her first western meal, she didn't know how to use knives and forks and clattered them on the plate. In her clumsy efforts to cut up her helping of chicken, it slipped on to the table, dirtying the white cloth and upsetting a glass of wine, to Zuo Wei's great embarrassment. But now, without Zuo Wei there, she had no qualms, though she didn't expect to manage much better this time. Weren't foreigners equally awkward using chopsticks?

The restaurant was very busy. Linger sat down at a table by the window where she had a view of the sea. She studied the menu.

"May I sit here?" a man asked.

She gave a start—he sounded so like Zuo Wei. She looked up and stared at him blankly.

"Sorry, but all the other tables are full." The young man, who was wearing a checked shirt, mistook her silence for unwillingness.

"Of course, of course you can." Linger relaxed.

"Thank you." He sat down. "Are you here for a conference?"

"Yes. And you? Are you on holiday?"

"No, I'm here for a conference too."

" His generation was lucky. He had finished at the university at a good time. Unlike her generation, who had wasted the most creative years of their lives and could never make up for the time they had lost.

"May I ask when you graduated?"

"In the fifties."

"Ah, you people are in key positions now."

The soup was served.

"Is there any pepper, please?" Linger asked.

"Get it yourself," said the waitress icily.

"Don't get up, I'll get it," offered the young man.

"Thanks."

Fried pork chops came next.

"Have you got some chilli sauce?" Linger asked.

"Get it yourself," said the waitress again.

Linger smiled at the young man, who winked at her. "Get it yourself!" they both said, then burst out laughing.

It was an enjoyable meal. Though her companion was so young, he seemed to be a mine of information. Talking with him Linger felt rejuvenated. She thought enviously how lucky he was to be young, with so much time ahead of him to work.

After lunch she went out to the beach, the ribbon on her new hat flapping in the wind. She took off her shoes and carried them as she walked along the beach. The tide was just coming in—it looked like a spring tide—yes, this was the first or second of the lunar month.

Waves pounding the shore soaked her trousers so that they clung to her calves and the wind chilled her. She stopped beside Tiger-head Rock where they had set off for a swim that year. It was still crouching there unchanged, buffeted by the waves. She wished the past could blow away like the wind or scatter like clouds, leaving her no memory of it. But she realized here that the past was still alive. Like the seeds in some ancient tomb, buried in the dark for centuries yet still able to germinate.

But . . . at least she herself had changed. She knew that what stirred her and filled her heart with love now was not Zuo Wei but the land where she had spent the best years of her life and dedicated herself so generously in service.

"Ardent."

That was an apt description of her life.

The bare soles of her feet could feel the sand being sucked out to sea by the receding waves. If she stood here motionless she might be carried out to sea herself.

She climbed up the rock and sat overlooking the sea, watching women poking about for rock-oysters, and an old fisherman. He seemed to be out of luck and to have lost patience. Each time he drew in his line he sighed and glanced around as if hoping no one had noticed his incompetence. Linger turned away to spare him embarrassment. Her father had been quite different, so self-confident that he never tried to cover up his mistakes.

The sky became overcast. Threatening black clouds loomed up in the south, darkening the sea in the distance and scudding towards the shore. Soon it might pour with rain. The women looking for rock-oysters made off. So did the old fisherman. Bathers swam swiftly ashore, and the people who had been sunbathing on the beach wrapped their colorful towels around themselves and went home. Linger remained seated on the rock watching the sea sweep in to break, foaming, on the shore.

When she arrived back at the hotel, completely drenched, it was dark. Her table lamp was alight, turned on no doubt by the attendant. On the table lay a note.

> Comrade Zeng Linger,
> I'm sorry not to have found you in. At 6:30 I'll wait for you in the restaurant downstairs, and we can have dinner together.
>
> Lu Beihe

Comrade Zeng Linger!
Lu Beihe?

She sank into the armchair by the bed, then sprang up so as not to wet it.

To be addressed as "comrade" amused her, reminding her how correct Lu Beihe had been, an old head on young shoulders. Was she still so circumspect?

Of course Linger would dine with her. She was longing for news of her former classmates. She hastily washed her hair, which was dirty after several days on the train.

Just as she finished her bath the telephone rang. "Hello, who's there?"

"It's us," replied the bridegroom.

"Oh, I've bought a pair of red candles. Would you like them?"

"Of course. Thank you very much."

"Splendid!" Linger laughed happily.

"Didn't we arrange to go swimming this evening? How about it?"

"I'm terribly sorry, an old classmate has asked me to dinner this evening. Besides. . . ." She glanced outside. It was still pouring. "In weather like this you'd better stay indoors."

"No, this weather's ideal for swimming." He must be a daredevil, just as she had been at his age. Perhaps he wanted to impress his bride. "Well, if you can't go, we will. We can swim together tomorrow."

"Where are you going to swim?"

"By Tiger-head Rock."

"No, not there!" Linger exclaimed.

"Why not?"

"It's dangerous. There's a whirlpoool four thousand metres offshore."

"Don't worry, I'll steer clear of that."

"If I were you, I wouldn't go."

"All right. Thanks for your concern. See you tomorrow." He hung up.

Linger went downstairs to the beauty salon.

"Do you want a perm?" the hairdresser asked.

"No, just a blow dry."

Why should they go to Tiger-head Rock? Linger was worried, remembering the fearful whirlpool.

That summer they had gone camping in E by the seaside. Each evening the best swimmers had swum out towards the moon from

Tiger-head Rock. The sparkling moonlight made a silvery track all the way from the horizon till it seemed just five feet away, and you thought that with just a few more strokes you could reach it. But after a few more strokes it remained the same distance away, tempting you to swim after it, to reach it and share in its radiance.

One evening Linger discovered Zuo Wei on her right. Each time he raised his left arm he turned his smiling face to her. Presently they were out of earshot of the others, could no longer hear the waves breaking against the shore, as if the two of them were alone in the world except for the bright moon at the horizon.

A wave suddenly towered over them. Linger took a breath and dived through it. When she surfaced there was no sign of Zuo Wei. She looked around anxiously: "Zuo Wei—"

No answer.

Another huge wave came crashing down like a mountain. This must be the edge of the whirlpool. She was afraid for Zuo Wei, not knowing how strong a swimmer he was or whether he would know how to cope with this danger.

"Zuo Wei!"

Still no answer. Linger burst out sobbing, like the fishermen's wives kneeling on the beach screaming for their husbands who hadn't returned from the sea, sobbing till they fainted.

Then she saw what looked like a black gourd floating not far away. She cut through the waves and clutched at it—it was Zuo Wei's soft hair. As she pulled him to her side, an irresistible force sucked them both down. If death hadn't been staring her in the face, that suction would have been enjoyable.

They had been drawn into the whirlpool. Zuo Wei, clinging desperately to her left arm, had drained half her strength away. She knew she should strike him so that he let go, or they would soon be drowned. Unable to bring herself to do this, she just struggled hopelessly, wasting her energy. Her feet and arms felt as heavy as lead. She was done for. But the thought that Zuo Wei too would be drowned suddenly cleared her head. She must save his life.

She hit him so that he let go of her. Then she caught hold of his hair again, forcing herself to calm down and relax, whirling up and down with the eddy. When they were carried close to the top of its funnel, she heaved herself to the surface and took a deep breath, thinking: There's hope for us yet!

Still tugging Zuo Wei by the hair, she swam with one arm. Her teeth were chattering, not with cold but with fear. She had a cramp now in her left leg and could only float with the current. She rallied her strength to strike out when they were on the crest of a wave, her mind set on saving Zuo Wei.

And so, with superhuman determination, she finally towed him ashore. Zuo Wei soon recovered, but Linger had strained her muscles and for a long time she limped.

"Is this all right?" the stylist asked.

Linger hardly recognized herself in the mirror. Her long shaggy mane was now glossy and swept back to reveal her broad, prominent forehead. The lock of white hair over her right temple added a touch of distinction.

"Thank you for making me look so smart," she said.

"You were good-looking to start with," answered the stylist.

Linger laughed, surveying herself closely in the mirror. "Heavens, that's the first time in my life I've been paid such a compliment."

She paid and went out. Since it was now 6:30 she made straight for the restaurant. Outside it was still raining. Again she felt a strange uneasiness. When would the rain stop?

* * *

They smiled at each other in silence. Linger looked warmly into Lu Beihe's eyes.

Beihe was scanning her from head to foot. She hadn't changed. Or perhaps had grown more attractive. Her short-sighted eyes had a gentle, dreamy look. Her dark green silk blouse with white polka dots was tucked into her white trousers. Though her clothes didn't fit her too well—they must have been made in that little town—the color scheme was distinctive.

How could Beihe have forgotten? Linger never looked ill at ease no matter what she wore. She had arrived in college in the short baggy pants of a fisherman's daughter, yet had worn them well. Her waist was still as slim as a girl's, making it hard for Beihe to believe what she had been through, according to her dossier. Only her serene expression showed that she had matured, had been through so much. She noticed Linger's ring. Strange, was it a memento?

Confronted by this Linger, Beihe suddenly lost her normal self-confidence. "So we meet again," she said, her voice conveying genuine pleasure as well as a touch of envy, which surprised her. How could anyone envy Linger?

Beihe felt she was not her usual self today. She even envied the gaily-dressed, flighty girls who were gliding between the tables with such self-assurance. She glanced at her own grey suit and felt depressed. Her whole life had been drab and grey.

"I'm so glad," said Linger calmly. The sight of Beihe had carried her back to her student days. She remembered a favorite song which she hadn't sung for a long time:

> Ah, moon,
> Tell me where, oh where
> Is the one I love?

"How have you been doing?" Beihe asked.

"All right. And you? What's become of our old classmates? I've not been in touch with them since leaving college."

Beihe fiddled with her chopsticks. . . . "In '58 Zuo Wei and I married. . . ." She watched Linger's reaction.

The news came as a surprise to Linger, but that was only natural since she had been cut off for so long. Of course Zuo Wei would marry, whether to Beihe or to some other woman. So she took this announcement calmly, having long since forgiven him for his fickleness. For over twenty years her common sense had battled with her love for him, so that now she could stand any test.

> Ah, moon,
> Tell me where, oh where
> Is the one I love?

The worst is over, thought Beihe. She went on, "We have a son, in his first year at college."

A son! Linger thought of Taotao. Had he lived he would be twenty-five now, the half-brother of their boy. "Does he take after you or Zuo Wei?" Linger was surprised how easily Zuo Wei's name came to her lips.

"Neither of us."

But Taotao had looked just like Zuo Wei. "He may have the good points of you both."

"The weaknesses more like!" joked Beihe. Well, now this unavoidable topic had been dealt with. "Let's order now. You are my guest. What would you like?"

"I like pretty well everything."

"Good, and to drink?"

"Sichuan liquor?"

"Whatever you say."

Linger had a hearty appetite and made appreciative noises over each dish. "The cuisine here is excellent. It's a long time since I tasted food like this. I wish I had two stomachs."

Yet Linger was still so thin, with a stomach like a "steel plate." Not with a middle-aged spread like her. Beihe asked with a smile, "Remember your nickname?"

"Of course I do. Steel Plate, right? I can still do two hundred sit-ups. Want me to show you?" Linger pushed back her chair as if for a demonstration.

"Sure, sure." Beihe caught her arm. "Have you had too much to drink?"

Linger picked up the bottle and looked at it. "We've drunk quite a bit but I have a good head for liquor. When I was still too small to feed myself, my dad would dip a chopstick in liquor for me to suck. If I threw a tantrum and the grown-ups stuck a chopstick dipped in liquor into my mouth, I immediately stopped crying. Dad had wanted a son to go out to sea with him and to drink with him. But he had a daughter instead. As I grew up, though, he told me he wasn't sorry, because in most ways I was as good as a boy."

Linger seemed in high spirits. Her eyes were sparkling, her cheeks flushed as she gaily chattered away. Perhaps this was a good time to raise the subject. "Comrade Zeng Linger. . . ."

"Call me Linger, please. I prefer it."

"All right. Linger. . . . You know why you were invited here?"

"For a conference."

"This conference isn't just for a discussion but to organize a new project. We want to keep you here as deputy head of the microcode group."

Linger raised her clasped hands to her breast. "What wonderful news, Beihe! That's just the job I'd love and have always dreamed of."

"You've loved too many things, worn yourself out." Beihe thought to herself that Linger must have dreamed of Zuo Wei too.

"Yes, I love everything." Linger smiled, thinking of the "ardent" in her horoscope. "But why should I be a deputy head? I'm not leadership material, you know that. In college you put me in charge of recreation and sports, but I wasn't up to it and you had to find someone else, don't you remember?"

"You won't be the head, just the deputy, the convener."

"Oh. . . ." Linger nodded. "Will the head be easy to work with?"

"Working with him shouldn't be difficult. But it may not be too easy either, that's what worries me." Beihe sounded embarrassed.

"Don't worry on my account. I'm quite content to fall in with his wishes so long as I can do this work."

"But . . . the group head is Zuo Wei."

Linger put down her chopsticks and stared wide-eyed at Beihe's lowered head. "What practical joker decided this?" she asked.

"I'm sorry, I did," whispered Beihe.

"Why? Don't you realize that's putting me on the spot?"

"I know. But surely you won't bear him a grudge for ever. Some people fall in love when they're young, then part and later, after they're happily married, can meet again like old friends. Forgive him, Linger."

Fall in love. . . .Part. No, Beihe had no idea of what had passed between her and Zuo Wei. Their secret would have to go to the grave with them.

Taotao! Had it been the fleeting romance of two young people? Like a morning glory which blooms only once? Taotao! Had she fallen in love with another one? Like a willow sapling which lives wherever it is planted? Taotao!

What was Zuo Wei to her now? She had finished with Zuo Wei. Once in a lifetime someone may fall passionately in love, but that need not prove the deepest, most enduring passion in his or her life. "There's no question of forgiving him, I don't hate him," Linger said. To tell you the truth, before I came back and even on the train here, I couldn't be sure that coming back might not rekindle my old feeling for him. But then I realized that all it rekindled was the memory of having loved him. I love the sea, the rocks, casual acquaintances, memories of our young days, and the love I had for Zuo Wei when I was young. I love super microcomputers, micro-codes, everything—except Zuo Wei. It was strange. I felt like Monkey King waking up one morning to find that the tight band around his head had been removed. For years I was incapable of love . . . you wouldn't know what that was like. It's frightening, the sensation that you've become a sour, dried-up lemon. I'm happy now because I can feel again."

"Is it because you no longer love Zuo Wei that you won't work with him?"

"Oh no, but it would be too embarrassing."

"He needs help. . . ." Beihe closed her eyes in frustration and propped her head on her hands.

Linger was amazed to hear how distressed she sounded. "How can that be? He's fully capable of doing the job."

Beihe opened her eyes. "You don't understand him, Linger. Though you were head over heels in love, what you loved was simply one side of him. I took over the whole him."

Beihe no longer seemed an insensate clay Buddha but an ordinary woman like herself, desperately worried about her irresponsible husband. This made Linger feel closer to her.

"Don't tell me these things." Linger didn't want to listen to her complaints.

"You don't understand him," Beihe insisted. "Please help him. You helped him out of so many difficulties before." Her voice was faint. When with ulterior motives she'd laid her plans, this reaction of Linger's had never occurred to her. The longer they talked the more at a loss she felt. What had become of her forcefulness and iron fist? She could only appeal to Linger's generosity.

In their third year at college Zuo Wei had contracted TB. He didn't want to drop out for a year, but the school doctor insisted for fear that he might infect other students. The third year is the start of the busiest period for college students, and for that whole year Linger attended classes, took notes, did her assignments and coached Zuo Wei—copied out notes for him as well.

She never went to bed before midnight and often had no time for a bath all week or even for washing her clothes. After sitting down beside her Zuo Wei would fan himself. "Why don't you wash your hair?"

Red in the face she would press both hands to her hair. "Oh, sorry—I forgot." She didn't like to explain that she had no time, in case that would make him feel guilty. Being ill had made him irritable. Sometimes when she drew a graph for him and explained it, he looked not at the graph but at her dirty cuff, and scolded her, "Can't you change your clothes?"

Linger would smile sheepishly and tuck the cuff underneath.

"What's the use of tucking it inside? Does that make it clean? I like girls to be immaculate, Linger. Do tidy yourself up a bit, please."

His loss of interest in her mathematical brilliance saddened her. It had been stupid of her to have thought the only way to win his love was by coming out first in mathematical contests. Before, when she had won, Zuo Wei had glanced at her with admiration. Now she'd lost his good opinion with her dirty blouse and hair. Linger despaired, because math was the only thing she excelled in. Apart from that she was beneath his notice.

She started going to bed even later. At meals she memorized her notes; while walking or riding a bike she practiced English words. Once she was knocked down by a car. When the driver offered to take her to hospital, she told him, "No, it wasn't your fault, I'm in a hurry. Never mind, I'm all right." She gritted her teeth and forced a smile, stretching and flexing her leg to show that she was not hurt, then washed the blood from her knee and her face under a tap by the road before hurrying to Zuo Wei's home to coach him.

Infection set in, so that for days she limped. She lost weight, sweated at night and had a hacking cough, but paid no attention. It never occurred to her that Zuo Wei might give her his TB.

Zuo Wei passed the end of term exams and didn't have to stay back a year. He was over his illness too. "How can I thank you?" he asked. When he was in a good mood he was an angel.

"Give me a kiss," she answered. "No, not on the lips, on my forehead."

"What's the point of that?"

"Don't you know? My forehead bulges because it's stuffed with wisdom. If you kiss it you'll do better next year in math."

"What wisdom? You're the silliest person I know."

Linger smiled and closed her tired eyes while he kissed her. She wanted to sleep for three whole days and nights, then have a bath, wash her hair and put on clean clothes. She would buy a bottle of perfume and maybe some cod liver oil because now she was sweating even worse at night. Finally she bought just the perfume that Zuo Wei liked best.

She went home to the seaside for the summer vacation. Her father was appalled by her pallid face and the dark circles under her eyes. "Do they have vampires in that school of yours? I sent you there fit and sturdy, but now you're nothing but skin and bones. Why don't they take proper care of you? I must go and sort this out with them."

"Don't talk nonsense, Dad." Linger went to flop down on the beach. She slept on the beach all through the summer vacation, as if catching up on years of missed sleep. The fresh sea breezes cleared up her TB. And at her father's insistence she gorged herself on sea food. When he went fishing he knew what to catch to build her up.

Her father put his foot down, made her take an extra month's "personal leave" and Linger recuperated. Just before returning to college she said to him: "Dad, I love you more than anyone." Linger's mother had died long ago and, out of his love for her, her father had never remarried. "When I graduate, I'll arrange for you to move into town."

"So you love your father. But your father knows you've got other things on your mind too. That's all right. Life goes on from generation to generation. As for going to the city, don't bother about that —if I leave the sea and my boat I'm afraid I won't last long. You just remember to come back often and visit me, and don't wait until you get into this sort of state before you do, looking as though you just crawled out of a coffin. It worries me too much."

But Linger never went back again. She didn't want to upset her father with the even more distressing events that followed. And they didn't let people sentenced to hard labor visit their families, so even when he died she wasn't allowed to go back and bury him.

"I seem to be running a relay race with you. You run the first two hundred metres, I run the last." Beihe gave a wry smile. She could feel a sadness welling up inside of her . . . What was happening? Maybe it was the alcohol. She ought not to drink any more, but she couldn't help reaching for the bottle and refilling both their glasses.

She felt that at some point she and Linger had changed places. And the person to be pitied wasn't Linger, but herself. It seemed as though they were on two boats brushing past one another at sea. One was a sumptuous white pleasure boat, all richly decorated in gold. Moving calmly through the water, it went wherever she wanted it to. The other was an old wooden tub, its tattered sails at the mercy of the wind, pulled this way and that. Linger was grasping the rudder, holding the oars. And the boat was being tossed about, thrown up and down on the waves.

Her boat swiftly caught up with Linger's, confidently moved in front, speeding to its destination. She was standing on deck looking back. The outline of Linger's boat, buffeted up and down, became more and more indistinct. But then the crewmen suddenly told her their boat had engine trouble, that it couldn't be fixed, that the boiler-room was taking in water. It was frightening. Why was it only today that she realized the truth: her life was aimless, would never have any destination to reach. She was only moving through a mirage. Wouldn't it be better to be an ordinary woman like Linger, to experience a woman's joys and sorrows?

"You are already above it all, because you are no longer in love. As soon as you stop loving, you have won." Beihe sipped her wine slowly and spoke calmly, as though what she was saying had nothing to do with her. I want to say something it may possibly upset you to hear. For many years, we fought for the same man's love, bravely sacrificed everything for him. But in the end we discovered it wasn't worth it. And he was totally unaware of our sacrifice, or perhaps thought it was what we ought to do." It was perhaps the first time since Beihe had become an adult that she'd exposed her true feelings. Long years of restraint had finally found an outlet. And it wasn't at all because of any special circumstance or need. Her boat had capsized, it was as simple as that.

"Don't talk like that. If you love, you don't describe it as a sacrifice." Linger didn't know what had happened in Beihe's life since they had last met. Could it be that she and Zuo Wei had been miserable together? "Have the two of you not been happy?" Linger asked sympathetically.

"No, we've been very happy. We've never quarreled, never fought. But it's the happiness of a master who does exactly as he pleases and a dutiful slave." Seeing Linger's eyes widen in astonishment, Beihe added, "Do you find that strange? Actually, you played exactly the same role in the relationship you had with him."

"What on earth are you saying? I never felt that way at all." Linger shook her head emphatically.

"Maybe it's not Zuo Wei's fault, maybe there's something wrong with me. . . . Can you still recite the names of the emperors and the great events in history?" Beihe laughed nervously, reminding her of the innumerable times she'd answered this when they were in school.

Linger thought carefully, then shook her head and laughed. "No, I can't, although I often used to get high marks for that."

"But people remember the poets Li Bai and Du Fu, don't they?"

Linger savoured the bitterness in her words. "Life gives us a huge variety of roles to choose from. You should cherish yours. Perhaps what I represent is just some kind of unambitious attitude. Think it over, some people want what you've got but never achieve it. For example, one woman perhaps becomes a professor of mathematics, but she never knows love, never experiences the joy of being a wife, and yet cannot help remembering that she is a woman. For everyone there is a point, a plateau they are destined not to go beyond. It's the same for everybody, it always has been, and you and I are no different. You . . . you shouldn't place such high expectations on Zuo Wei." She took Beihe's hand. It was very cold so she gently started rubbing her palm, trying to warm it up a little.

Beihe was flustered and distraught. "Let's . . . let's get this business settled."

"What business?"

"Zuo Wei."

Linger said nothing.

"I'm begging you, help me finish this last lap." She could avoid every danger, but she couldn't avoid Zuo Wei. Maybe what Linger had said was true, maybe there really were things in this world that people just couldn't overcome.

"Let me think about it. . . ."

"Let's forget everything that was said just now." Beihe smoothed back her hair and straightened her blouse. She seemed to have regained her composure, to have retreated back inside her grey suit. And so quickly! Linger admired her self-control.

"Of course. You didn't say anything. I didn't hear anything."

Linger gave her an understanding smile.

So Beihe had handed this difficult issue back to her. How could she and Zuo Wei work together? Beihe had told her that Zuo Wei would go to the first conference meeting the day after tomorrow. Linger had the courage to meet him then, nod, shake hands . . . but under no circumstances could she work with him face-to-face, morning till night. There were too many painful and difficult memories between them. There was Taotao between them.

She thought of the nights she'd spent studying, carrying Taotao on her back, thought of the countless times he'd made her back wet; for this day she'd endured all kinds of hardship and struggle, accumulated more than twenty years of skill and knowledge to contribute to society, had so many times rejected Taotao's demands to "play with Mummy for a little while. . . ." And now she would never be able to make it up to him. If one day she were able to make some contribution to society she thought, this contribution would include Taotao's effort too. Tears came to her eyes.

"I hate your mathematical problems." She remembered the note Taotao had left her. She'd originally promised to take him on a spring outing, then had been unable to go, so Taotao had left her that note, had gone by himself. Could it be that all of her and Taotao's efforts were destined to be blocked by Zuo Wei? Could she not overcome that obstacle?

She snuggled up inside the quilt. It was a magnificent night. She listened to the howling wind, the driving rain, the roar of the sea; she listened to her own heart, to the echo of distant waves. It was such a long time since she had been near the sea. And then it seemed as if she could hear muffled cries for help carried on the wind. Who was calling out? What were they shouting?

She couldn't sleep. She had told Beihe that she didn't hate Zuo Wei, and she knew that the whole business with Zuo Wei had finished long ago. So what was it that was stopping her? Linger hated her own weakness.

She switched on the bedstead lamp and looked at her watch; it was already a quarter past twelve. The wind had died down and the rain had stopped. As the muffled cries gradually became clearer, it seemed to be a woman's voice, howling and crying, terrifying to listen to. It was a sound Linger knew only too well, she had wailed in the same way, for Zuo Wei.

Linger jumped out of bed, went to the window and pulled back the heavy curtains to look outside. All she could see was the distant beach, and a lamp glimmering, flickering in the darkness. She gave a start. What had happened? She couldn't help thinking of the newlyweds downstairs. An ominous intuition flashed across her mind. She hurriedly dressed, slipped on her shoes and raced to the beach.

A young woman with dishevelled hair was frantically running back and forth along the sand. Running and uttering heart-rending wails. Linger ran up to her, saw that it was the young bride who'd come to the city for her honeymoon and imediately guessed what had happened.

She put her arms around the half-crazed young woman, tenderly clasping her to her bosom. Her clothes were already soaking wet and her teeth were chattering loudly. Every now and then she uttered an agonized howl. She struggled to break free from Linger's embrace. "It's me, Linger. Look at me, look at me."

The bride stared at her, seemed to recognize her. She silently raised her hand and pointed at the sea, then went limp and sank to the beach. Linger sat on the soaking wet sand, holding the girl in her arms. Motionless, they watched two speedboats shuttling back and forth, sweeping the surface of the sea with their searchlights.

Linger knew full well that it was all in vain, that the bridegroom who had ignored her warning had already been sucked into that whirlpool. And she knew that you escaped from that whirlpool only by chance. Only through a miracle, with the luck of the gods, did you escape. She remembered with absolute clarity the dread, the hopelessness, the powerlessness of being caught in that whirlpool. Then why did she not cherish things more, having been through that seemingly hopeless battle herself and having won her life? This precious experience should give her existence even broader horizons, give it even more significance. She gently rocked the young woman in her arms, thinking about death and about life, topics as old as humankind itself.

Nestled in her arms, the girl had stopped wailing. Every ounce of her vitality, her strength, had gone. Now it seemed as though only her eyes were alive, listlessly watching the two motorboats searching out at sea. Linger couldn't bear to tell her it was already too late. If she were going to accept what Linger had already understood and appreciated, she had to make her own way along this path to understanding. It was a unique, mud-sodden path.

Dawn was approaching. Out of the darkness the sea gradually revealed its incomparably solemn majesty. The light defining its contours seemed to come not from the sky, but from some enormous shining pillar piercing upwards from its depths, casting a shaft of pale yellow across the water. From the layers of clouds to the east, an exquisite pink hue slowly seeped, then became a golden light reflected from the sea. This golden light in turn burnished the sea surface and beneath its brilliance, the distant fishing boats seemed like tiny toys fashioned from gold foil.

As the tide receded, the waves continued to roar. With each roar they retreated a stage further, returning back to the depths of the sea. And, mouthful by mouthful, the sea disgorged all of the debris tossed into it by the previous night's storm. Branches, planks of wood, empty liquor bottles, tin lids and plastic bags—all were returned to the shore, to dry land.

The sea moved further and further out, becoming more and more calm. Clear and limpid, it shone with a serene brilliance beneath the morning sun. Pleasantly surprised, Linger exclaimed, "Our wise sea. . . ."

Suddenly she saw a few people who were out beach-combing start racing towards something. She helped the young woman up and ran over to the spot. It was him! He would never wake up again. Unwilling to accept anything from the land, the ocean had disgorged him too.

The young woman could neither speak nor weep. With both hands, she reached out and touched him. Inch by inch, she caressed his body from head to foot, almost as though she were trying to discern whether or not this bloated, bruised man was really her beloved husband. Then, uttering a shout, she ran towards the ocean. They caught her and helped her back to the hotel.

Linger removed the girl's clothes. They had somehow been torn to shreds—it was hard to tell whether in her anguished frenzy she'd done it herself or whether she'd snagged them on bushes while racing up and down the beach. She half-filled the bath with warm water and then gently helped the girl into it. Her circulation seemed almost to have stopped and her body was purple with cold. Linger stood watching over her, waiting until her color returned to normal. After rubbing her dry, Linger helped her into a clean set of clothes, then gave her two sedatives and put her to bed. The girl fell asleep, a deep, peaceful slumber like the sleep of the dead.

Emptying out the drawers and cupboards Linger gathered the husband's things together, then placed them in a trunk and locked it. She had an urge to take the trunk, or at least the key, and hurl it into the ocean, but she remembered what the ocean had taught her, something she could never forget—it rejected anything which was unclean.

She took a chair and placed it next to the window. Eyelids drooping, she stared out towards the distant ocean, the wise ocean. And just in that moment, she realized that somehow she had transcended yet another plane of human existence. She would be able to work with Zuo Wei. And it wasn't out of love or hatred for him, nor out of pity for Beihe. It was for this society, to do something that had some meaning.

She gently sighed, rested both hands on the window-sill and breathed in the sea air. She must wait, wait until the young woman woke up. And she would tell her that, as well as her dead husband, there were many other things in this world worth loving; she would tell the bride that her love had already been reciprocated, that she had already experienced the most profound love, the kind that is reciprocated, and that even one day of that love can be enough. So many people lived their whole lives without ever experiencing that.

Linger wanted to tell her about the meaning of the word "ardent".

That beautiful word.

Translated by Gladys Yang

The Time Is Not Yet Ripe

Breathe in—breathe out.

A pearly mist faintly tinged with green was hanging above the lake. The air was fresh and bracing.

Breathe in—breathe out.

All of a sudden Section Chief Yue saw before him a mass of lotus blooms. Had they opened overnight? He ran around this lake every morning, yet hadn't noticed them before.

Breathe in—breathe out.

The day had started out muggy and now it seemed as if it might be going to rain. Dragonflies skimmed the water; others circled above his head.

Breathe in—breathe out.

Yue had run half a lap already, yet his pace and breathing were still steady and even. He loped along, effortlessly overtaking one by one the elderly people who, though ostensibly jogging, were little faster than walkers.

Their ranks had expanded in the last couple of years. Some, you could see at a glance, were newly retired and slightly paunchy officials, who retained their old mannerisms. Jogging under the willows by the lake, each step they took seemed as weighty as solving some complex case. Some of them he came across every day. Each time he overtook them Yue would nod respectfully and smile. Their answering smiles elated him just as a green light at a crossing.

After passing the hexagonal pavilion, Yue saw Little Duan tottering along in front, his old blue gym shoes flip-flopping on the cement path, his lean flabby legs quivering under his baggy shorts. On the back of his faded purple track suit was printed the number 7. On the front was the name of their old univesity—characters indicating one of the most prestigious in all China.

There had been only twenty-one of them in their class, yet he seemed to run into them everywhere. There were three in his own bureau: Little Duan, Cai Depei and himself.

Well, no wonder. Having specialized in the same subject, most of them were naturally assigned to similar posts. Since their graduation in the 60s, their practical experience had equipped them to work independently; and now that the Central Committee set store by intellectuals they were doing all right, their social status had risen. Whenever he went down to a grassroools unit, he always found a couple of his old classmates in senior positions. Still, a section chief in the provinces could not compare with him, a section chief in a government ministry.

Yue had ascertained that he had done the best of their whole class. And now the Central Committee had a long-term plan for training leading cadres and intended to promote younger people, a "third echelon," aged between thirty-five and forty-five. As luck would have it, Yue was just forty-five.

His generation was fortunate. They had completed their formal education, and though sent to work in cadre schools in the Cultural Revolution, had come through unscathed. For over a dozen years there were no pay raises, but since 1978 they had received four increases. And now the CentralCommittee stressed the importance of middle-aged technicians, owing to the drastic shortage of competent leaders. The timing was just right!

Someone had intimated to Yue that he would be promoted to deputy director of their bureau. And this seemed to be borne out by certain events. He had recently been invited to attend enlarged meetings of the bureau Party committee, and he had been given responsibility for coordinating the designing of equipment for a major project, work involving many research institutes and factories. Though Director Chai was nominally in charge, the actual say was Yue's. Chai was nearly seventy. In a few more months he would no doubt join the ranks of the retired officials beside the lake.

These reflections made Yue assume a graver expression. Like an actor entering into his part.

He caught up with Little Duan. They had called him "little" in college because he was the youngest in the class. Though he was growing bald now, Yue still addressed him this way. Since becoming section chief he had taken to prefacing the names of many of his subordinates with "little." Apart from sounding fatherly, it also conveyed his own seniority.

Duan grinned at Yue.

"Jogging?" asked Yue, neither too heartily nor too coldly. Without waiting for an answer he loped on. This was deliberate. From now on he ought to keep his distance from his old connections. If he put off doing this till his promotion it would seem too abrupt and they might accuse him of putting on airs. For the sake of the work he must keep them at arm's length, or else they might sound him out about the intentions of the higher-ups, and that would never do. To tell them would be a breach of discipline; not to would hurt their feelings.

Duan had no understanding of this. Had Yue been promoted to deputy premier he would still buttonhole him for a chat, whether he had anything special to say or not. He did not notice Yue's calculated aloofness but put on a spurt to catch up. "Say, where were you yesterday evening? I came to see you but you weren't in."

"I was out on business." Yue didn't ask what he had wanted—it couldn't be of any consequence.

Undeterred by Yue's cryptic reply, Duan asked, "Didn't Huifen give you a message?"

"She was already asleep when I got back."

"Trust women to hold things up."

Yue shot him a sidelong glance. Little Duan's way of running was all wrong. Instead of moving backwards and forwards like pistons, his arms revolved like spindles in front of his chest.

"Did you hear? A few days ago two representatives from the personnel division came, apparently to check up on Cai Depei since our bureau has been considering him for deputy director."

At first Yue failed to take in this news, so at odds was it with his own wishful thinking. When it did sink in it nearly knocked him over; he had been so sure of getting that post himself. He sagged, unable to answer in his dismay, utterly crushed. No need to worry about the top echelon. In less than five years they would all have to step down. But the men appointed to the third echelon would stay put for twenty years, by which time he would be finished. Losing this last chance could drive him to distraction.

This shocking revelation left him more dead than alive, but he recovered sufficiently to analyze its credibility. He couldn't believe it, for the simple reason that it came from a bookworm with no real grasp of the overall situation. Little Duan was completely lacking in insight, entirely capable of turning things upside down. By comparison, Yueh, though not all that brilliant himself, at least had the experience of over twenty years in the Party.

Still, he couldn't help having misgivings. Two men from the personnel division *had* come. If it had been to check up on Cai Depei, Yue would surely have heard about it before Little Duan. Mind-boggling as this was, he had to behave as if nothing had happened. He said off-handedly, "I hadn't heard." Even if he had, he would never have casually spread such news.

Rifts suddenly appeared in the slate-grey sky, almost as though the roasting red sun inside had cracked it. Lurid sunlight shone through the clouds. The sultry humidity made Yue's scalp tingle as if with prickly heat. But one overriding thought made him calm down. This threat couldn't be averted by a fit of temper. He had to keep cool in order to further analyze the situation.

As soon as a "third echelon" was called for, Yue had reviewed all the members of their bureau aged between thirty-five and forty-five. He had assessed their political stand, qualifications, technical skill, qualities of leadership, the superiors' opinion of them, even the records of their family dependents. As to the speed and accuracy of this investigation, Yue as head of the technical section was every bit as good, if not better, than the personnel division. For he had carried it out completely on the sly. Not even his wife Huifen had had any inkling of it. In all previous political movements a lot of people had ended up in trouble through careless talk. As the ancients said: A loose tongue leads to disaster.

A thorough sifting revealed that the cadres who were professionally competent and had the ability to lead were, unfortunately, not Party members, while some Party members were lacking in ability. His own qualifications were seemingly the best. He might not measure up to the most skilled technicians, but at least he came from a first-rate university. Compared to comrades in the first echelon, his Party seniority was nothing, but he had joined the Party twenty-six years and seven months ago. He had steered clear of trouble in all the political movements, and no serious problems had cropped up in the section under him.

"Old Yue, Cai Depei has mass support, so I think he's got a good chance of being promoted. What do you think? The only possible snag is that he's not in the Party yet."

Breathe in—breathe out. Yue's steps and breathing, temporarily uneven, recovered their normal rhythm. Breathe in—breathe out.

That was the crux of the matter. Only in exceptional cases were non-Party members appointed to leading posts. It was unwritten law. A good thing too, or what a mess they'd be in. Yue now knew his best course of action. "Little Duan, the decision is up to our Party committee," he said.

Duan gave him an appraising glance, wondering whether this was official jargon or was what Yue really believed. It was the same look he gave pedlers weighing out vegetables in the free market; no matter how closely he watched the scale in their hands, they always managed to cheat him just the same. Deciding that Yue had spoken earnestly, he went on confidently, "So why don't you help him? He's under your Party branch; hurry up and get his application passed. In another three months he'll be forty-six, too old for the third echelon. As his classmate you know all about him, you were our Party secretary in college. Hasn't he been applying to join the Party for the last twenty-five years, ever since he was in college?"

Yue was disconcerted. Even Little Duan had seen the next move to be taken. Duan was watching him expectantly and had put on a spurt to keep up, his arms rotating like spindles, his steps even jerkier. Sweat from his forehead was dripping down his sallow cheeks. Strange, what business was it of his? What was he so worked up about? Still he had pointed out that the crucial thing was the three months' time limit.

"Precisely because we're classmates I can't butt in," he said. "The truth is, Little Duan, you still haven't overcome that old weakness of yours. We have to act in a principled way and pay attention to politics instead of being swayed by personal feelings. What does the Party Constitution say? We join the Party because we believe in communism, not for the sake of selfish interests or special privileges." Yue had spoken sincerely, his solemn eyes fixed on the winding path ahead. He only blinked when sweat dripped from his eyebrows.

Duan had nothing to say. He kept his eyes on the path too, listening to his shuffling feet. Compared with Yue's regular steps, his own seemed to reveal unprincipled liberalism. Yue was running along calmly, as if confident of a prize at the end of the track.

"You ought to know me better than that. Since our college days have I ever been swayed by personal sentiment?" Yue seemed to be appealing for understanding.

True, In their five years at college, Duan recalled, Yue had done his best to help all his classmates in turn to straighten out their thinking. Not for five days or five months but for five whole years he had sacrificed his own academic prospects to help them make progress. To this friend who gave them frank advice they had confided everything, even what love-letters they had been writing. But by graduation not one of them had managed to join the Party, a poor return for Yue's concern. Remembering this, Duan felt doubly contrite. Yue was right: he hadn't changed. Neither had Yue.

Once home again Yue sat motionless till his wife asked, "Aren't you going to have a wash?"

Huifen had already eyed him several times. He had to stand up then; if he sat there any longer she was bound to ask, "What's wrong? Aren't you feeling well? It's ten past seven, high time to get washed and have breakfast." His plump, easy-going wife never gave much thought to serious matters, and only concentrated on being a good housewife.

Yue could never relax at home or in the office, if there was someone else around. He went into the toilet and glanced at himself in the mirror. It struck him that he had suddenly aged. He moved closer to the mirror. Yes, the wrinkles on his forehead and round his eyes seemed much deeper than before. In dismay he reached up as if to smooth them away. The stubble on his chin pricked his hand. Maybe after shaving he would look less haggard.

He poured hot water into the basin, moistened his face with a towel, squeezed some shaving cream onto his brush and lathered his cheeks and jaw. Then he started to shave . . . three months . . . they were crucial, might make all the difference. He heaved a long sigh, thinking hard.

Damn, his wrist shook and the razor gashed his face. Blood reddened the lather. When he wiped it off he saw that the cut was a small one. He bent under the tap to rinse it with cold water, then quickly shaved around it and washed his face.

He must stall for three months, he thought. He picked up a comb to comb his thick hair, but stopped abruptly, holding it in mid-air. There was a white hair at his temples, very conspicuous among the black. What was the matter with him today? He'd found white hairs before, but they hadn't made him so conscious of his age and the passing of time. Now of all times he mustn't give the impression that he would soon be an old man.

Yue put down the comb and tried to pull out the white hair, but, slippery with cream, it eluded him. He tugged several times, but only pulled out some black hair. Never mind, he had plenty of hair, not like some of his colleagues turning bald.

His arm was beginning to ache, but he wouldn't enlist Huifen's help. Why should anybody else know about this. In any case, his wife was no more to him than a wisdom tooth one simply acquired at a certain age. Finally he pulled the hair out, flicked it angrily on the floor, then emerged from the toilet.

His wife and sons had finished their breakfast, leaving his share on the dining-table. He sat down, straightened his chopsticks then polished off the food. After wiping his mouth he took down his black, artificial leather briefcase from the clothes rack behind the door. "I'm off now," he announced, addressing no one in particular.

Huifen came out of the kitchen to call him back. "What's the hurry? Take these salted duck's eggs to Cai Depei." She thrust a dozen blue-shelled eggs in a net bag at him.

"Why take him those? He can buy some himself if he wants them." Yue stepped back frowning. What a fool he'd look, a section chief carrying a net bag of salted eggs to the office.

"What time has he got for shopping? A bachelor can't pick and choose what he eats." Again the net bag was thrust at him.

Yue could only say, "Then find a plastic bag, so that I can put them in my briefcase. I'd look a sight dangling a net bag of eggs."

"What does it matter? Everybody does it." Huifen rounded her big eyes. But being easy-going, she didn't insist and brought him a plastic bag. It had probably been a bag for milk powder. White powder dropped out as she shook it. "Did you talk to Sister?" she asked.

Wouldn't the plastic bag dirty his briefcase? "Forget it." Yue took a big envelope out of his briefcase, stuffed the net bag into it, then put it back, ignoring Huifen's question.

Wanting no part in that business, he hadn't proposed the match to his sister-in-law. His motives were strangely mixed. Should he marry his sister-in-law to Cai Depei? Could she be happy with him? He had divorced his first wife. If she agreed—and he could tell that she had a good impression of Cai—how should he treat him in future? Cai had recently been promoted to be a 7th-grade engineer. So what? Their outfit swarmed with engineers and technicians; but a 7th-grade engineer, if he had a Party card, that would be someone to be reckoned with.

"Little Duan came yesterday evening and said. . . ."

"I know, I met him out jogging."

"As secretary of the Party branch, can't you help Cai Depei join the Party?"

"He's still not up to it, so what can I do? I can't order our Party members to vote for him, can I?"

"What do they have against him?" she asked with concern.

"Well. . . ." Yue hesitated. "He just isn't ready for it yet." This was a valid pretext which could be used at any time about anyone. Everybody could be faulted in some respect. Who could claim to be a thoroughly remolded proletarian intellectual? But the fact was quite the opposite of what Yue made out. No one, in the Party or out of it, had anything against Cai, whose name headed the list of candidates to be admitted to their Party branch. Only Yue, Party secretary, kept putting off holding a meeting to discuss it.

"Well, for one thing . . . he's arrogant, lacks political consciousness and a good mass line. . . . And why did he get a divorce? Divorced his wife out of the blue without reporting the reason to our Party branch. . . . Oh yes, there's been plenty of talk." Yue could keep this up for hours. Practice makes perfect! Like a donkey turning a grindstone, plodding round and round in circles.

"Is that all?" cried Huifen. "Well, you can surely win over those Party members who hold that against him."

What nonsense! If everyone joined the Party it would cease to be a distinction. It would only produce more rivals. "You want me to drag him into the Party? I can't do such an unprincipled thing," he retorted self-righteously.

"Well, he helped you write your graduation thesis. If not for him you'd have flunked."

Ignoring this, Yue looked again at his watch—the third time in two minutes. "It's late," he said. "I must go now."

Huifen couldn't understand why, even to her and to his classmates, her husband should behave like a bureaucrat. She blurted out, "Seems to me your classmates are all making out better than you!"

This touched a raw nerve in Yue. You couldn't have it both ways. Who could have known that a time would come when technical proficiency was what counted? It was too late now. He couldn't go back to college to make up the classes he'd missed. Couldn't have the last twenty years back. Could only keep going on the path he had chosen. Cai Depei on his sunny highway was already heading for further promotion, so why should he squeeze Yue out? And he didn't mean to block Cai all his life, not after this appointment of new leading cadres.

"That's no way to talk," he answered her. "If I hadn't steered them the right way, would they have made such a good showing? I've done my best for the Party, training all these skilled technicians." Resentfully stuffing his briefcase under one arm, he marched out with an air of martyrdom.

In spite of the load on his mind, when Yue stepped into his office he surveyed every corner as usual. Because this was *his* office he examined it carefully, as if preparing to welcome some inspector.

Good, everything was just right, in its proper place. The little girl on the calendar was smiling, head tilted like a film star and looking out of the corner of her eyes. The caption underneath read: "I'm mama's only child." On another wall was the slogan, "Learn from Zhang Haidi," the current model Youth League member. The wall for an inch around this was slightly lighter in color, where a previous larger slogan, "Learn from Comrade Lei Feng," another model Youth League member, had been. It didn't look good, but never mind, he would probably put up a bigger one soon. Yue liked slogans because they showed at a glance, more effectively than circulars or reports, the central tasks of the time.

As he put his briefcase down on a chair by the window, the salted duck's eggs clinked against each other. He smiled at it as if he were contemplating his rival's skull.

He sat down at his desk rubbing his hands, then picked up the telephone, rapidly dialled a number, and asked Liu Danian to stop by. This done, he took from a drawer a *de luxe* edition of *Documents of the Third Plenary Session*, and put it in a prominent position on the desk. He then pulled out a sheaf of documents, putting some on his right, the rest in front of him. Next he picked up a red and blue pencil, lit a cigarette and made a show of going through this material carefully.

There was a knock at the door.

"Come in," called Yue without looking up. He greeted Liu Danian with a nod. "I'll be through in a minute." Having underlined certain passages in red he put down the pencil and turned to ask Liu to sit down, offering him a packet of cigarettes. "Have one. They're from Yunnan."

Liu lit up. "Recently the price of cigarettes has come down. They thought raising prices was the way to make a profit, but then found people stopped buying. . . ."

Normally Yue made no response to remarks like this. Today, however, with a tolerant smile, he commented, "After all these years of a planned economy, we still lack experience in market adjustments. . . ."

Liu took a deep drag on his cigarette. Yes, it was good tobacco. "As you can see, I'm up to my ears in work." Yue indicated with a vague gesture the documents and notebooks on his desk. "So I never got round to asking after your father."

Liu stopped smoking and sat up straight. "He's in a bad way," he said in a worried voice. "After his operation last year he picked up, but recently my mother wrote saying he's had a relapse. I'm afraid the cancer is spreading. And it's not easy to get him hospitalized."

Yue nodded sympathetically, then switched on the fan and turned it in Liu's direction. "Don't worry. I've got an idea, see what you think. A few days ago we received a report from one of the plants manufacturing equipment for our new project; but we still need to know how long it's going to take them." He took the report from a drawer and handed it over. "There seem to be some problems they need our help with. Could you go there and see what's going on? You might also meet with the other units involved. It would take you at least three months. And during that time you could help fix up your father. My wife has a classmate, a doctor there who's a hospital director. I can write and ask him to help. I don't know, though, if it would be difficult for you to leave home?"

Liu rose eagerly to this bait. "What could be better! A trip for the bureau combined with family business. How considerate of you to think of it."

"How else could you manage? With your father's illness dragging on, your mother needs help. You can't ask for a long leave of absence, and someone has to visit that plant. Only. . . ." Yue hesitated, looking troubled. "This business is rather urgent. Since this is a key project, the ministry keeps calling and asking for progress reports. I just hope there's no hitch through any fault of ours. Can you set off in the next couple of days?"

"No problem, don't you worry."

"Good. Then hand over your work today, and go home to get ready. I've got to attend a meeting now on housing. It's going to be another rough session. We've made a fair allocation, but there's no satisfying certain people," they're demanding flats for their children and grandchildren. Old Wen in our section still only has two rooms for his family of five—three generations and a grown-up son and daughter. It's just not good enough! If he doesn't get a flat this time, I'm going to take it up with the Party committee."

Everyone in the section knew that Yue had worn himself out, talked himself hoarse, trying to get Old Wen a flat, though he himself, a section chief, still had only two rooms. Luckily both his children were boys, which simplified matters.

After seeing Liu out, Yue equipped himself with a notebook and went off with an easy mind to the housing meeting. After the meeting he announced the outcome to his section: He had at last managed to get a three-room flat for Old Wen. The latter nearly kowtowed in his gratitude, as if Yue had personally built the flat and given it to him.

Old Wen's delight bolstered Yue's self-confidence. He told them earnestly, "This is the result of implementing the Party's policy on

intellectuals. We must all work harder to speed up modernization." He returned to his office exhausted yet elated, as if he had
just run a marathon. Having brewed himself a mug of excellent
jasmine tea, he settled down contentedly to skim through the
round-up of foreign news and the *People's Daily* . . . .

The telephone rang. He picked up the receiver, his eyes still on
the paper. He never missed out on a single day's news. Even
towards the end of the Cultural Revolution, when everyone was
disgusted by the lies of the "gang of four" the papers were full of,
he had still read them conscientiously.

"Hello, who's there?"

"Chen Jinghui speaking."

"Oh, Director Chen! What can I do for you?" Yue asked respectfully, putting down the paper."

"I want to know what you've done about admitting Cai Depei to
the Party."

Yue's scalp seemed to contract. So Duan hadn't just made it up!
Director Chen was in charge of personnel. If he asked specifically
about Cai Depei, it must be after discussion with the Party committee. What was the best way to handle this? He'd better watch
his step. "Yes, we mean to accept him. . . ."

"Right." Chen cut him short. "I understand he has a good
record."

Yue's heart contracted. "Yes, we've given him a form to fill in."

"When was that?" The director sounded rather displeased.

"Oh, six or seven months ago." Yue had to give an honest answer.

"Why haven't you discussed it then?" Chen was no novice in this
kind of thing; he got to the point.

Yue laughed apologetically. "We haven't been able to convene a
meeting of the whole branch. The work keeps us too busy because
we're so short-staffed. There's always somebody away on business, stopping us from having a quorum. The committee member
who's sponsoring him is out on business again at the moment." He
secretly congratulated himself on sending Liu Danian off first
thing that morning.

"How long will he be gone?"

"About three months."

"That long?"

"Yes."

"You must expedite matters so that we can make better use of our middle-aged intellectuals, according to the Central Committee's directive."

"Yes. As soon as his sponsor comes back we'll call a branch meeting."

"What's Cai's attitude?"

"Quite correct. He says that in spite of the delay he'll work as hard as he can for the Party. . . . In fact in our section we treat him just like a Party member."

Director Chen laughed. Was Yue trying to teach his grandmother to suck eggs? "All right then, see to it." With that he hung up.

Putting down the receiver, clammy with sweat, Yue stared blankly at the slogans on the wall. Well, he'd managd to get by this time, but what next? Was he one up, or was Cai? It was hard to tell what the next three months would bring. If only this nerve-racking period would flash past.

The three months passed uneventfully, with no further pressure from Director Chen. And Yue heard no more talk about Cai's promotion. The weight on his mind lessened with each passing day.

At last Liu Danian came back and reported that the problems had been solved and the equipment would be ready on time. But his father's illness was going from bad to worse.

"Don't worry," Yue told him, "we'll find some other way out."

Liu couldn't understand why Yue looked so grateful and patted him so cordially on the back. He had only done his duty, hadn't he? Strange!

Yue did not convene a branch meeting immediately, but if pressed by Director Chen he intended to say, "I've notified everyone to attend a meeting the day after tomorrow. We hope you'll come to it too." But the director appeared to have forgotten all about the matter.

One Wednesday morning in October, Yue was summoned to an enlarged meeting of the bureau Party committee. He went there confident that he would soon be a full member of that committee. After a discussion of the current major tasks, Director Chen announced, "All Party committees have instructions to waste no time in appointing younger and better qualified cadres to their leading bodies, to speed up modernization. Our bureau Party committee has considered the situation. After examining a number of comrades, we all agree that Comrade Cai Depei comes closest to the Central Committee's criteria. He has been well educatd by the Party, is of good political caliber, is in his prime and has rich practial experience. He has a sense of responsibility, works very hard and is one of our key cadres. We should recruit him as a reserve cadre for the third echelon and train him systematically for eventual promotion to the post of deputy director. . . ."

Finished, done for! Yue gave up all hope. His cigarette burnt his fingers. He darted a glance at Director Chen, afraid the latter might know what he was thinking, then tried to look indifferent, listening intently. Chen went on, "Comrade Cai Depei is just over forty-five, but the age limit isn't too rigid; and though he's not a Party member that's not because the time is not yet ripe for him, it's because we have let things slide." He glanced sharply at Yue.

Hell, if he'd known non-Party members could be promoted and that the age limit wasn't a strict one, he needn't have worried all this time for nothing!

He'd been taken for a ride! Fuming inwardly, Yue impassively accepted this *fait accompli*. What else could he do? He'd muffed it, missed his chance. When had he slipped up? He couldn't figure it out. Perhaps it was because of his carelessness, because he'd had too much faith in his past experience.

Straight after the meeting he told Liu Danian to convene a Party branch meeting for Friday morning, to discuss Cai Depei's application to join the Party.

Before the meeting Cai met Yue in the toilet.

Yue told him confidentially, "Relax, there's no problem, I've seen to it that everything will go smoothly. Whatever criticism the comrades raise, your attitude should be to correct any mistakes you have and guard against those you haven't. . . ." After a moment's thought he added, as if passing on a precious tip, "On no account try to justify yourself. Take along a notebook and write down everything that's said. Oh yes, and in conclusion promise that whether you're passed or not, you'll go on trying to remold your world outlook and to measure up to the standard of Party membership. . . ."

Cai nodded nervously and thanked Yue sincerely. "I will. You've shown so much concern for me over twenty years, since our college days, all the help you've given me...."

"Don't treat me like a stranger, we're old classmates," Yue retorted. "I'm really pleased that your application is finally going to be passed. I only wish our whole class could have the honor of joining the Party." He didn't mention a word about Cai's coming promotion, as if it had never been proposed.

As they left the toilet Yue said cryptically, "Oh, I nearly forgot, come to my place this evening—Huifen's preparing a meal to celebrate, and her sister will be there too. We've got a private matter to discuss with you." This said he walked with solemn dignity into the meeting-room to cast his sacred vote.

Translated by Gladys Yang

An Unfinished Record

I know that I will never come back to this place again. As I close the window, forcing my old cat, The Grand Historian, outside for the last time. He grows cross with me for the insult of this rough treatment. Yet he's far too tolerant and dignified to scratch or yowl at me. He merely springs back onto the windowsill, crouched, staring at me through the pane, with those apparently all-seeing eyes.

The sighing of the poplars, the clamor of the traffic, the neighbor boy playing his mouth-organ are all muffled now, more distant, removed. I wonder if the lad is growing tired, attempting the same tune over and over again since this morning. But I am finished with these sounds by now and with the pain they make deep inside my ears.

I decide to be thorough and lock the window, but it's been broken for so long that the frame is coming apart and is too misshapen to shut properly. No matter how hard I try, it cannot be bolted. It is not the fault of the maintenance staff for not doing their job properly, rather I'd call it one more symptom of my hopeless indifference to making my life more comfortable. Usually I managed by tying up the frame with string, making raising the window a terrible nuisance, but luckily I've rarely opened it. I've long been as delicate as a premature baby and the night breezes or the slightest change in temperature cause me the most mysterious complaints. I'm always wishing our hospitals had insulated cubicles for decrepit old wrecks like me to find rest in.

From being shut off so long my room has always had a musty atmosphere, like that of a cellar, the desiccated odor of a room where an invalid has been enduring for a long time. But for the last few nights I've kept the window open, wanting the flower-scented spring breeze to drift into every corner and whisk away all traces of my life which has impregnated the room for all these years. It was a warm, lovely breeze but it started me off coughing, my throat thick with phlegm, like a chimney clogged with soot. If only, like a chimney, it could be swept clean.

This is probably the last thing I will be able to do for anyone else. Or is it the first? The best thing, of course, would have been to give these walls a good new coat of whitewash, but now it's too late. Sooner or later some new tenants will move in, and I don't wish them to resent any lingering part of me. But even if they do resent any hold I may have on the place, I will be beyond hearing them.

The hospital called me the day before yesterday with the message that I should come there today. The boy who spoke to me had a voice like a singer in a musical, melodious, as though he were singing a solo. He might have been urging me to go to a rendezvous with someone who'd be waiting for me, under a silk tree or by a little bridge. But instead I'll be going through the door that leads to . . . who can say what.

After that phone call I began looking back over my life, the way people who are about to die find themselves doing. It surprised me—why hadn't I done this before? Do we really have to wait until it's too late to do anything, before we remember all those countless old debts great and small that we've no way of settling now? Each of us can only experience the mystery of death once and it seems cruel to enter this mystery feeling unsettled, with a sense of guilt. But, in fact, my life has been pointless and dull, the most ordinary life possible, containing absolutely nothing of interest for a novelist—no dramatic tragedy, no peaks of joy. Poor soul who must write my eulogy, perhaps the shortest eulogy ever, read in two brief minutes.

My very name seems to have been designed to make things awkward for everyone. It's graceless, hard to pronounce, a stiff and commonplace sounding name. Even though it appears on the spine of books on Ming history every couple of years or so, those thick tomes of four or five hundred pages costing well over a yuan are usually found on the bottom shelves of the bookshop. I always know perfectly well that when my next book comes out the previous one won't have sold out, but I can't help going to the bookshop from time to time to look and see if there are any fewer of those unsold volumes. Even one less would be a welcome sight. Then I slip away like a thief, afraid someone will discover that I'm the author of those unsold books. I've wasted all that paper, I feel, and tricked all my readers into giving me their time. It makes me heavy-hearted. I know I have little talent, but it's as if I had been bewitched into devoting all my thoughts, my soul and even my body to the study of our ancestors' history. I could not stop myself from writing. What else was there for me to live for, all alone as I am?

A moment ago Li, my neighbor, asked with some concern whether there was anything he could do for me while I was in hospital. Should he take letters and cables straight to the hospital, or wait till he could bring them along when he came to visit me? They could wait, I told him. He could get someone to take them along when it was convenient.

Apart from letters to and from publishers, magazines and a university journal which takes my articles, and very occasionally a hand-written note from another simple-minded bookworm like me wanting to argue about just where a battle was fought during some dynasty, I have virtually no private correspondence. And since I have done no work for a long time because of my illness, even letters such as these have become few and far between.

Now that I think of it, there is something to be said for having no private life: You have few attachments, and nobody has to feel distressed when you begin to fail. Still, if I do get to heaven I shall feel sad that no one on earth will be grieving for me. It's not that I don't get along with people, but that I simply haven't had the good fortune to make any friends. My colleagues in the research institute regard me with great respect and kindness. People usually treat me well, but I tend to frighten them off, or to mistake their ordinary courtesy for an expression of interest. I'm afraid I have gone on for hours and hours citing evidence to show that the Qing historian Xia Xie's *Universal Mirror of Ming History* is full of wrong judgments, not caring whether my listeners are interested, how busy they are, or if I'm trying their patience. Whenever I have to return a visit, my mind stays back with those manuscripts piled on my desk and I hope that the person I am going to see will be out. Then, by leaving a brief note I can meet the requirements of courtesy with the minimum waste of time. If I find them in I always make meaningless remarks, such as "It's gradually been getting a bit warmer recently," then repeat myself three times over. These social performances generally exhaust me, and my boorishness and lack of manners leave others at a complete loss as to how to deal with me. When I get up to leave, my host's face shows relief and gratitude that he will not have to prolong this mutual torture.

My everyday life is totally organized around work, and on public holidays when I can't go to the institute cafeteria, I'm never sure about when to eat breakfast, lunch or supper. No one has more enthusiasm than I have for the development of China's food and clothing industries: I'm eager for the time when the whole business of eating can be reduced to the simplicity of the astronaut's toothpaste-tube meals. I await anxiously the new clothing to be made out of paper, as well as the quilt-covers and pillowcases, so mine won't always be like soiled rags. Of course, I like clean clothes and quilt covers the same as everyone else, but I've had neither the time nor the inclination to bother with them.

But now these minor irritations are history and I ask myself: Has there been nothing else interesting to review from my life? Is there no more than the few yuan I owe here and there, or the call I've forgotten to return? In a fairy tale of Hans Christian Andersen, one cold, winter's night a lonely old man on the point of death sees the whole of the past through one of his cloudy tears. And it reminds me that there has been just one tear in my long, monotonous life. Not an old man's cloudy tear, but a unique tear from my youth that had the luster and the color of a pearl. It is only now, when it is about to be buried with me, that I can bear to bring it up from the deep well of memory.

It was a warm summer morning. She was laughing as she came into our office which was dark and sombre from the shadowy green vines on the wall outside the small windows. From the moment she arrived it was as if there had been another window in the room. How could she laugh so much? Whenever she laughed I laughed too, and I discovered to my delight that this made her laugh even more. I never knew what I looked like when I laughed, but from then on I was full of confidence that my face looked fine when I laughed, and that confidence made my writing suddenly speed up from one to two thousand characters a day.

I'm always losing umbrellas, one after another. It only has to rain for me to lose an umbrella—on buses, in little restaurants or bookstores I chance upon, or by newsstands. The day I left my umbrella at some academic conference, she came running after me, calling and laughing, and handed me my umbrella back. I drank in her laughter with such pleasure that I forgot to thank her.

Listening to her voice, to her laughter, and feeling that the office had an extra window in it had become the most important thing in my life. Any day on which she did not come to work might just as well have not happened. Her lightness, her conversation, her losing a button, her touch of irritation because she had been unable to buy a pretty pair of shoes all slowly infused the historical data I read and the words I wrote. I longed to share everything I had and everything I did with her.

My life seemed a lot more complicated than it had been before I knew her. I was always showing her books that I found interesting and useful, and whenever I talkd to her about our admirable forebears and the history that had ebbed like a tide I felt an emotion I had never known before: happiness.

I even started going to the pictures. I recall one film. At the time everyone said that it was a thoroughly boring film, the sort you forget all about before you're even outside the cinema. But that film, with an actress who reminded me of her, turned my heart upside down. I found a new boldness I didn't know I had. I took out paper and pen and I wrote to her, asking her to meet at nine o'clock by a little bridge, just as in the film. Even the words I used were borrowed from the film. I was drunk with the image of her running to meet me under the silk tree.

I arrived an hour early, to be there ready, to see her as she arrived. Nine o'clock passed. By ten o'clock she had still not come and I thought that I must have written the wrong date or time. That was very possible, even though I had taken the letter out of the envelope many times, read it through and put it back again before I posted it. I could not be sure that my mind had been clear enough at the time, or whether my nerves had been dependable. That sort of thing had happened to me before. Back in middle-school math, for example, an exam question asked what 50/2 was equal to. I wrote it correctly: 50/2. I don't know how many times I checked through my answers, but for its own reasons my mind stubbornly held onto 50/3, a fraction that could not be reduced any further. Could I in the same way have written midday or 8 P.M. instead of 9 A.M. ?

I became hungry, but I dared not leave the little bridge to have some lunch. I kept taking my glasses off to wipe clean the lenses, so I wouldn't miss seeing her, but they stayed as hazy as ever. I wished I had not always thrust them into my pockets with keys, nailclippers and everything else, or carelessly thrown them lens-down on my desk, until they were like frosted glass. Why did they seem now even worse than ever?

I began to wonder whether she had suddenly fallen ill. I felt so anxious that my heart was hurting. Perhaps she had an accident on the way there. If something like that really had happened I'd never have been able to forgive myself, not even if I could have gone to hell and been punished ten times over.

The bustle of traffic and people gradually died away with the day. The street lights came on in the distance and generously cast their gentle orange glow over me, as if to soothe away my disappointment. I walked home alone, among the shadows, as if the happiness of the morning had never been.

Even before I got into the office next morning I heard her laughter as I walked on the path among the green trees. Thank heavens! She was still alive, healthy and happy. For a long time I stood under the eaves of the building, not wanting to go inside in case some other impression might weaken the happiness I had lost and now recovered. My eyes were filled with tears of gratitude, even though I did not know who I should be thanking or for what.

Laughing as sweetly as ever she spoke to me, "Please meet my fiance. We would like you to come to our wedding on Saturday evening." He was strong, tall and good-looking and shook my hand heartily.

As she spoke she handed me a heavy parcel, wrapped in strong brown paper and tied with string. It was the book I had lent her. As I watched them I thought happily about their wedding, and of how well-matched they were. It was just as if my agonies of self-reproach by the bridge the day before had never happened and the letter I had tortured myself for so long over sending had never existed.

The wedding ceremony was informal, with a very free and jovial atmosphere, like a group of friends meeting spontaneously. That was very much her way of doing things. It was the first time I had been in a crowd without feeling awkward and uncomfortable.

The bridegroom sat down right next to me and told me he was a geologist. He explained to me with great gusto how the stress that caused earthquakes is built up, and how infra-red remote sensing was going to replace the geologist's compass, hammer and magnifying-glass in prospecting for the earth's natural resources. He talked to me not as if he were the groom, but as if he were a guest who had come along to offer his congratulations.

I smiled. His way of making conversation without bothering whether he was killing the person he was talking to was a bit like mine. He was very fond of his work and believed that geology was definitely very useful to the world and a truly wonderful science. I admired him and even started wondering whether I had made a mistake in studying history instead of geology all those years ago. He casually handed me a cigarette. He was evidently too happy and enthusiastic to care about such details as whether I was a smoker or wanted to smoke.

Of course I accepted the cigarette—I couldn't turn his kind offer down. He was the man she loved, and on top of that I liked him myself. I didn't know whether I was meant to swallow the evil-smelling fumes or to inhale them. From the health posters I had seen in hospitals about smoking causing lung cancer I guessed that you had to draw them into your lungs. I could not have remembered wrongly; the hospital was a place I knew very well, the place I went to most often apart from my office and my room. I choked on the first puff, but tried as hard as I could not to cough although the effort made my eyes water. It did not go at all well and I was afraid all this would alarm him and make him blame himself for causing one such misery.

She came over to us smiling, her eyes dazzling. She handed me an exquisite crystal glass and wanted me to drink a toast to them. I accepted the glass of wine and at once a humming started in my head. The drink was so strong, yet my heart remained light. It was very odd that I should have felt that way, but I was as happy as if I were getting married myself.

It was late at night when I left the place where those two people had surrounded me with happiness. It was mid-October, still quite warm, and I was in a cheerful frame of mind. I flung my jacket over my shoulders and strolled back through the moonlight. I didn't know whether it came from the cigarette or the drink, but I felt as if I were floating through the air. In a gust of light breeze I seemed to hear people whispering or laughing quietly from the locust and poplar trees by the roadside.

I remembered the Schubert Serenade stanzas the bridegroom had just been singing:

Softly my songs
Cry to you through the night

And I remembered her expression as he sang.

A pale longing welled up in my heart. I longed to have a soft shoulder beside me, longed to have someone leaning her adorable curly head against my shoulder. I would have put my jacket around her like a gallant Spanish knight wrapping his woman in his cloak.

I tripped over a stone, and looked down to see my shadow on the ground, the shoulders as narrow as a child's. I looked as if I had three less ribs than anyone else, and seemed to be painfully bent forward. It suddenly occurred to me that I was an old fool—no woman would ever want to rest her head on a shoulder like mine.

Oh my dearest, a cry to the beloved is carried on the
wind, on such a night as this . . .

As soon as I was back in my room I flung myself across my little bed, stretched out to the side of the bedside table and on it wrote the first letter of her name: S. I felt no particular misery or grief. Gradually my eyes misted up, and the letter seemed to turn into a winged angel flying lightly above my head. I closed my tired eyelids. I must have had a happy dream that night, but it was such a long time ago that I can no longer remember it clearly.

She soon left our institute and started traveling all over the country with her geologist. And the years passed. I realize that by now she must be as decrepit as I am, but as long as I don't see her again I'll remember her as she was when we parted, always laughing for no good reason, radiant and cheerful like someone who has slept and dreamt well the night before.

People say that love is endless longing, heartache and madness, wild exhilaration, pain like hell frozen over, cruel sleepless nights. I've never in all my life experienced such complicated and bittersweet emotions. But I am very grateful to her. Even though I never stood in front of her window night after night waiting for her shadow to appear, she still brought me good fortune. Because of her I knew the delight and felt the brightness that emanate from an extra window, and was happy even with just her single initial by my side.

I suppose I should be going, but there is still so much unfinished business to be done. Why am I trying to sort it out now in this last minute? I had intended to catalogue all the books now shoved into the shelves at random, and to arrange them by period so that they will be easier for their next owner to refer to. And I haven't yet corrected the proofs of the article on Zhu Yuanzhang, the founder of the Ming dynasty, and the Red Turban Army of peasant rebels.

All I managed to complete last night were two small tasks that were within my powers. I rubbed out the initial written on the side of my table, and burned that sheet of brown wrapping paper—so brittle it went to pieces at the touch—and the piece of string. I didn't want those things I've treasured for so many years to be casually thrown away as rubbish when my effects are sorted out after I'm dead, and I wasn't prepared to let a stranger's hand rub that initial out.

As I watched the last spark fly away I thought of all these years, of how I kept them as treasures because she had breathed on them and touched them. It was as if I had been a thief all these years, a thief who had stolen what she had never given me, what had never belonged to me—a tiny fragment of her life. It was probably the most shameful thing I have ever done. If I could I'd kneel before her and beg her to forgive me. She is so good and sweet and generous that I'm sure she'd have forgiven me and said, "In a long life everyone does something wrong."

As I lift the net bag with my washing things in it my toothbrush slips out through a hole and when I lean over to pick it up I take another look around the room that has shared half a lifetime with me. My old table stands isolated in the middle of the room, there irrelevant and unconnected, like some obscure island in the Pacific that not even the most third-rate explorer would bother with. The springs of my folding bed gave out a long time ago, and it sags very low to the floor. The yellowing and blackened walls have an air of decrepitude, just like my dried-up face, as they lean feebly together around my jumble of furniture. Even the books on the shelves look sick and crippled, without even one fine leather volume with gold lettering to give the bookshelves a touch of distinction. All the large soft cover books lie on their sides, drooping out over the shelves like wilting foliage taken too long ago from a tree. Dusty cobwebs sway from the ceiling and in the corners of the room.

The sight of this dispirited room fills me with regret, as if I have wasted its youth for nothing. It could have been as clean, bright and tidy as other rooms. And as I see this, a new nameless feeling begins to overwhelm me. I cannot give it a name, but from it I sense that my whole life from beginning to end has been lacking in something.

Lacking what? My eyes sweep the cluttered bookcases, across the books I've scrimped and saved for a lifetime to buy, or written with my own sweat and blood. I realize that I have all of these things to leave to a lot of people, but no one unique thing to leave to one special person. And this is the lack, this is what is missing.

I know that Dong from the personnel department of the institute will finally sign in the space on the operation form where the next of kin's signature is needed. But if only there could be one beloved face, wrinkled like mine, sitting on the bench outside the operating theater, anxious for me, quietly sobbing for me. If only on my bedside table there could be good things to eat prepard by her own hand. My head, which has worked through mountains of waste paper like a mechanical recording machine, has at last shown its boundless creative genius in imagining the food. These delectable treats look, smell and taste delicious as I eat them from the aluminum canteen that's been scrubbed till it shines.

But, in fact, the time for these imaginings is finished. Soon my ashes will lie in their urn which will be placed on an obscure shelf to gather dust for three years, until at last they are flung away. Nobody will want to keep them. And even less will anyone want to mingle her ashes with mine.

There is a soft noise at the window. The Grand Historian's ugly face is pressed against the glass, his expression one of concentration and bewilderment. His usual coldness and superiority have vanished. I look away at once, not wanting him to see the loneliness in my heart. We have seen many things together and he should not feel bereft as I leave him. He scratches at the pane with his front paws like someone knocking at a door.

Years ago I picked him up in the street and brought him home. There wasn't an uglier, lazier cat in the world. His short tail was like a piece of rag. His greyish, dull fur was so dirty that you couldn't tell his true color. He had been sitting in the middle of the road, not moving or making a sound, while the torrent of bicycle, lorry and car wheels flowed past him. He just sat there like a pile of rubbish that had been dumped on the road, as if he had stopped caring whether he lived or died. It would only have taken a small turn by a single wheel to squash him flat.

I gave him a bath in my foot-bowl and I'm inclined to think he failed to understand my good intentions and reckoned that I was trying to skin him aive. He drew blood where he clawed the back of my hand as he jumped onto my radio, which was playing at the time and felt warm to his paws. He stared at me with caution and silence. After several days of very close observation he acknowledged me as a friend, but even then, with a touch of condescension. Whenever I sat at my desk writing furiously he always looked at me with a certain superciliousness. His manner said: "What you're scribbling is all useless nonsense, old friend." When I read my articles aloud to myself, wagging my head, he lazily shut his eyes and purred rhythmically. And when I gazed with adoration at the letter written on the side of the table every night before going to sleep he sat by my pillow with his head on his front paws and stared at my face with a pitying, mocking stare. I am still covered from head to foot with little red flea bites, just as I was when he first came to me.

Every morning he used to stroke my thinning white hair with his paw, telling me to stop lying in bed gazing vacantly at the ceiling. Whenever I sat down to take a rest and shut my dim old eyes he'd spring onto my lap, or lick my hands with their protruding blue veins and slack, wrinkled skin, or grasp my wrists and nip my fingers, but very carefully so that he never hurt me.

It was because of him that I finally started paying some attention to feeding us properly and sometimes treated us with cold meat. I would spread it out on the greasy wrapping paper, and as he crouched on the other side of it facing me, we would take our time savoring the meat together. Sometimes my imagination would run free and I'd think that if we could both have had a drink we would have clinked glasses and drunk to each other. Thank God for sending me an animal soul, so patient and understanding, never using its tongue to harass or harm me. I am praying that the next tenant will adopt The Grand Historian and that maybe even he will liven up a bit. I'm sure he can, and that someone will take him in, but I can't be certain.

I have been silently hoping that the next tenant will be someone full of life who will decorate this room like other rooms with sheer white curtains, a gleaming crystal fixture hanging from the ceiling, a woven table-cloth, a beautiful landscape painting on the wall and a vase of pale yellow roses. . . . A girl would be best. She'd be bound to have her boy friend mend the window bolt so she could open it wide and allow the moonlight to come flooding in, the breeze to waft in the scent of locust blossom in May, and perhaps even strains of Schubert's Serenade. Then the room will have the joy and pleasure I was never able to bring to it.

What else is there left? Oh, yes, so many longings I still feel, vividly, acutely, now that the time is used up. They have not faded but hang suspended in my heart.

I used to think that all my emotions belonged in the past, to history, but I know that I yearn for the future just like everyone else. Even as life draws to a close, I realize that I have never understood myself completely . . . If only. . . .

But now it certainly is too late to do more, to be more in this lifetime.

Translated by W.J.F. Jenner

Under The Hawthorn

How did the song go? Wu Cangyun's thoughts drifted back in time to his youth when he was filled with fresh hope, when the words had little meaning . . .

Hawthorns, hawthorns, little forest,
Covered with your blossoms white,
Why do you hold such sorrow?
Hawthorns, my hawthorns, my delight.

The solitary bench in the orchard where Wu Cangyun spent his days had been set under the hawthorn. It puzzled him that only this one was there. If a bench would be good for people to rest upon here, why hadn't they placed one under every tree? The upper boards were warped so that the bench resembled a cripple with a twisted shoulder. Two of its legs had sunk deep into mud at one end and its white paint had long since vanished, except for the traces still noticeable at the joints. It must have been a pleasant sight once, a broad white wooden bench, in the shade of the green trees.

This was an orchard of apple trees with just the one hawthorn among them. Perhaps the nursery had carelessly sold a hawthorn sapling along with the apple saplings, and the planters had not noticed that it was different from the rest. The boughs of the apple trees, unpruned for many a year, had been allowed to run riot, growing where they pleased. A few tiny green newly-formed apples, which looked as though they would never mature, were scattered on the branches. It would have been difficult for any passer-by on the path outside the orchard, who was not looking out for it, to discern the old bench where Wu sat, hidden as he was, as if behind a thick green curtain.

But between the many branches one could, with effort, observe the patients standing on the balcony of the sanatorium's first-floor ward. Forty minutes remained until visiting time, but already they were crowding onto the balcony, gazing at the path from the main gate of the hospital. As they pressed against the balcony railings, thrusting out their chests and craning their heads forward, they looked much like penguins. Their faces were all turned, as if they had just heard the order, "Eyes Left!"

Wu Cangyun never looked toward the gate. With no wife or family, and with most of his old friends sick or gone, none were left to write or visit him. Old Juru was the only one who came there occasionally. Like the old hawthorn, Wu Cangyun's history was obscure, dim. He had lived a narrow, almost invisible life, one which became devoid of meaning, leaving him no comfort, desire or will. He no longer even questioned why he was there.

He knew in great detail the life stories and the hopes of the other inmates. But he had no story of his own to tell. Whenever a nurse came to the ward to call someone to the telephone or to deliver the patients' mail, he always turned away as if he were ashamed. He constantly felt the inmates' hard stares at his back, stares which humiliated, even frightened him. All because he had no story to tell. He had nothing to interest anyone and over time he seemed to become a completely silent being, a grey mouse hiding in his corner.

One morning at eleven when the attendant came in to deliver the mail as usual, he had been sitting alone on his bed. She ignored him but he observed her, and after she finished putting the letters on the bedside cupboards and he heard her steps receding down the hallway, he cautiously picked up a letter. He examined it for a long time, lightly running his fingers over the image of the Great Wall on the pale blue stamp and carefully deciphering the hazy date of the postmark. He felt an extraordinary intimacy with the rough envelope which had on its back a picture of a graceful woman, clothed in ancient garb. He guessed at and could almost see the words inside which warmly described all the important and trivial family news. The strange thing was that the letter, which was obviously meant for him, had by some conjuring trick suddenly been turned into a letter to someone else.

On a day which appeared as numbingly empty as all the other countless days which had preceded it, the attendant stepped into the ward and called out Wu Cangyun's name. She was calling him to the telephone. He looked at her with hesitation, not knowing whether he should respond. Could it be a mistake?

"It's a lady," she urged him, with a touch of congratulation in her voice.

The other patients stared at each other, then became very excited for him. "Go on . . . Answer it!" they said. They eagerly watched him leave, much as if they were watching a chicken go off to lay her first egg. Maybe now he would be like them, qualify as one of them, and finally gain their recognition.

The woman on the other end of the telephone was weeping. "Is that Wu Cangyun?" she asked in her grief.

It really was a woman! He studied the telephone in his hand, stupefied, as if he did not comprehend what it was. "Yes," he finally replied, "may I ask who is speaking?"

"I'm Juru's wife. I thought you might want to know . . . Juru is dead. The farewell is tomorrow morning. . . ."

He understood nothing more she said and finally he heard only her sobs. He was shocked and unable to speak at first. He fought off a sickening moment of panic while a cold, sinister chill rose up from the soles of his feet. But then he came back to his senses when he was struck by how incredible it was: How could someone die who'd always been virtually non-existent?

Juru, his friend, hardly more than a voice, sometimes distant and sometimes near, but always a voice with integrity and clarity, like a French horn playing a low-pitched round. The image he carried in his mind was of Juru listening intently, his head turned to one side as if he heard sounds inaudible to everyone else, sounds not only from without but from within his own heart.

"Did you say that Juru has passed away?" he asked, uncertain that this wasn't a dream, a trick.

Again all he heard from the other end was crying.

"How . . . ?" he began to ask.

"Suicide. Hanged himself."

A rage came across him, then a paralysis. He replaced the receiver. How could it be? he asked himself. Could Juru have killed himself? Never! He would not believe it! Juru must have slipped his head into a noose without realizing what he was doing. Yes, that was it. He understood Juru. Of course . . . a man who lives his life as quietly as a shadow does not do anything so conspicuous. There was no question in his mind, these were lies, more lies about good men, about his loyal friend Juru.

But how could his wife say it was suicide? She of all people knew the truth—she was closest to him. Unbelievable that she would even say it. How could she be fooled, lied to? It made things look very bad for Juru and he was appalled.

The other inmates had smiled expectantly at him when he came back to the ward, but when he sat sullen and silent, and the minutes passed, the lines on their faces had stiffened up again. He saw that their interest had waned, but how could something like this be turned into a story to tell them? Like the rest of his life, this too was senseless and vacant, futile to speak of. Unspeakable.

The farewell to Juru's body had been so horrifying that Wu Cangyun had not been able to bring himself to go to the memorial meeting, leaving his grief disorderly and unexpressed. At the farewell he was first startled to see Juru's face thickly plastered and covered with garish colors, made up like a circus clown at a masquerade party, instead of as an old cadre on his way to the crematorium. Juru's face in life had been so colorless that one had had to look carefully to detect his eyebrows and eyelashes. His body looked so strange that Wu Cangyun wondered if the undertakers had made a mistake. This was not Juru but some temptress or seducer they had put on the bier to fool him and have fun out of his alarm and distress. Any minute he expected her to sit up with a wink, slap her thigh and throw him an enchanting smile. He almost shouted, "Get that witch out of here! Who is she? Why do you torment me?"

If Juru's wife had not been weeping so bitterly beside him he might have remained confused. But her crying, too long and too loud, was inappropriate for Juru and disconcerting to Wu. When other people arrived, their coments had stunned him, too:

"Why did he do himself in?"

"Well, he was a failure." Or "He was a fool."

How cruel and ridiculous!

"His wife wasn't good to him."

That was wrong. Juru's wife had cared for him, even though she was now saying his death was suicide.

"He certainly had some dark secret."

What dark secrets might Juru have had? Not long before his death, Juru had said, "Cangyun, I feel as though I have no more life left in me."

"Don't imagine that," he told him. "It's just that you haven't been feeling very well recently."

Juru had thought for a moment before answering. "Perhaps you're right." They had never brought up the matter again. Surely this did not amount to any dark secret which could have driven Juru to take his own life. No, he understood Juru and he must make them understand, too.

Their whispers and mutterings continued, louder, disrespectful, contemptible. . . ." It wasn't suicide!" he protested indignantly to everyone as they entered or exited. . . ." Juru didn't know what he was doing when he slipped his head into that noose."

Some who passed him looked blankly at him or averted their eyes. Others laughed disdainfully as if he spoke utter nonsense. Those who would stop and speak told him that no person or illness drove him to his death—say what you like, Juru himself made the decision to put his head into that noose and choke himself to death.

Wu Cangyun was beside himself, livid. "No, you can't prove it. . . ." He gasped out his words. "I tell you it was his illness that put him in a trance . . . you know cancer is fatal—it can't be beaten—don't you realize . . . the trance made him put his head in the noose."

They seemed unmoved by his words. "Look," he said, trying to calm himself, "by your logic people killed by the fumes from their coal stoves commit suicide because they fail to seal their stoves properly. . . ." He waited to see their response.

"Ignore him," they said. "He's a mental case."

Of course, Wu thought, this must be what they say about Juru, too. They were going too far. They were lunatics, not he. Why couldn't they see? They twisted everything around. Juru was the last of his friends and they would have him scandalize his name and leave him in dishonor. He argued with them until he was red in the face, until no one was left, parting with them all on bad terms.

Wu Cangyun came again to sit on the bench, once more to resume his vigil beneath the solitary hawthorn. And there he thought of Juru, although the memory was fading. The only thing he had to remember him by was a tape of his voice, recorded from the radio broadcast when Juru read his story, "The Gravestone." He had listened to it so often that now it played through in his mind. Juru's voice seemed to emanate not from the vibration of his vocal chords but from a deep, unhurried flow within Juru's very body. He was especially moved by one passage, although puzzled at whether it was Juru himself speaking, or the old stonemason narrator as he carved his own tombstone. It began after a long pause.

> *Whenever the north wind blew,*
> *the pounding of the waves*
> *as they broke upon the rocks*
> *carried up to the church.*
> *I pulled back my hammer,*
> *put down my chisel, to listen*
> *to the rhythmic, monotonous sound.*

Was it the lonely old carver, listening intently, or was it Juru deep in his trance? Wu Cangyun could never be sure now.

He would always believe that Juru could not kill himself. If Juru died, it was certainly by some other cause, for some other reason. Juru's life would end finally, only when all of his spirit had flowed away, departing slowly and unhurriedly. Death could not stop his spirit from wandering everywhere, utterly fascinated, listening intently to the noisy world he had left behind. And when he'd finished listening, when he had heard everything, he would exclaim in his deep calm voice, "Beautiful! Oh, beautiful!"

From the poplars on either side of the path came the chirp of the first cicada, uncertain, breaking off then starting again, ending as suddenly as it had begun. He heard the swish of footsteps on the grass and the whisper of branches being pushed aside. A little boy whose hair had not been cut for a long time was walking towards the bench. His pajama jacket was so long it hung below his thigh, like a short overcoat. The boy appeared to be seeking shelter behind the curtain of green.

He asked cautiously, "May I sit on this bench for a while, please?"

Wu Cangyun had thought he would always be alone here, that no one would ever come to sit beside him again. He moved to one end of the bench and patted the empty space beside him. "Take a seat, lad," he said.

"I'm not a lad—I'm a girl!" she corrected him, in a high voice filled with embarrassment. She seemed distraught, as if she had been holding herself back as long as she could bear, just waiting to speak this out.

He felt confused. "*Are* you a girl?" he asked, looking at her carefully. He was uneasy since he could not tell whether she was or was not.

"Yes, I'm a girl. They keep giving me medicine and injections I don't want—that's why I look this way." Her mouth puckered up and she started crying forlornly.

She worried him. Had he upset her with his question? "There, there . . . poor child. Don't cry. Shall I tell you a story?" He regretted his offer at once since he could not tell stories. Even those he might have known once were forgotten now. The most he could do for her, if she really wanted to hear it, would be to meet her again one day and play her the tape of Juru reading "The Gravestone." But could he be sure that she would enjoy it? What could it possibly mean to her?

So there they were: She wasn't a boy and he couldn't tell a story. She looked so dejected and he wondered why someone so young was in the sanatorium. "What's wrong with you?" he asked.

"Nothing," she answered in her high-pitched voice.

Had he put his foot in it again? "Then . . . why are you here, in this sanatorium?"

"Who knows! I don't. One day in school the physical education teacher told me to do a somersault. After I did it my head started aching. When it ached for days and I saw things upside-down, they said I was ill and took me to a hospital. They gave me injections, medicine and operations too. All my hair was shaved off

—it still hasn't grown back properly. Oh, it looks horrible.

He began to speak, "No, it's . . ."

She leaned over and interrupted him, "Mind you, I don't always see things upside-down; it was just that once or twice."

"Yes, I know how that is and I believe you. I'm sure you see things correctly."

A lizard ran out of the grass and with its long jaw stretched out in front, looked to either side. After a moment of philosophical reflection it climbed across Wu Cangyun's slipper to the top of his right foot. Despite the itchy sensation, Wu stayed absolutely still. The lizard blinked, suspicious of the unfamiliar terrain, then had a flash of enlightenment and opened its mouth. If Juru were there he might have been able to hear what the lizard was saying.

"Uncle, do you want to hear more?"

"Yes, of course."

"My parents have no money left. They had to borrow to pay for my care. First 600 yuan from Grandmother, and then 800 from my aunt. . . ."

This child, at so tender an age to have so much hardship, Wu Cangyun thought. "Don't worry about this; these are your people, your family. They love you."

"They won't let me go home." She began crying again, covering her face with her hands. "How I miss my family." When she took her hands away she didn't wipe her tears but let them drop one at a time to the ground.

He saw one tear fall onto a blade of grass, and the weight of it was more than the stalk could hold. It bent over, allowing the tear to roll down its side and soak into the earth. Perhaps Juru would have been able to hear the sigh as the tear vanished into the earth. It seemed as if Juru, in his death, had taught him more about how to see and feel life."

"Are you listening, uncle?"

"I hear you."

"We live deep in the mountains and no one ever comes to see me because of the train fare. I was so homesick I begged Father to buy me a ticket so I could go home just once. When I walked in Mother and Grandmother cried—everyone cried."

"Surely you will go home soon again," he told her. "Can you believe that?" He was silent about his own doubts.

"After the first hospital I told my father I wouldn't have any more treatment, but here I am again. The money is spent and they say I'm still not well. And sometimes I do see things upside-down. . . ." She caught her breath and looked panic-stricken. "You're the only person I've told that to. You mustn't ever tell the doctors."

"Come, come . . . your secret is safe with me. I, like you, know how it is to wait and to yearn." She seemed to have an endless flow of tears which fell rapidly, as rain upon the grass. The blades dipped down and touched the earth, and almost like Juru, Wu Canguyn thought he heard the green blades rustling against each other.

But what of this child . . . what could he do for her? How could he comfort her? She needed to start all over again. "Listen," he said, looking directly into her face, "I can see very clearly that you look just like a little girl."

"Really? Can you see that?" she asked with a calmer voice. Her tears and sobs stopped at once.

"Yes," he said with great conviction. "There is no question: You are yourself, a girl, and you can see perfectly well. You can be strong."

She looked up. Her red, tear-stained face was transparent, like a clear sky after rain. She folded her arms in front of her chest and peered through the openings in the branches at the patients still watching so eagerly from the balcony.

"They're waiting for their visitors," she explained quietly.

"Yes, they're waiting," he replied softly.

They were no great distance from the balcony, yet far enough to see the path which had brought them both to the bench beneath the hawthorn. They stopped to listen. . . .

And without even being aware of it, Wu Cangyun had found at last, within his compassion, the beginnings of his story.

Translated by W.J.F. Jenner

Who Knows How to Live?

There was a new ticket-seller on the Number 1176 bus. She was thin and fragile, like a piece of delicate glasswork. She might have been labeled "handle with care." Every time she pushed and squeezed her way through the crowd, Shi Yanan couldn't help worrying: She's going to break to pieces. Wu Huan, on the other hand, would think: What's one more ticket sold? A few extra cents won't make or break the bus company. Why does she have to be so meticulous about selling tickets?

Her mouth was slightly upturned at the corners, as if in a perpetual smile. The deep, penetrating eyes on her thin, pale face never seemed quite focused on the person or thing directly in front of her. They wandered instead somewhere far off giving people the impression that she was forever deep in thought or lost in a dream.

But when those pensive, dreamy eyes rested gently on you, when she politely asked you where you were going, whether you needed a ticket, you could not help being reminded of good manners once thoroughly cultivated, now totally disregarded. Rain or shine she did her job with equal perseverence, whether it be checking for tickets or standing outside the bus using her frail arms to help passengers squeeze on.

But it was evident that her physical strength could not support her strenuous task. During the padded coat stage of early spring, the tip of her cute little nose dripped tiny beads of sweat while strands of hair, as if also wanting to get in on the action, persistently slid out of her hairclip, covering her eyebrows and blocking her vision. If it weren't for the fact that the passengers were all perfect strangers, someone on the bus might have put the lock back in place for her.

Young men seemed to feel uncomfortable around her. Only Wu Huan seemed unaffected, carrying on as usual with remarks, for instance, about a kid who had just climbed in through the rear door: "Look at that hick. He probably got his suit from the commission shop."

His friends thought it was funny. Moreover, they were appreciative of the fact that Wu Huan had temporarily relieved them of their uneasiness.

Shi Yanan glanced at her. She hadn't heard a word Wu Huan said but was concentrating on counting tickets and returning change. Her nylon gloves were obviously well-worn. There was a hole in the seam, exposing a slender thumb and forefinger.

If Shi Yanan saw right, Wu Huan also managed to steal a quick, almost imperceptible, glance at her.

The young workers in the factory all belonged to their own "cliques." The combinations they formed were the result of life's naturally sifting processes. Shi Yanan's clique was definitely not the same as the hick's. They wouldn't be caught dead whistling at girls from behind, or teasing them, or hooting. Shi Yanan and his gang weren't like those who went around wearing ridiculous clothes either. Compared to those young men they had a lot more class.

After all, how many people would carry around a book by Spinoza as Wu Huan did? Not that anyone would necessarily know why Wu Huan was reading it. The main reason was simply that it was obscure and erudite. Therefore, people would think he was a man of refined taste and profound thought. Wu Huan was the kind of person that no matter what happened in this crazy world of ours, he would never get excited or moved, or alter the set patterns in his life. You could never make him lose sleep or spoil his appetite, never catch him shedding a tear for anybody. If Shi Yanan were to lament the fate of a hero in a book or a movie, sometimes fighting back tears, Wu Huan would simply yawn even more loudly, shrug his shoulders and ask disapprovingly, "Why are you taking it so seriously?" Even with Vietnam's invasion of Kampuchea, it seems he knew about it for years. "I could tell it was going to happen all along." That was all he had to say. The practical, daily matters of life only evoked in him a reaction of disgust, or contempt. He was a hard-core cynic, and nothing escaped his biting sarcasm.

In the company of Wu Huan, Shi Yanan always felt unrefined, a philistine, because he could never copy Wu Huan's cool, carefree, almost transcendental manner. Shi Yanan loved sensations like light, color and sound; he loved the little things in life like the marathons during the Spring Festival, lining up in front of the post office to buy the broadcasting timetable, even eavesdropping on the bantering in an unbearably crowded bus. Also, he didn't care for Wu Huan's tapes of the Hong Kong star Miss Fragrant Dream singing popular songs like "Blue Earring," and "No One Else Like You." To him, each note sounded like a vengeful bite out of a tough turnip. But he could never bring himself to speak his mind. He certainly wouldn't risk Wu Huan mocking him for not being "sophisticated," not being cool.

Cool? Cool! Why, when Wu Huan brought him his letter, did his face suddenly turn the color of lobster that had just been thrown into a deep-frying pan. He felt embarrassed to death. Why did he have to blush? What would Wu Huan think?

Looking at his blushing face, Wu Huan asked nonchalantly, "Who's it from?"

Shi Yanan tried in vain to brush his question off with a vague excuse.

"A love letter? How come I didn't know you had a girl-friend?"

Shi Yanan gave a noncommittal smile. Letting him think it was a love letter was certainly better than his knowing the truth. If Wu Huan found out that he was secretly writing poems, well, that would be enough for him to be made a laughingstock.

Shi Yanan waited until he was alone before he fished the letter out. He stared at the powerful strokes of the handwriting on the envelope. It was as if everything he worshipped about this writer was right before him. He was pleased, but nervous. He had read some poems of this author in a magazine. The poems were like a breath of fresh air that vibrated a harmonious chord in his own heart. Lest this chord dissipate in the breeze, he immediately recorded his thoughts and mailed them off to the author. He never thought his blunt, impulsive letter would receive such a cordial response. He could visit at his convenience so that they could discuss poetry. But the thought of actually presenting his poetry to the talented writer terrified him; it was like being caught naked. He wasn't sure his courage would hold up.

The bus suddenly seemed packed. One old lady wanted to buy a ticket to the Xidan Market. The ticket-seller mulled over her request, trying to remember how much it cost. A sharp-tongued rascal by her side beat her to it, "ten cents!"

With so many people buying tickets, the ticket-seller couldn't think straight and was about to tear off a ten-cent ticket when Wu Huan whispered to her, "It's only five cents, not ten." She blinked a few times, then blushed and said apologetically, "It's so busy, I almost sold the wrong ticket." She looked at Wu Huan gratefully and her mouth turned up at the corners even more than usual.

The sharp-tongued rascal smiled cockily. Wu Huan moved towards him. Seeing Wu Huan coming his way, and noticing the man's huge, athletic physique, the rascal immediately sucked in his smirk.

Shi Yanan couldn't help admiring Wu Huan. Everything seemed to come so easily to him. Even getting a girl to like him was for him a breeze.

Now why was Wu Huan smiling in such a smug, show-off way? It seemed Wu Huan was always extremely status-conscious. His condescending smirk depressed Shi Yanan.

The ticket-seller got to know them better with each passing day. If someone was missing, she wouldn't say much, but her eyes expressed her concern. They seemed to ask, "Where's the one with the leather jacket? Is he sick?" When it came to checking tickets though, she never compromised; she remained as stubborn as ever.

Wu Huan tried to crack her stubbornness. He never showed his monthly pass right away, but would always wait for her to say, "Comrade, your ticket?" Only then would Wu Huan reach into his pocket reluctantly. Sometimes he would bluff her with his employee's card, or wave his wallet instead. In any case, he always fumbled about for quite some time before finally cooperating.

When Wu Huan was in the right mood, though, he could really be a saint. He would help maintain order on the bus, transfer money and tickets for her, and make sure everyone getting off had a ticket. He did it all so very naturally, casually, that it put all the other men who wanted to help her but were too afraid of losing their masculinity to shame. To Shi Yanan, this chivalrous behavior was all a game, like a skit put on by some students at a drama institute.

In order to ride her bus, Wu Huan, who used to be late every day, started getting up especially early and waiting at the bus stop. After work he wouldn't rush home as usual but would stand in the wind and let bus after bus go by until 1176 arrived. The rest of the gang started teasing him. They all thought that Wu Huan had fallen head over heels in love, trapped just like so many others. Not only did Shi Yanan not find this funny, but he felt a kind of ambiguous resentment. It was as if they were all diminishing the reputation of this fine young lady.

Wu Huan asked him with a chuckle, "What's the matter with you?"

"Nothing. You . . . what do you want from her?"

"What do you mean what do I want from her?" And then, like an adult teasing a child, Wu Huan asked, "What do you want me to want from her?"

Shi Yanan remembered one summer when he was young and his father took him to the seashore for a vacation. In the ocean water's ebb and flow, one particularly beautiful shellfish was continually carried ashore. Perhaps it expected that it would always get swept into the ocean again, but that last time never came. Instead, it was picked up by a playful youth, Shi Yanan. Nurtured outside the ocean waters, the beautiful shell quickly lost its life. A feeling of guilt for having killed such a beautiful thing stayed with the child for a long time. Shi Yanan might have spent his whole life harboring an unexplainable depression if there had not been an incidental event that relieved him.

Just as Shi Yanan stepped away from one of the museum paintings to appreciate its effect from a distance, a young woman blocked his line of vision. He moved to the side a few steps and adopted a new angle. Then he glanced at the woman's profile and recognized the ticket-seller. He couldn't say for sure what prompted him to follow her stealthily around all afternoon. She evidently liked simple, pastoral landscapes; open fields under a silvery moon; small calves eating grass in the dense shadows of trees; weeping willows brushing the surface of the river; rain-cleared skies through which petals of a dandelion were being carried by a light breeze. The paintings gave her an indescribable pleasure. Her expression right then and there would have made a beautiful painting. And nobody else's presence in the painting, not even Wu Huan's, could have spoiled it.

After she left, Shi Yanan examined those paintings she seemed to like best. One just doesn't expect an ordinary ticket-seller to have such a refined sense of aesthetics. He thought of her getting on the bus every morning still chewing her last mouthful of a fried breakfast cake. He could always spot Wu Huan's involuntary, but sympathetic smile. From that smile, Shi Yanan thought to himself Wu Huan probably just had a breakfast of bread and butter, milk with cocoa or some other beverage. Was it necessarily more noble or elegant than her fried breakfast cake?

Wu Huan felt out of sorts all afternoon. He had no idea how she reacted to his message yesterday, and he couldn't believe she would have no reaction at all. Hadn't life for him been an uninterrupted series of green lights?

He thought of the silly question Shi Yanan once put to him, "You —what do you want from her?"

Well, what? If he said he loved her, it was really more of an uncontrollable desire to conquer her. Why did she have to treat him in the same way she treated everyone else? Why was she always so kind, friendly, courteous? Why was she always helping people on and off the bus, finding a seat for that crippled boy who got on at Prosperous Lane and got off at the Xidan Market? Why, from the first day he saw her, didn't she pay any attention to his efforts to attract her attention? Wasn't life supposed to afford him far more privileges than others?

As soon as they got off the bus, Wu Huan quickly got rid of Shi Yanan by saying, "You go first. I think I left a book on the bus yesterday. I'd better go and look for it." As soon as he saw Shi Yanan get on another bus, Wu Huan bounded back to the 1176. The ticket-seller was sweeping out the bus with a broom. She raised her head to meet Wu Huan's burning stare.

"Did you find a book on the bus yesterday?"

"What book?" she asked in a business-like manner. It seemed she had prepared herself for this scenario.

"A *Dream of Red Mansions*, Volume I."

"Did you have your name on it?"

"It was stamped Wu Huan."

"Ah, yes." She walked to the front of the bus and fished the book out from a bookbag hanging on a hook. She handed it to Wu Huan and then continued sweeping.

Wu Huan opened the book instantly and found the unaddressed, unsealed letter still stuck inside. He pondered for a minute. Had she or hadn't she read the letter? If she hadn't, why didn't she give the book to the lost and found office? Ah, so she must have read it. And she purposely kept it, knowing that he would come for it later! If that was the case, why didn't she take the letter?

"Excuse me . . ."

"Is there anything else?"

"Why didn't you place this book in the lost and found?"

"I thought maybe someone would come and get it."

"Didn't you notice? There's a letter for you inside."

She didn't become shy or embarrassed as other girls might have in this situation. She didn't avoid his stare but instead looked straight into his face. Her own face, ordinarily so gentle and serene, suddenly became terribly stern. Her tone, however, remained very relaxed. "Really, now. Don't you think this is all a bit ridiculous? If you don't respect yourself, which you definitely should, then can't you at least respect other people? Keep in mind that no matter what, you must never disgrace yourself. Look, maybe I've said too much. But try to understand that I only mean well."

Wu Huan was, after all, more "high-class" than the "hicks." So he was still going to help the ticket-seller as before. There was only one problem, his enthusiasm was a pretense. He couldn't cover up his frustration and depression. Who was provoking him? No one.

It was he who wanted to provoke her, but in her presence he suffered unparalleled defeat. It was as if all his efforts had bounced back at him like a rubber ball. Sure there was plenty he could get with minimal effort, but then there were things he couldn't get, like her honor, her adoration, her attention! He couldn't take it. He couldn't figure out what it was that was making her resist. What could he do to come out on top? He was determined to reverse the situation that made him feel so defeated.

Well, maybe he would have to get her angry. It might be a victory of sorts; he might ultimately get something from her. At least he might get her anger.

There must have been some demon playing tricks inside him. He had forgotten to maintain his typically "cool" self.

Everyone knows that at the beginning of each month the ticket-seller checks for tickets even more carefully than usual. When Wu Huan got off the bus, he ignored her request for a ticket. So she ran after him shouting, "Your monthly pass please. . . ."

He answered in a deliberately offended tone, "I don't have one."

Shi Yanan couldn't hold in his anger, "Who says you don't have one. You just bought it."

Wu Huan ignored him. He didn't even look in his direction but only stared aggressively at the ticket-seller.

She immediately understood what was gnawing at him. She tried to mollify him with soothing words, "Are you sure you don't have one? All you have to do is take it out and let me have a look. Everyone who gets off the bus has to have their ticket checked." But her good intentions were only met with resistance. He continued to insist stubbornly, "If I say I don't have one, it means I don't have one."

The ticket-seller's tone became much more serious. "Then you'll just have to buy one now."

"How much?"

"Fifty cents."

She had to fine Wu Huan who insisted on saying that he didn't have a ticket. Wu Huan rustled through his pockets and came up with a large handful of coins. He must have been planning this fuss all along.

She didn't catch it all. It wasn't clear whether this was intentional or not, but the money landed all over the ground.

It was the first time in Shi Yanan's life that he wanted to hit somebody. He wanted to grab Wu Huan by the neck and make him pick the money up from the floor coin by coin.

An old man wearing a pair of thick glasses hobbled over on his cane. He stood in front of Wu Huan and, as if reading aloud a scientific paper, declared, "Young man, I pity you. I pity the fact that your heart isn't as beautiful as your face."

Now that beautiful face of his twitched nervously, and wore a scornful smirk. He watched the ticket-seller diligently counting out each coin, like a philanthropist in the old society giving alms to the poor. Shi Yanan didn't know where Wu Huan picked up this perverse mentality, but it thoroughly disgusted him. It also filled him with the utmost respect for the target of his attacks. If this weren't her job, she wouldn't have to subject herself to such humiliation.

The ticket-seller lifted her head from the pile of coins. "You gave me seven cents too much." With that, she handed over his change.

"I don't want it."

"Well, that's your business!" She promptly placed the coins on the curb of the road and climbed back onto the bus.

He had acted according to plan. But why didn't he feel the pleasure and satisfaction from a job well done? Why, instead, did his whole body—from head to toe—feel utterly drained?

Despite Wu Huan's silence, Shi Yanan could tell that he knew, too, that in this last sparring match the lovely young lady came out victorious.

"Why did you do that?" Shi Yanan asked Wu Huan.

Wu Huan pulled himself together and said, "Isn't it worth spending fifty cents to watch her in a vulgar display of frustration?"

"Vulgar?" In the past, Shi Yanan wouldn't say anything to jeopardize his rapport with Wu Huan. But now, he was beginning to flare in anger. He couldn't hold it in. "If there's anyone vulgar, it's us. You think just because we lounge around on the sofa all day discussing philosophy and music, playing the guitar, listening to tapes, being genteel to the point of not eating fried breakfast cakes sold on the street, it means we've got class? It's all sham. It's all a camouflage to cover up our own petit-bourgeois vulgarity. We think of ourselves as being sophisticated, when inside all we are is rotten and dec- adent." As soon as he saw Wu Huan's expression, he halted his torrent of speech. If Wu Huan were to witness the sun turning into the moon, or the moon becoming the sun, he'd probably still wear that same blasé expression!

Up till now, Shi Yanan had always considered his relationship with Wu Huan to be built on a firm foundation. But he was mistaken. The truth of the matter was that they had always been standing on ice. With the spring's gentle breezes, the thick layer of ice on the river beneath them was already beginning to crack. Now they were standing on two separate pieces of ice, and the more it melted, the further apart the two pieces of ice would drift.

It was getting dark. They walked in silence toward the circular bus depot. Neither of them had anything to say. They knew that their worlds, their feelings, like the severing bond between them, were breaking apart, disappearing.

Shi Yanan suddenly stopped short. He was never again going to be afraid of being called "chicken." All the strength that he had been wanting to use in his fist was suddenly concentrated in one simple word, "Disgusting." Then he promptly took leave and headed for the bus depot. He wanted to tell the ticket-seller something. Tell her what, he didn't know.

Wu Huan had said it before. Women are frail creatures. Pretty women are even more so.

Shi Yanan saw her sitting there in the empty bus, waiting for another shift. Her head hung low in the twilight. He thought for sure she would be crying and even thought he heard sobbing sounds. If he weren't afraid that she'd get the wrong idea—that he was a rascal who wanted to take advantage of the situation—he would have dried her eyes and said, "There are many people who respect the ordinary but necessary work of a ticket-seller."

A bus silently drove by. Shi Yanan could see her face clearly in the light of the bus. Not only wasn't she crying, but she seemed to be lost in her own dreams. Her facial expression attested to a train of thought that drifted to somewhere beautiful and far-off. . . . Just then, Shi Yanan understood. Personal will and determination are completely dependent on one's attainment of inner peace. It wasn't the ticket-seller who was frail, but Wu Huan . . . and maybe even himself. Silently he left.

He wandered aimlessly in the drizzling rain, listening to the pitter-patter of the raindrops beating against the wide and white poplar leaves. He thought how different people were, and how different people found different things in life. He suddenly had a burning desire to share this thought, realized belatedly, with that esteemed writer of poetry.

Late Sunday afternoon, Shi Yanan walked along the rows of simple houses. It wasn't often that he had a chance to frequent residential areas like this. The sewage system hadn't been perfected, so pools of dirty water collected between the dwellings. Little boys were screeching at the top of their lungs.

That someone living in this environment could still produce writings that were original, deep, full of life and rich in philosophy was really quite remarkable. It took a very special kind of person. . . .

He quickly found the address he was looking for.

The door opened. He didn't understand what the ticket-seller was doing in front of him.

She smiled a greeting. "Oh, it's you? How are you? Whom are you looking for?"

He stuttered his reply. "I'm looking for Tian Ye."

"I'm Tian Ye."

No matter how rich or wild his imagination was, he couldn't match the image of the poet with the image of the ticket-seller. He expected the poet to be an elderly professional writer. He never thought that the writer would be someone as young as she, writing in her spare time.

"Is there something I can do for you?"

Shi Yanan didn't know why he told such a foolish lie. "I'm a friend of Shi Yanan's. I happened to be in the neighborhood on business, so he asked me to bring you a message. He wants to come and visit you in the next few days. When are you free?"

Her intelligent eyes were full of understanding and patience. "Next week I work the morning shift. I'll be home in the evenings. Tell him he can come any time. Don't you want to come in and sit down for a while?"

Shi Yanan just got more flustered: "Ugh . . . No, no. I'll come some other time. Bye."

"Good-bye."

Splash. His head got washed with a cup of leftover tea someone upstairs poured out of the window. He didn't dare raise his head to see who it was, much less wipe the water off his head. He hurried away like a fugitive.

It wasn't until he got home that he realized how stupid he had been. She must have known all along that he was Shi Yanan. Hadn't Wu Huan called out his name before on the bus?"

He never wanted to ride the 1176 bus again. He didn't know exactly why, but he felt that he had played a part in Wu Huan's behavior. It didn't matter that the factory was far away from his home, he decided to ride his bike to work from now on.

He could see the 1176 bus go past every day. Every time it did, he would say to himself, "Dear friend, wait till I'm a little more like you. Then I'll go and see you. I'm not ready right now."

Translated by Janet Yang

The Ark

"You are particularly unfortunate, because you were born a woman. . . ."
　　　　　　　　　　　　　　　　　　　　　　　—*an old saying*

Not *another* cloudy day! Cao Jinghua feared that the clouds might bring rain and then her back would become more painful than ever. The doctor had warned her of the danger of arthritis in the future. But what of the future? Jinghua had no wish that she would live a long time. Doctors busy doing research to prolong lives should realize that what torments people most is not the brevity of life, but the discomforts of an endless old age. Once she was no longer of any use, she hoped she would be discreet enough to fade away before she became a burden to others. If people only realized that the meaning of life lay not in longevity but in opening one's heart to generosity, then the world would be a much better place.

After spending the whole night stretched out on her bed, her legs had become quite numb. She reached for her watch—not yet five o'clock—so the sky was not really overcast, only still dark. Jinghua tried to raise herself up, but her back was as stiff as a board and she couldn't turn over yet. Luckily she could prop up onto her arms without too much effort. Her years of labor in the countryside had taken their toll on her back, but left her arms strong. Perhaps in the future she would have to use her arms in place of her legs, like the cripples she had occasionally seen.

What would she have done without those two strong arms of hers? But just imagine if every woman had arms like a weight-lifter and lacked feminine grace and beauty. Even Jinghua thought that it would be a shame, and of course men would be outraged. Jinghua believed that it might soon be time for "the mare to pull the cart." If it were really true that the world developed in cycles, then wasn't a return to the matriarchal society inevitable?

She reached for the diathermy machine on the table and plugged it in, watching for the indicator light to illumine the milky yellow plastic. Those people in Shanghai were clever enough to make even a diathermy machine look attractive. But for Jinghua the convenience and style of this machine served only to emphasize that she had few luxuries. Such luxuries were temporary, not a part of her life. The machine began to grow warm and as Jinghua placed it against her back, a stream of warmth flowed through her, driving out the chill which she felt all year round.

She was truly grateful to Lao An, her co-worker, for asking someone to bring the machine back from Shanghai for her. He had spoken more rapidly than usual as he handed it to her, not giving her mind a chance to wander in all directions as it often did when he was speaking. "I'm just like you," he had said. "I hate other people's pity." Then, almost as if he were having an argument with Jinghua, he had added angrily, "I'm certainly not giving this to you out of pity!"

Jinghua had always felt that Lao An was quite unlike a Party Branch Secretary. Even his proper name, An Tai, meaning "Peace and Stability", gave one a sense of his quietness, his gentleness.

The potted plant on the windowsill cast a sharp shadow on the curtains, its withered leaves hanging limply downwards. Had another plant died? Why was it that they could never succeed in growing plants like other people? Someone once said that plants take after their owners. What could be the matter with them? When they first bought that plant it had been healthy enough, with thick juicy leaves and plenty of buds. But before long the leaves had become thin and yellow and the buds fewer and fewer, and now it appeared feeble and hopeless. The room got plenty of sun and Jinghua had given the plant sesame paste and other kinds of foul-smelling fertilizer until the odor permeated the entire room. But to no avail. All the balconies opposite were packed with plants, but theirs alone remained bare, like an old crone in a crowd of pretty girls. Perhaps the air in their flat made it impossible for plants to grow—even during the hottest days of July the place felt as cold as a mortuary.

Perhaps this flat was a bit too large to be warm and comfortable. Jinghua had done her best to outfit the room—both her's and Liu Quan's—with furniture which she had made herself. Perhaps it did not look like the kind of furniture one can buy in the shops, but it was functional. There probably wasn't a single person at work who would have thought Jinghua capable of doing carpentry, but then everyone has their hidden talents. After a while, though, she had lost interest, so the furniture remained bare and unfinished. The sofa had no proper cover on it, just a cheap piece of yellow fabric. Everything had an incomplete look about it, exposing Jinghua's often lack of dedication. Many people had pointed out this character trait to Jinghua throughout her forty years. Jinghua laughed aloud at this thought. Maotou, the cat, jumped down from the sofa and miaowed twice as if to ask. "Are you awake yet?" Jinghua stretched out her hand, but Maotou waved her tail and went back to the sofa to sleep.

Since it was still early and today was Sunday, Jinghua could have gone back to sleep too, if she wanted to. But she did not feel like it. She had a lingering memory of an unpleasant dream, about rain and snow, wind, mud and bitter cold . . . about that window in the post office, with its peeling green paint, where the tattered ten-cent notes had lain scattered on the floor. Every one of those notes had borne the mark of her suffering. She had been saving the money to send to her father and sister, but then that man came and tore it from her hand. What had he said? She couldn't remember clearly now, but it had been something like, "Why did you have to go and have an abortion? Just so you can make money to send to that father and sister of yours? You killed my child! Why in hell did I marry you in the first place? Well, now I'm going to get a divorce!"

She had asked herself many times if it had really been just for the money. In those days it really would have been wrong to bring a child into the world. She had never imagined that a time would come when the "Gang of Four" would be overthrown and life would return to normal. And what had he wanted—to have chil-

dren, to sleep with her, to make a family? But unfortunately
Jinghua could offer him none of these things. And what of her
father and sister . . . shouldn't they also have been his responsibility? No, Jinghua had not seen it that way, she had taken on the
burden herself. Jinghua's father, an intellectual, had been branded
as a reactionary at the time and her younger sister had been left
helpless. Hadn't it actually been for their sakes in the first place
that she had gotten married and then, later on, been forced to get
divorced? Why was it that people gave her no understanding then
and only criticized her? Those who are more fortunate should try
to be more magnanimous.

Jinghua finally was able to turn over. No, she would not sleep
and return to that dream, nor to the one about those forests. The
forests, like so many things, were only beautiful and poetic in the
artist's imagination; in art even darkness and cruelty can be made
to take on a wild sort of beauty. But having to live in those forests
had been a cruel fate for any woman as frail as Jinghua. The
temperatures in that small wooden hut would fall to minus 20° C.
in the winter, cold enough for her to feel frozen stiff as an iron rod.
Whenever she came to her wits' end these days, she would think of
how she used to spend winters fetching water, mixing plaster and
repairing the holes in their roof, standing atop the wobbly ladder
she had pounded together herself. She was learning to be contented with her lot now, but she feared that the experiences, the
hardships of the past, were too deeply branded on her.

Uncanny, how she remembered distinctly every blow he had
landed on her face, every insult he had shouted at her. She could
even recall every word of the big character posters he had pasted
up on the wall of the school where she had been teaching, accusing her of being unfaithful. He was forever shouting the latest
slogans: "There is no love without cause, neither is there hate
without cause." "We can have no common ground with the bour-
geoisie." "The East Wind is blowing, the red flags are waving." She
could never forget the powerful odor of garlic which he always
carried around him. But, odd to say, she could not recall how he
had looked, though she had slept on his heated brick kang and
eaten at his table for six or seven years. If she came face-to-face
with him now Jinghua doubted whether she would recognize
him. Everything, the suffering, the humiliation had all turned into

memory, but his face had grown cloudy and obscure.

Jinghua forced herself to think of something else. Today it was her turn to do the cooking, so as soon as she got up she should go to the market. Usually they turned a blind eye to the cooking turns but today, being Sunday, she should cook two proper meals.

In the next room, Liu Quan started crying. Maotou let out a loud "miaow!" as she jumped down from the sofa, then she rushed into Liu Quan's bedroom, tail erect, as if about to do battle. "Just don't push me too far, or else I might do something desperate!" Liu Quan yelled. Then she began crying again and the shouting decreased into a soft, indistinct sobbing.

Jinghua sighed, Ah, well! It must be a dream—a nightmare. Why was she always having nightmares? Maotou slunk back and returned to her place on the sofa where she lay, staring at Jinghua quizzically, as if to say, "What on earth is the matter with all of you?" Jinghua smiled at her apologetically. Even for a cat it had to be rather trying to live with them. No wonder all those men wanted to get divorced!

Their apartment was like a "widow's club." She found it curious over time that she met more and more women like them. Someone might do some serious research on why the divorce rate among women of their age was so high—not just dismiss this phenomenon as a result of "bourgeois ideology." Could such a superficial judgment presume to sum up their actual suffering and courage during those terrible years? The three of them had all been schoolmates together at the same primary school and then at the same girls' middle school, only splitting up when they had gone off to the university. One after another they had got married and then, as if they had arranged it beforehand, they had one by one gotten separated or divorced. After that, thanks to Liang Qian, she and Liu Quan had moved into the same apartment. Sometimes Jinghua felt as though there had been some kind of time-warp and that this apartment had, indeed, become the dormitory of their old school. She remembered how she had taken advantage of her schoolmates' afternoon nap and poured drops of cold water on each of their eyelids as they had slept. After that, Liu Quan would become grown up and say sternly, "Comrade Cao Jinghua! You should realize that what you have done is very, very wrong!" Liu Quan had been their class monitor at that time and felt very self-important, quite unlike the wrinkled old persimmon she was now. If only she could hear that old school bell once again . . .

Bang, bang, bang . . . came a heavy knocking on the door, as if someone were trying to alert them to a fire. The knocking set Jinghua in a fluster. She scrambled to get her blouse on, only to find that she had it on inside out.

"Who is it?" Liu Quan shuffled out of her room doing up the buttons of her blouse. Bang, bang, bang! No answer, but the heavy knocking continued. Liu Quan pulled open the door angrily. Oh no! It was him again, the "cultured" Bai Fushan. He was wearing a grey summer suit, white leather shoes, and his hair was certainly longer than that of an average civil servant or university lecturer. Every inch of him shone with the confidence of a first-rate violinist, without the slightest suggestion that he might, in fact, be just some sort of cheap performer. People like him can always impress others and never feel the least bit of embarrassment or self-consciousness. Why on earth did Bai Fushan choose a moment like this to march in so brazenly, upsetting all their plans for a peaceful Sunday at home? His presence always made them feel angry and put out, and he couldn't have come about anything important.

Bai Fushan wrinkled up his nose and told them their apartment smelled like a zoo, that the cat had probably gone and made a mess somewhere. Jinghua came to the door and raised her arm as if to block his way. "What do you want?" she asked. Bai Fushun surveyed the dishevelled figure before him, not understanding why Jinghua would not let him in. Since this apartment belonged to Liang Qian, his wife, then surely it was his too. Those two women were no more than guests in this home and he could enter whenever he pleased, no matter whether they were in the middle of washing, or still fast asleep in their beds.

"I'm looking for Liang Qian," he said, smiling ironically. Sometimes the peculiar behavior of these two women with their odd cat made him furious.

"You don't pay us to keep track of your wife for you!" Liu Quan, too, felt furious. Over the past few days Bai Fushan had come here at all hours of the day and night looking for Liang Qian. She often stayed at the film studio dormitory when she worked late. But even when they told him that she was not there, he would still come spying around the apartment as if they were hiding some secret there. This was really getting to be too much!

Not in the least put out by his cool reception, Bai Fushan tried to push his way in towards Liu Quan's room. "I'd happily pay someone to take charge of her—and the whole lot of you, as well!" he shouted at Liu Quan. But what he really meant was: who would want anyone as old and hideous as you—or Liang Qian, for that matter?

"You've got a nerve!" Liu Quan was at her wits' end and shoved him back out the door.

"It is 6:30 now," Jinghua spat out, slowly and deliberately. "We will receive visitors from 9 A.M. to 8 P.M.. If you have any important business, please come back at nine." She slammed the door shut. What a way to begin the day!

A large pile of dirty dishes had collected in the sink over the past two days, and not a single clean bowl remained in the cupboard. If they were to have breakfast Jinghua would have to do some washing-up first, a job which none of them enjoyed. They got around to doing it once all the plates and bowls were dirty. They should have a rotation system for washing-up, as they once had for cleaning their dormitory. Cooking was much more pleasant and creative. Jinghua put a spoonful of soda into the boiling hot water and stirred it around with her fingertips. The water quickly turned murkey, with a layer of oil bubbles floating on the surface. Everything was filthy. They always seemed so busy, yet how was it that they never seemed to do anything properly?

Crash! Liu Quan was banging on the table, scolding her son, Mengmeng, who lived with his father but had come to spend the day. "You're really useless! How do you ever expect to get into a good school? And if you don't get into a good school, how on earth are you going to get to the university? Doesn't your father help you at all?" Mengmeng had probably failed to solve some math problem and he started howling. Times had changed and this was not their old dormitory after all.

Any other mother who only saw her child once a week would surely do all she could to encourage him, make him happy. Liu Quan seemed like a pretty unreasonable mother, on the surface, but in fact she had tried for nearly five years to get custody of him. The dilemma was that if you wanted a child, you shouldn't then have got divorced. Or if you wanted to get divorced, you shouldn't have had a child in the first place. Mengmeng had become a hostage, torn between his parents, and Liu Quan had practically reached the point of distraction. Marriage, seemingly just a private matter between two people, became such a complicated business. Liu Quan and Jinghua both felt instinctively that they would never enjoy such a union ever again after their unhappy experiences, and that divorce, as to most people, was an affair associated only with hatred and suffering. Some people, those who cannot tell black from white, try to persuade others not to get divorced, even when it is perfectly plain that the marriage cannot be saved. Love is reciprocal, and if one side stops loving then, whatever the rights and wrongs of the case, very little can be done to save the marriage. Yet anyone wishing to divorce must be very courageous, must be prepared to lose all dignity in pleading their case. Their choice may seem irrational to others, but for them it is a life and death matter, with their very integrity at stake.

Jinghua had finally convinced Liu Quan of Mengmen's own ability to choose the best place for him. Mengmeng would soon grow up and be able to leave his father. Then nothing would be able to constrain him from coming back to Liu Quan. People are not objects; even if you place them under lock and key, you cannot control their minds. How foolish to think that one can destroy the natural bonds between mother and son. His father had no way of preventing him coming here more often, not being willing to lose a day's wages to stay home and look after him. So, in the end, his father was just an out-and-out materialist, caring more about money than about his son's upbringing.

Now Liu Quan had started crying too. She had not been in a good mood lately. At work, Manager Wei had been aggressive with her again. For the last few days he had been calling her into his office after work. "Now then, Liu Quan, tell me something about production over the last fortnight," he'd say. Why on earth couldn't he discuss this during working hours, or with her section head? Before Liu Quan could open her mouth to answer, he would begin to get excited and say, "Those clothes you're wearing look really good. You're really looking quite . . . " Then he would give Liu Quan's waist a pinch. She'd act as if she hadn't noticed and move to a chair nearer the door.

"I thought you wanted to talk about work," she said, her face flushed. Manager Wei's expression changed to one of disappointment. "Eh? Oh, yes . . . well . . . if you want to talk about it, how about coming to my place for a chat this evening?" Then he would laugh nervously as if he had just stepped on a slippery frog. God! That man's mood could change as fast as lightning—a really tricky fish to deal with.

"I'm too busy," she said in a flat tone. Why couldn't she have just said outright, "I can't be at your beck and call all the time, you know." That would have felt really good. Why couldn't she be like some of those self-assured women who can rely on their status and never got trodden underfoot? But since she had no status she could never enjoy such freedom. Her life had taught her always to be humble and self-effacing. Why had she ever been born a woman, carrying around with her the burden of feminine beauty? Most people think it is a misfortune to be born ugly, but few people understand the misfortunes of beauty. And on top of this, why did she have to be a divorcee who, because she belonged to no one in particular, could become the property of everyone? There seemed to be no way to handle her present predicament, except to escape it, so Liang Qian and her influential father were now trying to arrange a transfer for her which, with good fortune, they might just accomplish. After that things should be a bit better.

Jinghua picked up the oil bottle. It was nearly empty and she must remember to get it filled. She must not forget again today, otherwise they would have no oil to cook with. She poured the remaining oil into the pan, but there was barely enough left to fry a *mantou* bun. Mengmeng was still crying; so was Liu Quan, in what was the first movement of the regular Sunday concert. Jinghua called out, "Mengmeng, come and tell auntie whether you would like your *mantou* sweet or salty."

"Sweet!" Mengmeng was still sniffling, but once he started thinking about his breakfast he would surely stop crying. Why was it that children always liked sweet things most? It was only when they grew up that they learned also to appreciate spicy and savory things.

There was another knock at the door and Jinghua glanced at her watch. It was nine o'clock; could Bai Fushan really have been waiting there all that time? He must have come about something urgent, since he had never been known to persist for so long before.

"Mengmeng, go and open the door," Liu Quan said. Mengmeng could not get the door open at once—he still hadn't quite mastered the lock. But he could learn by himself. Liu Quan really did too much for him and if her face had not been so red from crying right now, she would surely have run over to help him. Over-attention like that could only produce a timid child. So few intelligent mothers today, just as there are few intelligent wives—which probably helps explain the reversal of sex roles people are always talking about. That, however, is a problem for the sociologists to solve.

At last the door was opened. "Auntie," she heard Mengmeng say,"What do you want?"

Not Bai Fushan? Jinghua laughed at herself. How could she have imagined that Bai Fushan would wait outside all that time. It was the voice of Mrs. Jia, head of their neighborhood committee. "Are there any adults at home?" There was a trace of suspicion in her voice at seeing the door opened by a child. Who else might be in there? Liu Quan could not possibly have come out to meet her, since in that state of emotion she would have aroused even more suspicion. So Jinghua took the pot off of the stove, took the half-fried *mantou* out of the oil and went to the door.

"Oh, hello, Comrade Cao. You're in," said Mrs. Jia warmly, though she still peered suspicously along the corridor.

Mrs. Jia lived next door, so she must have heard Bai Fushan's knocking earlier that morning. When the "Gang of Four" were still in power, people used to come around investigating residence permits, never failing to check on Liu Quan and Jinghua, as if they were hiding some wild man in their flat. At first they used to check every household, but later on they narrowed down their targets, and divorced women were an obvious enough one. No wonder Manager Wei still treated Liu Qan like that.

The more suspicious Mrs. Jia became, the more Jinghua tried to block her way. "What is it?"

"Has our cat by any chance come over to your place?"

"No," Jinghua replied quickly. "Why should it come here?"

"Oh dear, Comrade Cao. Don't you know? Your cat has been playing court to all six of our toms . . . And she tittered sarcastically.

Could single cats really evoke the same disapproval as single women? Perhaps they ought to marry Maotou off as quickly as possible! Jinghua laughed aloud. "Well, I'm very proud of her. She's lucky to have so many admirers!"

"Er, yes . . . ha . . . ha," Mrs. Jia retreated slowly.

"Won't you come in for a while?" Jinghua had suddenly become quite hospitable, and opened the door wide.

"Er, no . . . no," Mrs. Jia backed away from the door as if their flat contained lepers.

Jinghua closed the door but then, on a sudden impulse, opened it again and called in a low voice down the corridor. "Mrs. Jia, just one thing. The other day after supper, did you doze off on your balcony?" Mrs. Jia's balcony was adjacent to theirs and every evening, between ten and eleven, they could hear the sound of her fanning herself. As the rhythmical sound of the fan beating against her body got slower and slower, they knew she must be dozing off.

"Er, yes."

"Well, I heard you talking in your sleep," Jinghua paused, a grave expression on her face.

"What did I say?" One look at Jinghua's face told her that she had said something she should not have. Good heavens, what could she have said? She searched her memory, as if trying to find some trace.

"You said something about politics, something rather serious. So serious, in fact, that I'd rather not repeat it."

"Me? No, it's impossible. No . . ." she stammered. Her double chin began to tremble—she was bewildered. Perhaps she had let slip some political remark overheard during a private family discussion. Dreams can contain our daytime thought. Her face was blank.

"No? Think about it carefully." Jinghua closed the door.

Liu Quan, her eyes still red and swollen, came out and asked. "Did you really hear something?"

"I only heard her farting! I was just getting back at her."

"You really went a bit far, scaring her like that."

Yes, this joke had been a bit cruel, but who ever came here who showed any love or compassion towards them? Earlier it had been Bai Fushan looking for his wife. Now it had been Mrs. Jia looking for her cat. It was all just too much, being treated like the lowest caste in society. Everyone felt free to come and vent their anger on them. And in return she had learned to behave cruelly toward people. She wished she could be like ordinary women, loving and loved by all around her, instead of finding herself a target.

* * *

Everyone had left and Liang Qian remained alone in the recording studio. Just a moment before the room had been crowded and noisy with the sound of chatter and musical instruments, but suddenly it had become quite empty. Liang Qian could even hear herself sighing, but sighing was not enough. If only she had had a drop of strength left in her, she would like to have rolled around on the floor to vent her anger, as she had done when she was still a child. She stood in the center of the studio with arms crossed, as if she were in the middle of a wilderness. The bulb hanging from the ceiling cast a cold white light on her desolate wooden features. Narrow lines of weariness ran across her face like fine rivulets. A sudden cool draft brought her back to her senses; she must not go on standing around in such a distraught fashion. She turned out the light and went into the sound booth next door, a small room which looked like the bridge of a ship, with all its recording equipment arranged in rows. Liang Qian sat before it like the skipper, peering into the blackness of the recording studio beyond the soundproof glass. She started up the playback of the soundtrack. The studio now gave the impression of infinite depth and darkness, adding to Liang Qian's feeling of isolation. She remembered reading one of Jack London's stories, "Sea Wolf," about the lone skipper of a ship who had eventually died like a maddened wolf. She looked about her and aimlessly picked up a small paper swallow from the sofa behind her, a swallow someone had made from an old cigarette carton. When she pulled its tail the wings fluttered up and down, pathetically, absurdly . . .

She had needed a lot of resolve to utter those last few words before the technicians, musicians, conductor and composer all left indignantly, leaving Liang Qian alone here like the manager of a factory whose workers have gone on strike. Fixing her eyes on the ceiling she had said, "Tomorrow, we start at 9 A.M. O.K.?" But someone had shouted, "Nine thirty!" and she hadn't had the courage to argue, and dared not look at their faces. Originally she had intended to say 8 A.M., but could not bring herself to do it. As the director of the film, she should really have been firm with them and said, "Comrades, tomorrow we start at nine. Please be punctual."

What unnerved Liang Qian was the remark she had pretended not to hear. "Hell! Has that old bag finished yet or not?" No, they had not finished and could not finish until they put more life into the music. She had tried to tell the conductor what she wanted from the music, but lacked the confidence to express herself clearly. The conductor had glanced arrogantly down from the rostrum at her and tapped impatiently on his music stand. He clearly thought little of Liang Qian's muddled instructions and paid her no more attention than he would some young bassoonist in his orchestra. But in the end, whose fault was it that she couldn't command the respect of others, as great directors always should? Surely the main responsibility lay with herself.

"You really do make a fuss about nothing," Bai Fushan had said sarcastically. "Haven't you seen the films being made these days? Most people will take whatever you give them. And in any case, nobody takes any notice of the director—it's only the actors they're interested in. Can't you see that you're getting on everyone's nerves, demanding so much?" Well, at least he had expressed some interest in her—after all, he was still her husband. But she did not like his tone at all. She wasn't stupid and could see the problem perfectly well herself. As they left, nobody had taken the slightest notice of her, just as if she had been some old woman living dementedly in her past.

Liang Qian stood up and looked at her reflection in the window between the booth and studio. She looked worn and dishevelled, with a hard, stubborn streak in her face. She tied the loose hair back from her face with a handkerchief and tried to force herself to relax. But her face muscles seemed taut and rigid, like those of a chicken. No wonder she could evoke so little affection in others. She was only forty but already looked like an old woman. What had happened to her youth? She had passed it by so quickly, with barely a moment to enjoy its beauties, to love or be loved. She thought about that young violinist who had remarked so rudely about her . . . Liang Qian had admired the woman. She must have been about twenty-one with long shiny hair, bright eyes which had probably never shed tears, red lips, and not a single line across her forehead, which might mean she did little thinking, or at least, worrying. The only thing about her appearance which seemed out of place was her cheap jewelry.

Of course, as all women do, Liang Qian wanted to remain young and beautiful for ever, but how could she find the hours needed, as some foreign women did, to fiddle around with face creams, make-up and massage? She knew that in the end she must just resign herself to the inevitable and let her brow become dry and parched like a weathered old piece of wood. She had once bought herself a couple of bottles of beauty cream, but it had done no good: once youth had flown there was nothing one could do to recapture it. In any case, if she chose to follow a career, then she had to be prepared to sacrifice womanly pleasures, that was an irreconcilable truth. Women, like Mrs. Thatcher, who manage to combine the job of prime minister with baking cakes for her children, must be few and far between.

Although she had never really found anything which exactly suited her, Liang Qian had finally chosen a career. Maybe it had all been a mistake. She had always imagined that her love for directing would automatically transform itself into an ability to direct. Now she knew that even though she might have produced a few films, none of them would even be remembered. It was a tragedy similar to that of the lover who receives no response from his loved one.

One conductor had already quit, knowing full well that Liang Qian couldn't continue very well without him. If only she had the powers of Sun Wukong, the Monkey King, and could transform her hairs into enough Liang Qians to do all of the jobs in the studio, then she could have things as she wanted them. A film should be the product of its director, not the conductor who has other opportunities to display his art. Ever since she had started this film Liang Qian had had to go around pleading with people, suffering their insults and humiliation. First of all she'd had to get the script approved, then select people for the production team. She had been made to feel like a beggar, even hearing it said that she was just trading on her father's name. But had it been her father who had suffered for the last ten months while they had been filming on location? Had it been her father who had suffered the disrespect, as if she were some country quack in the midst of qualified surgeons who waited to see what miracles she could perform? But none of this indignity really mattered; what she wanted most was to be able to pursue her art as fully and effectively as possible.

The music stopped, leaving only a solitary drumbeat. It filled her with a sense of impending doom. She felt trapped, suffocated, unable to break out. She was as inadequate, solitary and helpless as the crippled little tree in one of the scenes of her own film. If only she could break out . . . She could not stand it any longer. She rushed into the pitch black recording studio, pushed the heavy door closed and began crying hysterically. It gave her a sense of relief, her cries melting into the darkness. Here at last she could find momentary peace. She sat down heavily on the sofa and closed her eyes, the tears still trickling down her face as she wept for her lost youth, for her shattered self-confidence . . .

Who was that tapping on her foot? Was this some sort of joke? Liang Qian gave a start and opened her eyes. There was Bai Fushan, cheerful and confident as ever, sitting at her feet. He must have wanted something important, since they rarely communicated these days. Even if some disaster had befallen her, she doubted whether he would have come to her assistance. Liang Qian got up quickly, straightened her hair and went to sit on another sofa. She did not want them to be seen closely together for fear people would start to gossip. To her, Bai Fushan was like a stranger and she must be careful around him. They had not seen each other for about half a year and Liang Qian was not quite sure how to treat him. He still looked youthful and might almost have passed for thirty had it not been for the dark circles under his eyes from his excessive drinking and smoking. She wondered if he could still play the iolin well, though what was that to her? Perhaps Liang Qian had too great a reverence for "artistic talent"; art was meaningless unless it contained the artistic spirit.

So in the end which of them, herself or Bai Fushan, had really suffered most? Perhaps if he had married someone else he would not have lost his artistic spirit so quickly. She had loved it once and had wanted him to love her. After they were married she would often try to dress herself to look beautiful for him, though now those same dresses were stuffed into her trunk as though she had never touched them. She dared not give them away in case they might infect others with her own misfortune.

Questions she has asked herself since:
Do you know how to receive a man's affection?

No.

Can you appreciate the music of Debussy?

No.

Do you know where a man's vanity lies?

No, I don't know.

The questioning should have taken place before they got married. But their feelings had come so fast, just as they had vanished later, just as a passing summer shower. She had been too young, a mere girl of only eighteen or nineteen, unable to cope with the rigors of married life.

"You want to get divorced? Divorced! What on earth for? Divorce just isn't done, you know. But I am quite open-minded and would be willing to come to a 'gentleman's agreement,' so that each of us can go our own separate ways without losing too much face."

Bai Fushan had said this without the least sign of agitation, just as if he had been haggling over the price of fish in the free market, something at which he was most adept. And while he acted out this new role in public, he had managed to keep absolutely calm and self-possessed, maintaining his false sense of morality, surprising even Liang Qian with his skill. Perhaps he had been right after all. Liang Qian must consider the social position of her family. Yet outsiders could never realize what hardships this situation had inflicted upon both of them, the deadening effects on the soul of living a lie. In some ways she must take the blame for how Bai Fushan had changed, and feel some sympathy for him. She might not love him, but at least she could be fair in her judgment of him.

Preserving the family status was a continuous burden. Even without a divorce, they drew people's attention. All her father's old comrades watched Lian Qian's every movement and they would have raised a storm if she had tried to get divorced. A divorce would threaten them all and they would use every argument they could to dissuade her from such a course of action, in trying to protect her father's image. Bai Fushan was as aware of this as she was. So all they could do was to let things remain as they were. In any case, she had no lover waiting for her.

"I couldn't find you anywhere. How have you been lately?" He took a packet of cigarettes out of his pocket and handed one to Liang Qian.

"Not too bad, thanks." Liang Qian looked at the "555" sign on her cigarette. Foreign cigarettes! He really knew how to live.

"How about the film?"

"Not going so smoothly, I'm afraid." At least he was still concerned enough to ask her that.

"Are some of them making trouble for you?"

"No, not particularly. It's just me." Liang Qian did not feel like chatting with Bai Fushan, though she knew that she must at least go on making polite conversation, as with anyone else. She casually slipped off one of her sandals, accidentally revealing a hole in her sock, which Bai Fushan noticed at once. How had she gottten to this state? She had enough money. He noticed her thin, stick-like legs and her wasted hips. Then, following his gaze upwards, he saw her sunken chest and her thin yellow face. He could no longer find anything lovable or even interesting about her. How on earth could she have become so haggard, so pathetic?

Bai Fushan could never understand why Liang Qian always kept him at such a distance. Even if there were no love left in their relationship, couldn't they at least be like good business partners, continuing to help one another in various ways? If only she could get her father to do a few favors for Bai Fushan, then she need no longer go on struggling like this and he would see to it that her life was more comfortable. What was the point of plodding along like this? In the future, no one would take the slightest notice of what she had achieved, just as he himself would never be remembered as a violinist. Why sacrifice all material comfort for something one could never hope to achieve? In this world it was necessary to fight for everything. Bai Fushan already had a bit of money stashed away in Hong Kong and as soon as his father-in-law was no longer around to help him, he planned to go abroad to open a restaurant somewhere, or to sell silk. There would be little point in him staying here once the old man had passed away, for without that connection he was nothing. If Liang Qian liked, he could take her abroad with him. Then she could write her memoirs and make a fortune. After that they would be able to live the rest of their lives in comfort. Thinking of this, Bai Fushan suddenly felt a small wave of affection towards her. He came over and sat down beside her, his shoulder just touching hers, though he was careful not to sit too close and chase her away.

"Why do you push yourself so hard?" His voice sounded as affectionate as ever and Liang Qian could feel the warmth of his shoulder against her own. She remembered the first night of their marriage, how he had held her tight as they had whirled round and round the bedroom. The light had been switched off and the moonlight streamed in through the window, enveloping both of them. Each time he spun her round to face the window, she could see the small translucent clouds, lit silver and gold and purple by the moonlight. Her heart had been filled to overflowing by those clouds.

"Play me a song on your violin," she had whispered. That had perhaps been the best performance he had ever given. If only she had known, she would have recorded it. She wondered how it would affect him if he could hear it now. Liang Qian glanced at him and noticed the red streaks in his eyes which had lost the glimmer of their old brilliance. He had sold his soul to drink long before and had probably been drinking the night before. One is a fool to try to recreate the past. She felt herself overwhelmed by a sense of numbness. If only she could sleep here alone for a while so that she could regain her sensitivity . . .

Bai Fushan could feel that his presence was unwelcome and decided to get on with what he had come for. "Could you take me to see your father?" he asked.

Liang Qian gave a start. Bai Fushan rarely made such a request. If he wanted to get something done it was usually enough just to say that he was so-and-so's son-in-law, like so many people do nowadays, rather than going through the official channels. Bai Fushan's request was unusual this time. "What for?" she asked him.

"I want to go abroad."

Go abroad! Lately people had caught this craze, as if "abroad" were some kind of treasure trove where anyone could go and help himself. What could he do, anyway, play the violin? His playing wasn't much good anymore, though, she supposed, he could always become some sort of street musician. Liang Qian wondered why he had thought of going abroad in the first place, unless he was in some sort of trouble. "Are you running away from something?" she asked. "What is it, problems with a woman? Or have you been getting involved in some sort of illegal activities, like smuggling?"

"What do you mean?" Bai Fushan was angered by Liang Qian's response. He rested his arm on the back of the sofa, making Liang Qian feel as if she would be suffocated by the warmth of his body. She quickly moved aside and said hoarsely, "I can't take you to see him. He hasn't been well lately and I won't disturb him."

"In that case I'll go and see him myself." Bai Fushan had begun to tremble with irritation; it had always been like this—her being as obstinate as an old witch—and he knew there was nothing he could do to persuade her.

"I could phone them and tell them not to let you in," she said.

She would have done it too. What an infuriating woman! Bai Fushan's cheeks were already becoming pouched and unsightly. She felt like telling him so, but before she had a chance he blurted out, "You really don't give a damn for me, do you?" His voice sounded almost threatening, as if to say, "Don't push me too far."

Liang Qian had used her father's influence to solve problems in the past, but she had always been careful not to take advantage or manipulate him. And she had never used it to her own advantage. After Jinghua and Liu Quan had finished their divorces she had used it to help them find somewhere to live. Could she have chosen not to help them? Could she have refused to assist another friend when it came to settling his father's rehabilitation case? For herself she had waited more than ten years to have a chance to direct a film and had to struggle along just like everyone else. So who could accuse her of trading on her father's name? She had certainly never exploited him as much as Bai Fushan had. And now he hadn't even had the common courtesy to show concern at her father's illness. He only thought of himself.

"How selfish you are. Do you want to kill him?" Liang Qian asked. "You can't imagine how my father has suffered because of his position. Everyone has tried to squeeze something out of him. You haven't done badly out of him yourself, flaunting your connections left and right. But what have you done in return? You haven't even bothered to visit him. And now you ask me to . . . " Liang Qian jumped to her feet and pulled open the door.

Bai Fushan looked at her. Hysterical woman! He threw his cigarette on the floor and, as if taking the last curtain call, he rushed out of the room. Disgusting! Even at a time like this he paid careful

attention to his every movement, but he ignored the lighted cigarette, still smouldering on the floor. Liang Qian went over and
stamped it out. Bai Fushan sent his parting shot echoing through
the corridor, "Don't forget, you are still my wife, your dad is still my
father-in-law, and Chengcheng is still my son!"

Liang Qian felt like pasting up a notice stating clearly that her
father was her father, she was Liang Qian and Bai Fushan was Bai
Fushan. Each should be responsible for their own actions. She
pitied her father. Everyone thought that someone in his position
must enjoy boundless privilege, how lonely he must have been
and how much he had suffered. He had no one to whom he could
give vent to his true feelings as she could with Liu Quan and
Jinghua.

Chengcheng was Bai Fushan's son too! Well, he was overdue in
realizing it. People who lack a sense of parental responsiblity
should never have children, children who always become subject
to the fortunes or misfortunes of their parents. If Liang Qian's
father had not had such high status, no one would ever have been
able to say that her achievements were purely due to him. When
would she be allowed to be herself? When would society begin to
recognize her own struggles? Liang Qian beat her fists on the back
of the sofa, but felt no relief. She decided to try to telephone Xie
Kunsheng to find out whether Liu Quan's job transfer had come
through yet. She tried dialing several times, but could not get
through. Since starting this filming Liang Qian had had more than
her share of telephoning to do, and with so few lines available she
could waste half a day trying to get through. After about ten
minutes, she managed to get the number.

"Hello?" A coquettish young voice answered the phone. It must
have been a woman called Qian Xiuying. Liang Qian felt a mixture
of scorn and admiration for people like her. Her voice contained
the soft, relaxing warmth one felt while soaking in a hot bath. Why
could none of them, she, Jinghua or Liu Quan, ever be like that?
Their voices were so coarse and unfeminine, though they were so
accustomed to each other that they hardly noticed it. But what
must men have thought of them? A man who spoke with an
effeminate, high-pitched voice evoked only revulsion in most
women, so presumably their heavier voices must have had a
similar effect on men.

"Hello. Is Director Xie there, please?"

"No!" The sweet voice suddenly turned icy.

"Could you please be kind enough to tell me where he is?"

"Click!" Liang Qian heard her hang up. She felt a wave of fury sweep over her. Didn't that woman have any manners? Liang Qian had seen her in Xie Kunsheng's office, painted eyebrows and lips, a little too plump. She picked up the receiver angrily, only to hear the busy signal again. But she had to get through.

"Hello?" The same sweet tone again.

"This is Liang Qian speaking," she said in an almost threatening voice.

"Oh, Comrade Liang Qian. How nice to hear from you. We haven't seen you for ages here. Why don't you come over sometime? And how is your film getting along—very well, I'm sure. We're all looking forward to seeing it."

Liang Qian could not help gazing at the receiver in her hand in wonder. Was this really the same one she had spoken into just a moment before? She really knew the trade, that woman! She must have realized that it had been Liang Qian she had cut short so impatiently a moment before, so now she was pouring out the compliments one after another, barely giving Liang Qian a chance to recall the first cold reception. Much as Liang Qian detested using her name, she knew that at times it was the only way to get things done.

She softened her tone and said, "Please could you be kind enough to call Director Xie for me?"

"Yes, of course. Wait a moment please, don't hang up . . ." She sounded almost as if she were pleading with Liang Qian.

Liang Qian could hear Director Xie's voice indistinctly in the background. " . . . So don't you worry about it, I'll have a word with them and all will be settled . . . "

"Hello. . . ." he drawled over the phone in a bored voice, as if he did not know it was Liang Qian at the other end of the line. Liang Qian was sure he knew perfectly well.

"This is Liang Qian!"

"Oh, hello!" His tone at once changed and became cheerful and familiar and he laughed. "What can I do for you . . . Have you got some film tickets for me?"

"Film tickets? Well, that shouldn't be a problem. No, I want to find out what is happening about Liu Quan's transfer. You said I should wait, but it's been a month now and I wanted to remind you in case you had forgotten about it."

"What do you mean? How could I forget about it?" This at least was probably true. Director Xie's position as head of the Foreign Affairs Bureau was much sought-after and he had only got it thanks to Bai Fushan who, as usual, had been ready to flaunt his connection. Xie Kunsheng had no doubt done some good turn for Bai Fushan in return. "Is Xiao Bai back from his concert tour of Hong Kong yet?" he asked. "I haven't seen him. What did he buy himself there? Do you know if he can manage to get me a cassette recorder?"

Damn him! Why did he bring up this musician who had nothing to do with their business? Liang Qian cursed under her breath. How could anyone be so brazen? If he was like this with her, God knows how he must have behaved with other people. "That shouldn't be a problem either," Liang Qian laughed coldly. "But right now you should attend to this matter. Just tell me when you can fix the transfer, and no more delay!"

Xie Kunsheng dared not argue, not only because of Liang Qian's father, even though he saw him seldom and he was not likely to take much notice of someone like himself, but also because he knew that Liang Qian herself was a strong force to deal with. She was quite unlike any woman he had known. Her moods were unpredictable and at any moment she might turn round and do something vicious to make one lose face. If all women were like her, what would the world come to? What would men be able to do about it? He glanced at his secretary, Qian Xiuying, sitting at his side with her pretty made-up face. He would far rather deal with a woman like her than with Liang Qian, who was as dried up and stale as a piece of old cake. Hearing Liang Qian's determined tone, Xie Kunsheng became more serious and said, "How about next week?"

"Is that a promise?"

"Yes."

Liang Qian hung up and laughed to herself bitterly. How many roles had she been acting out that day? She had always been a poor student in the drama class at film college, but life was a greater teacher than any textbooks, and people must adapt and learn far more than they realize. Life is the only stage on which one can experience real human suffering, and knowledge.

The little paper swallow was still lying on the sofa, shining faintly beneath the overhead light. Liang Qian was reminded of her time in primary school when they used to fold paper into clumsy little swallows, boats, monkeys and miniature jackets. What had happened to all those earnest, innocent little girls? She stayed deep within the memory, trying to remember their appearances, their faces, but she could recall nothing, not even how she herself had looked back then. All she could bring to mind was the way they looked now, haggard and prematurely grey, forever chasing after dreams they could never realize.

She had often told Liu Quan and Jinghua that they couldn't go on at this pace. They all should take the day off sometime and bicycle out into the countryside with a picnic, but they were always getting themselves bound up by one problem after another and kept putting this plan off, year in and year out. When would they be able to have a proper rest and stop saying later, after this and after that? At the moment they were saying, "Wait until Liu Quan gets her transfer"; "Wait until Liang Qian finishes her film"; "Wait until the controversy over Jinghua's article has blown over." But none of them could say when that time would come.

* * *

Liu Quan counted the cigarette butts in the little blue and white saucer from the cafeteria which she used as an ashtray. She knew that she should not go on smoking. She had smoked seven cigarettes that afternoon and now she took her eighth from the packet. She blew out a thin column of smoke which spread out and hovered before her eyes in the form of a large, wavering question mark. What was the question? To whom was it addressed?

Qu Yuan, the great minister of the Warring States Period (403-221 B.C.), had once written "Questions to Heaven," and after that had drowned himself in the Miluo River and was transformed into its waves which lapped against the silent banks day in and day out. That character for "mi" 汨 in the river's name, although quite clearly a "mi," always reminded Liu Quan of the character meaning "tears" 泪, lacking only a single stroke. This always made her think that the Miluo River must be a river of tears. She felt thankful to the Creator for giving people tear ducts, so that they could wash away their misery.

She blew lightly and with a sense of relief watched the question mark disappear. She had learned not to ask questions a long time ago. All answers lay with fate, and who could say what that might bring? Could she ever have imagined that she would start smoking like this? Believing in fate was a kind of anesthetic, a comfort when faced with daily reality. When she had been a healthy young student of English, with long, thick black braids, a woman who smoked did not fit with her ideal. But now she was merely a divorcee working in the office of an export company.

More than the other two, Liu Quan was probably the most proletarianized and wherever she was, in her office or in the street, no one could have told from her speech, her bearing or dress that she had once received a higher education. As Jinghua had said, when one reaches the end of one's rope, a change must be in store. Through some fluke the Foreign Affairs Bureau had finally agreed to give her a job. Had Liu Quan really fallen so far? She dared not be too optimistic.

As an intellectual, Jinghua was fond of discussing such philosophical subjects as dialectics and materialism. Liu Quan knew that a woman who talked about such things would surely scare men away, pretty as she might be. What a man wanted was a wife, not a lecturer in Marxist philosophy. But for Jinghua to have broken this habit would have been like taking the legs from a runner or severing the vocal chords of a singer. And when would Jinghua's fate change? At the moment, Jinghua was subject to various kinds of indirect criticism for her views, and since most of the articles attacking her were just signed "critic," it was hard to say at what level the criticisms originated.

Liu Quan had completed all her tasks that morning. She had put all the company's reports in order, drawn up charts of their liaison work with subsidiary companies and made a record of their work over the last month. She should really have been able to go home by now, but she knew that she was obliged to remain here smoking until it was time to leave. Her transfer would only be temporary, so for the moment she must leave a way back. After all, Manager Wei might attempt to ruin all her efforts to leave.

"Xiao Liuzi, Xiao Liuzi!" Manager Wei's driver, Tie, boomed at her, bidding her to come, as if he were ordering a servant girl around. Why had she bothered to study English at the university? If she had simply become a driver, she would be able to order everyone around like that too.

Liu Quan stubbed out her cigarette and stood up. Opposite, Lao Dong, the head of her section, raised his snowy white head from a pile of forms and looked at her anxiously. Whenever Manager Wei called her to his office, Lao Dong would always look at her in this way, as if he felt concerned for her safety. She did not want Lao Dong, a kindly person, to worry on her behalf. Such people lack the ability to fight or defend themselves and are easily hurt. The older they get, the more they become like young children. Liu Quan smiled kindly on and supported people like this as if danger, like a ferocious wolf, were always lurking outside the door. She might have been cheating them by doing so, but she couldn't really be blamed. Liu Quan reassured Lao Dong with a nod and then left the office.

As she walked along the corridor she wondered why she hadn't said anything to manager Wei. She felt terribly nervous and feared that he might raise some unexpected problems about her transfer. When she reached his office she found driver Tie leaning against the doorway, a pair of plastic sandals on his feet and a large palm fan stuck in the back of his trousers. Without waiting for Liu Quan to enter he waved a piece of paper at her and said, "Hey, can you translate all these squiggles for me?" He thrust the piece of paper before Liu Quan's face. She walked past as if she hadn't heard and went straight into Manager Wei's office. Driver Tie always behaved like this with Liu Quan and from this she concluded that Manager Wei probably made obscene remarks about her in private.

Manager Wei was reclining on a red sofa, one leg over the armrest and the buttons of his trousers undone to reveal the kind of colorful underpants usually worn only by women. He was pretending to read some report and appeared not even to have noticed what Driver Tie had been saying. Only when Liu Quan was standing right in front of him did he look up. At first Liu Quan had tried to fight against these sorts of insult, but she found that the harder she fought, the tougher her life had become. Finally it had seemed that self-respect was as fragile as an egg shell.

Liu Quan's voice trembled as she asked, "Manager Wei, what do you want?"

Manager Wei put down his report, stretched himself and then, eventually, took his leg down from the arm of the sofa. "Hasn't Mr. Tie told you?" He sounded very impatient, believing that since he had authority over Liu Quan then anything connected with him, down to the paper he wrote on or his teacups, carried the same authority. For Liu Quan to have ignored Driver Tie was an insult to him personally.

Driver Tie chuckled triumphantly and thrust the piece of paper into Liu Quan's face once again. "Translate it!"

Liu Quan glanced at it without taking it. It was a telegram in English, probably from some foreign company. "I can't understand it," she said frankly.

"Can't understand it? And you want to get a better job?" Manager Wei laughed dryly. He was not happy about Liu Quan leaving, as if it had been a personal affront which he must counter by humiliating her in some way. He hadn't imagined that Liu Quan could have been capable of arranging a transfer. What on earth did the Foreign Affairs Bureau want her for? Liu Quan? He had never imagined that anyone would help her in this way. Whenever he was asked about her, he remained noncommittal, neither recommending nor criticizing her. He couldn't think what sort of person Liu Quan must have got herself involved with.

He wanted to see Liu Quan one last time to try and size her up. She was wearing a pair of blue trousers, a black and white check blouse and black plastic sandals. Her face was deeply lined and there was nothing attractive that he could find in her entire figure. But if you looked at her long enough you could discover a charm which reminded Manager Wei of the Buddha's hand, which was a kind of plant his grandmother used to place on their family altar when he had been a child. In that dark, oppressive room, that Buddha's hand had given him the sensation of mature trees and gardens. For the past few years Manager Wei had been trying to find ways of dealing with Liu Quan, but to no avail. He couldn't figure out why she did not obey him. She seemed to have no goals or ambition, making her extremely hard to control. And now she was suddenly trying to stretch her wings and fly. Both of them knew perfectly well why she wanted to leave though neither of them would admit it. For Manager Wei this kind of insult was more than he could bear and so he hoped to have the satisfaction of delivering a final blow to her.

Liu Quan could sense the same implied insult in both Driver Tie's voice and Manager Wei's laugh. She was reminded of the cruel games Mengmeng would play with ants, drawing a circle on the ground with a mothball and trapping an ant inside, so that it ran around frantically, unable to escape. She felt like that ant, flaying her limbs about in the hopeless belief that there must be some way out.

Manager Wei began preaching to her:

"All work is for the revolution. There's no distinction between 'high' or 'low' work. The leaders have arranged it this way in accordance with an overall plan."

Liu Quan had to fight back her anger. But the image of that ant struggling for freedom kept floating before her eyes. She no longer noticed what Manager Wei was saying. Was it really his fault if she couldn't get transferred? Was he really responsible? Was anybody . . . ?

"Liu Quan, telephone!" Lao Dong knocked on the door of the office, with this very timely interruption.

"Anything else, Manager Wei?" Liu Quan asked.

"Go and answer the phone first." Manager Wei frowned.

As she left the office, Liu Quan felt the back of her blouse; it was soaked with perspiration.

Liu Quan picked up the receiver, only to hear a single mournful note, like the whine of the wind. "Hello, hello . . . "

"Never mind. They've probably hung up," Lao Dong said.

"Didn't you ask who it was?"

"No."

Liu Quan replaced the receiver and, noticing Lao Dong's faraway expression, suddenly asked, "Was there really a phone call for me?"

But Lao Dong's flat, expressionlss face remained as blank as a carved Buddha. Was he really as naive as she had thought? Last year, she remembered, he had managed to get her out of having to attend a Commodities Fair with Manager Wei, saying that she was occupied with some other work.

Liu Quan had never spoken of Manager Wei's insults to others, except Liang Qian and Jinghua to whom she poured forth all her life misfortunes. Often in the evening the three of them would sit beneath the lamplight, the remnants of the evening meal still scattered over the table, none of them feeling in the mood to clear it up. Two of them would usually listen, while the other explained her latest grievances, or raged about the way in which she had been treated, banging her fists on the arm of the sofa. But none of them could really give a word of comfort, so what did all that talking really amount to? Why did they have so many grievances, so many misfortunes? What evil could they have committed in their former lives that they should now, as it seemed, have to atone for the sins of all women?

Liu Quan lived in constant dread of being sent off on business with Manager Wei, of having to make a report to him, or of even having to squeeze onto the same public bus with him. The year before she had had to go on business to Hunan Province with him and he had squeezed close against her on a bus. It had been summer, so their clothes had been thin. In desperation Liu Quan had pushed towards the man on the other side of her, almost pressing her head into his chin, so close she could smell the odor of cigarette smoke coming from his nose and mouth. Luckily, the man must have realized Liu Quan's plight, for he quickly made space for her and put his bag between her and Manager Wei. Liu Quan had given the man a hasty, pitiful look of gratitude.

During the May First holiday their company had held a dinner at which Lao Dong had gotten a bit tipsy and said,"Why doesn't she get a raise, eh? I thought the whole division had already agreed to it? It seems that even if you've got a pretty face, life can still be hard. Liu Quan, you should get married, then you'll have someone to look after you."

Get married! That wasn't such an easy matter! Nowadays, even young girls found it hard to get themselves married, so how could a forty-year-old divorcee like herself even dare to hope? And she had a son. As people get older they become clearer about some things, and one realization is about how difficult marriage is. They begin to see marriage as a tragedy or, if not a tragedy, a lottery in which only a few meet fortune.

But women, unlike men, must always find some object for their affections, as if loving were their sole purpose in life. Without love their lives would lose all joy. And if they have no husband or child to dote on, even a cat may become the object of their affection, or for that matter, a piece of furniture or cooking in their kitchen. In Liu Quan's case, of couse, none of this was necessary since she had a son. But Liu Quan had surrendered her right to bring Mengmeng up because she did not have an apartment of her own. Living under someone else's roof made her feel constantly indebted to others, even if it was the roof of her best friend.

Thank heavens her son was neither like his father nor like Liu Quan herself. He was not irritable or forgetful as his father was. But perhaps he would change when he grew up; Liu Quan, too, had been open-minded as a child. Mengmeng had a round little face, glowing with health, like a shiny round loaf of bread straight out of the oven. Mengmeng was open and naughty, unlike his narrow-minded and stingy father. When his father bought tomato paste he would always get the large three *jin* tin, saying that this came cheaper than three six *liang* tins at 75 *fen* each. He did not have a refrigerator in his house either, so for every meal they had to eat either tomato and egg soup, potatoes in tomato sauce, fried rice with tomato sauce, or noodles in tomato sauce . . .

After she had gotten married, Liu Quan's relations with her family were strained since her father couldn't stand her commercially-minded husband. But then eventually, when she had decided to get divorced, they considered such behavior immoral, a disgrace to the family. So ultimately it seemed as though the ancient customs, handed down over thousands of years, dictated that she should stick to her husband, for better or for worse. Although her father had studied in England, returning with all the regalia of his Western education, his thinking was still bound up by these traditions. We learn wholesale from abroad: electronics, Coca-Cola, Trident aircraft, fashion, but we still retain our basic traditions. In this respect, at least, we have not yet conquered Confucius.

In Liu Quan's eyes, her father was like a great encyclopedia, full of dignity in its place on the bookshelf, with a sober brown cover and gold lettering down the spine. Precise and comprehensive, it contained all the information the ordinary person needed to know. But it could not tell her what kind of person she should marry, since the older generation can never dictate such things to the younger generation and, in any case, life is complex and each person must discover those personal, intangible answers herself. If one does everything according to convention and custom only, they will forever carry around with them the heavy, restricting burden of such an encyclopedia.

After getting divorced, Liu Quan had lived a nomadic existence for a while, staying in a friend's house here, an old classmate's there. Luckily her mother had brought her up to be adaptable and practical, so wherever she had stayed she could be of use as a baby-sitter. She always made sure that she wasn't a burden to others. In her worst moments of misery she would even make toys for their children or listen patiently to her host's own woes, though these had usually been less tragic than her own. But how she had wanted an apartment of her own! She had applied to her company for one, but Manager Wei had just looked away and said, "What do you want an apartment for?"

"Don't you know I'm divorced?" Liu Quan had replied.

"That makes no difference," he had retorted. "There are married couples waiting for apartments, you know. And now divorcees want them too! It's getting quite ridiculous. People shouldn't be allowed to get divorced in the first place!"

"What should I do then, live on the street?"

"Who's telling you to live on the street? Just settle where you are now." He laughed.

"That's no good. The flat belongs to someone else's work unit."

"Well, you could always put a curtain up in between, couldn't you?"

"How . . . how can you talk like that?" Liu Quan had felt more and more furious.

"Oh, I've seen a lot in my time. Plenty of people live together like that." Manager Wei's expression had shown that he saw Liu Quan as one of those women who can't survive for a day without a man.

Since that time, Liu Quan had never brought up the question of housing with him again. All she could do was ask for help from others, not such an easy matter when she had no money. Society is still full of those people who can solve any problem for you, be it transferring from a job, finding an apartment, buying a tape recorder or color TV from Hong Kong. But they will cheat you in a flash if given half a chance. Balzac could easily find enough material today to write another *Le Pere Goriot*.

At last she seemed to have found a flat in the suburbs. She had spent three or four hours a day, before and after work, searching for a place. Now at last she heard about a place she could have, a nest of her own, where she could hide away from the world. No longer would she have to go home tired and force herself to be cheerful and show concern for things which did not interest her in the least. She quickly phoned Jinghua, who had just returned to Beijing from a trip to a nearby province. "I've found a flat," she burst out. "Now we can live together."

It had taken them the best part of two hours to get there by bus. What a shock! Was this an apartment? You could see patches of grey sky through the holes in the roof, as well as the grass which grew up there, thick and abundant as a small forest. The wind blew through every crack in the wall and chipped bricks showed through the peeling plaster. The beams and rafters had been eaten away by woodworms, so that they looked as lined and pitted as an old man's forehead. Liu Quan said to Jinghua, "I feel like a survivor of an atomic explosion, standing amidst the ruins."

Jinghua, however, was rather more optomistic. "Don't worry," she said. "I know how to plaster ceilings and walls; I had plenty of experience with that when I was living in the forests."

"It's not just a matter of plastering," Liu Quan replied. "These walls need to be completely rebuilt. Do you want us to be buried alive in here?"

Liang Qian's appearance on the scene, with enough influence to get them a place, was like a gift from the gods. She had just been released from prison and her head, which had been shaved, was just beginning to sprout bristles, like a hedgehog.

"Damn the bastards!" she had said, rolling up her sleeves as if getting ready for a fight.

Jinghua had looked at her, dumbfounded. "Good heavens, when did you learn to swear?"

"I've not only learned to swear," Liang Qian replied, "but I've learnt a lot more about the world besides. Don't worry, though. Isn't the policy in favor of people like us now? I'll find some way to get an apartment."

Liu Quan laughed aloud, but her laughter sounded hollow, like the stylized mirth of a singer in a Beijing opera. She slipped her hand into her pocket and pulled out a packet of cigarettes.

Liang Qian raised an eyebrow. "You smoke?" she asked.

Jinghua came over and said, "I smoke too."

Liang Qian silently took the cigarette from Liu Quan's hand, produced a lighter from her pocket and lit it. She took a puff, watching the smoke as it curled upwards, and then said wistfully, "I smoke too."

Liu Quan had felt her muscles go slack with exhaustion. Where else did they have to go now?

The three of them had been together since primary school. At that time Liang Qian had been a tough little character. She was as plump as a freshly filled sausage, her flesh tight and firm, unlike the dried-up, creased figure she was now. When they showered she would sit cross-legged, guarding the exit of the shower room, and each of them would have to ask for her permission to leave, to which she would graciously nod her head. If she went to the lavatory, she would never take her own paper with her, as the other girls did, but would always call through the partition, "So-and-so, bring me some paper!" And then so-and-so would always have to run back and push some paper under the door for her.

But this habit was later broken by Jinghua. One day she ganged up with two other little girls and, catching Liang Qian off guard, pushed her into the shower bath. Liang Qian had started screaming at the top of her voice, and a furious water-splashing fight had ensued. When it was Jinghua's turn to take paper to her in the lavatory, Jinghua had refused, leaving Liang Qian howling there for half the class session, until their teacher heard her screams. After these incidents, Liang Qian had refused to speak to Jinghua for a whole week.

During the Korean War, Liang Qian had spent a lot of time with a spiked stick collecting wastepaper in the rubbish heaps, and then selling it. She had handed over every penny she made to her teacher for the "support of the front line." Later, during the public-health campaign to get rid of the "Four Pests," she had spent all her midday rest period squatting in the lavatory with a fly swatter. She had taken everything seriously, intensely, whether it was work or her relationships with her friends. And now she was helping Liu Quan to transfer to the Foreign Affairs Bureau.

Liu Quan sighed. Well, a person's life was as changeable as the weather. Wouldn't she be starting a new job in a new environment the day after tomorrow? She was searching for something, not just struggling to break free. Every illusion she ever had, had been extinguished by bitter experience. What remained were her authentic feelings of social responsibility and conscience: she must justify the 56 yuan she earned each month.

Whenever a dull or miserable day had passed and the sighing and weeping and cursing was over, she would sit alone beneath the light cast by a solitary reading lamp, her heavy head propped on her hand, idly reading some English magazine. Then she would suddenly come to her senses and think, what was she doing? She had always received high grades in her English exams at the university, but what use was that in her present job? Then she would stare at the panda design on her table lamp and finally, when no solution presented itself, she would give a long sigh, take off her clothes and climb into bed.

It seemed as if Manager Wei had wanted to threaten her, deliberately emphasising that her transfer was "temporary," as if to imply that she would forever be within his grasp. So could it be that nothing would change? Still, Director Xie had told her over the telephone, "Come and report here on Monday. We've got an American delegation coming on Tuesday and we're short of interpreters. We'll arrange a full transfer later."

But Lao Dong had warned her, "You should be patient. What's the use of a temporary transfer? You must make sure the Foreign Affairs Bureau actually has the transfer notice before you move." However, Liu Quan was in too much of a hurry to leave. She couldn't wait to get away from the sight of Manager Wei's balding head, floating like an egg on the far side of the half-frosted glass of her office window. Usually all she could see was an indistinct shape, but if she happened to move across the office the top of his head would come into view. She had a good feeling that everything would be all right. Her English was up to par and she worked steadily enough. So why should the Foreign Affairs Bureau have any reason to change their minds about her?

* * *

Ten long, slender fingers, blackened by sawdust and dirt, tightly gripped the plane as it slid evenly back and forth over the surface of the wood. The shavings rolled off like locks of curly hair, as the grain in the wood became more and more apparent. The simple beauty of the pale yellow wood, with its pattern of light brown grain, beckoned Jinghua to stop for a moment and feel its smooth, warm surface. She felt very pleased with herself, with her own hands; she had produced something as good as any carpenter could make on a lathe.

She had learned this skill while she had been living in the forests, in order to drive away the feelings of hopelessness and loneliness during those bitter days. Sometimes she would do a carpentry task for that reason alone, not to make anything in particular, just taking any scrap of wood and planing it down until it became a smooth, pleasing shape. Later she would use the wood shavings to light a fire.

But after being transferred back to Beijing she had given up carpentry altogether. Luckily her tools had no thoughts or feelings of their own and could not accuse her of resorting to them only when she was in the depths of despair. So long as she took up her tools they would reward her with any article of furniture she chose to make and would never catch her off guard and bite her. This kind of work was far easier and more beneficial than writing those articles which were always receiving criticism. So why did she have to go on writing? But if no one had any sense of social responsibility, what would the world be like?

Maotou stood at her feet, looking up at her and miaowing. What did she want now? Just a moment ago Jinhua had boiled some fish for her, before eating herself, despite the fact that her own stomach had been rumblng furiously. Then she had eaten her own food half-raw, too hungry to wait for it to cook through. Maotou jumped up onto the rough work-bench which Jinghua had knocked together from a few chunks of wood, and from there onto Jinghua's back, where she swayed about until finally she got her balance. As Jinghua moved back and forth with her plane, Maotou had to move up and down, digging her sharp claws into Jinghua's blue overalls. She probably felt lonely and depressed too, needing people to comfort and caress her. Poor weak creature. Ultimately, it seemed that human beings were the strongest creatures in this world. But then, what about that man at work whom she always nicknamed "The Knife-face"?

Last year, after that controversial article of hers had been published, Jinghua's ideas had been praised by many critics and analysts and there followed endless reprints and interviews. Then "The Knife-face" had said to her, "Comrade Cao Jinghua, your elaboration of Marxism is a superb contribution to our overall understanding. I'd like to see you on the Party Central Committee!" He didn't mean this as a joke. In his excitement, he wriggled his thin body like a worm.

Jinghua had felt goose bumps all over her body and had replied. "I've never been so ambitious. And you'd better be more careful when you make jokes in the future!"

Jinghua felt quite sure his comment was a danger signal. From that time on, Jinghua always had to be careful to keep her distance from "The Knife-face". She had seen enough tragedies before, highly talented people who found themselves trapped, lost their objectivity and integrity, and were eventually swallowed up piece by piece, like a mulberry leaf being devoured by a silkworm. Jinghua didn't want to make a name for herself. All she wanted was to work steadily according to the Party spirit. Recently a fresh wind had been blowing through the oppressive world of political theory and academic research had become more rigorous. A new spirit of reform made it possible for her to express more of her thoughts and observations as well as her high communist ideals.

A whole year had passed after her article had been published and then, for some reason, "The Knife-face" suddenly remembered her again. Perhaps the pen name she had chosen to use when the article was published had been a mistake since some people confused it with that of a well-known theorist. Such misunderstandings, which spread rapidly and involved so many other people, gave Jinghua a strange feeling of sadness. At last she was using her talents, but she felt that the article she had written had been shallow and unaccomplished and did not deserve such attention.

What had "The Knife-face" said at the meeting that morning? Watching his mouth opening and closing as he talked, Jinghua was startled by how huge his mouth looked and how narrow and wedge-like was his face. It seemed to slice its way into everything decent and harmonious around it. He wanted Jinghua to "correct her attitudes and conscientiously remove the mistakes in her political thinking." How could he have forgotten that only a short while before he had wanted to nominate her for such an exalted position as member of the Central Committee?

Jinghua had made a speech right then and there, giving a general summary of her ideas and quite forgtting that Liu Quan had warned her against public speaking. She had felt touched by Liu Quan's concern, but how on earth could she just remain silent? Wasn't she also a member of the Communist Party? A member of the Party should serve truth alone, and not only his or her own personal needs. If there were no struggles or contradictions in the world at all, then how could they move forward? When it came to matters of principle she could not back down. What did a little misunderstanding like this matter anyway. Ultimately history would be the fairest judge of all.

Jinghua could see that her speech had been like a stream of warm air, driving out the cold discord struck by "The Knife-face's" criticisms. His type of behavior had become less common after the Cultural Revolution. Was it not a sign of progress that political life now bore signs of normalcy? People must be straightforward and honest, not always swaying with the wind. One might lose all earthly possessions, but one could not afford to lose one's integrity, for this gives one a foundation to build upon. Jinghua did not believe that bitter people like "The Knife-face" could ever live a happy or contented life.

Shortly after the criticism of Jinghua's article had appeared in the newspapers, a certain leader came to her organization to hold a meeting and called on everyone to help transform the "negative elements" into "positive elements," and to improve their attitudes toward work.

It had happened that Jinghua had a headache that day and had planned to ask for leave, but if she did that it would seem as if she were just trying to avoid criticism. Just before the meeting she had quickly swallowed a pain-killer which "The Knife-face" had offered her. This had stopped the pain immediately, but it also made her very sleepy all afternoon. She sat in the front row and remembered later that someone kept nudging her to keep her from dozing off. But try as she might she just couldn't stay awake; everything blurred and all she heard was distant murmuring. Her limbs became numb and she felt like some formless object floating in space. After the meeting, the leader made a point of shaking hands with her and said with a concerned tone, "Comrade Cao

Jinghua, as a member of the Communist Party, you must develop a serious attitude towards any unhealthy thinking. And when it comes to criticism from one's comrades, you should always be modest and thoughtful. Ha, ha, ha! Of course, if you disagree with anything we have said, naturally you may give us your opinion, eh?"

In a daze, Jinghua had laughed too and nodded mechanically. It was only after two days had passed and she had recovered that she asked "The Knife-face," "What was that pain-killer you gave me the other day?"

"The Knife-face" looked down, as if trying to hide something.

"I wonder what made me think it might have been a sleeping drug."

"Well, pain-killers can calm you down and make you feel tired."

Jinghua considered him pitiable—that he needed to resort to such a measure. "The drug you gave me could only put me to sleep for a matter of hours, I'm afraid. Why didn't you have the guts to give me some arsenic!"

"The Knife-face" suddenly changed color. "What on earth do you mean by that?"

"Oh nothing. Just a joke. Didn't you know that I like to play practical jokes? If you don't have the guts to give me arsenic, I'm sure somebody will give you some, sooner or later!" Jinghua laughed.

"What's funny? You really are behaving very strangely today."

"People with no feelings at all are the ones I hate most," Jinghua replied, pulling out a cigarette. "Here, have a cigarette. They're Dazonghua brand."

From that time on, every time he drank a cup of tea he would glance suspiciously in Jinghua's direction and then at his cup, go rinse it out and take fresh tea leaves. Jinghua would laugh to herself and admonish him, "What a waste of a good cup of tea." He was scared of that arsenic. But why was he not afraid of losing his integrity and conscience? What was the meaning of life to him without these two elements? How could anyone be so low and shameless?

After Jinghua had spoken at the meeting, the Party Branch Secretary, Lao An, had given a speech in support of Jinghua. Jinghua had seen "The Knife-face" take out his notebook and pen once again and jot down notes.

Lao An had continued, "Why do I support Comrade Cao Jing-hua? Because she speaks the truth. What is meant by liberalism? Isn't it rejecting leadership of the Party and no longer working toward socialism? Comrade Cao Jinghua's article does not propose this. Her article is simply a piece of academic exploration. We must not go around labeling and accusing comrades in this way. Just think back and remember those intense early days, when we used to work underground in the areas controlled by the Kuomintang. At that time people felt free to express any conflicting ideas they had, even reactionary ideas. And what could we do? Well, we could simply rely on the facts, on reason and on our own experience to convince them to join the revolution. I remember how many false ideas I had before I joined. An old comrade used to come round to my dormitory after work whenever he could, squeeze onto my bed and patiently talk sense to me the whole night through. At the slightest sign of a breakthrough his face would light up into a happy smile. Why did we act like that in those days? Because we were small and weak and needed more people to swell our ranks. To have angrily pressured people would only have frightened them away. Now that our numbers are great and we are strong, some people seem to think it no longer matters if a few people get persecuted. But think carefully, we not only lose one or two people; others follow and we lose a whole multitude . . ."

Jinghua could not bear to hear Lao An speaking any longer and did not wait for him to finish. She got up and left the meeting room and hid herself behind the curtains in the auditorium. His words had brought the tears welling into her eyes and she could not have faced him. It was strange: one could no longer find any trace of vitality in the body of this weak old man, with his trembling hands and shaking head, his dull tired eyes and his white-streaked hair. But that inner power of his remained, like some great surging force.

When the meeting was over, there was Lao An waiting for her in his office. "How was my speech?" Jinghua asked, hearing something a little artificial in her own voice.

Fortunately Lao An was not overly sensitive to such things. "Very good."

"Really?" she exclaimed. She could not hide her real feelings from Lao An.

"Yes, everyone thought so. Very good indeed!"

She relaxed, even smiled at him. The trust between them endured. At last he reached into a lower drawer and withdrew a bundle of letters tied up with a yellow ribbon and placed them on Jinghua's table. "These are the letters she sent me," he said, gently stroking the bundle of letters as one would caress the hair of a loved one. Jinghua knew who "she" was; Lao An was in love. It might have seemed rare for someone in his sixties to fall in love, but Jinghua sincerely hoped that someone as fine as Lao An might still experience the happiness love could bring.

Lao An's family life had been unfortunate. His wife had fallen in love with another man and asked for a divorce. On their way to the local government office to apply for their divorce, Lao An had urged her over and over again, "Just tell them that our feelings for one another are no longer as good as they were and that we both agree to a divorce. Don't mention that anyone else is involved. It will only make things more difficult." He had not expressed himself more explicitly as this might have offended his wife's dignity. Later he told Jinghua, "I was born in the old society, when women suffered the most terrible oppression. So now I have particular respect for women."

"Can you give me some advice? I am just about to make up my mind," said Lao An, "but I have two fears: first, that she is too 'foreign' and, second, that she is too emotional. These are her letters, in the order that she wrote them. Have a look at them and see what you think."

Jinghua was not sure that she could face reading through all those letters. She would always remember this Party member, branch secretary and leader, Lao An, just in the way he remembered that old comrade who came to his room and gave him so much inspiration in his early days. Jinghua wondered if that old comrade was still alive and if he knew what qualities he had instilled in his student.

There was a rumbling outside and downstairs someone called, "The coal cart is here!" Jinghua quickly put down her wood plane and ran downstairs. By now, just about all the households in their block had given up using coal briquets and changed to gas heat. But they had never managed to buy a gas cylinder, and now the price of a cylinder plus cooker had gone up to more than 100 yuan, far more than they could afford. But burning coal was really tiresome. The coal deliveries were so unreliable that sometimes for days they had no coal left to burn; yet if they had wanted to buy more coal at a time, they would have had nowhere to store it. The people in the local coal depot refused to sell to them if they went there themselves. Liu Quan had tried to call over and over again to ask for an earlier delivery and it was only now that they had finally agreed to come. The person Liu Quan had dealt with on the telephone had always been a man, but it was a woman who made the delivery, a small, feeble-looking woman. What had happened to all the men? Probably they were left in charge of putting off customers who came or phoned in.

It was just about to rain and a westerly wind blew the black clouds in rolls across the sky. The coal dust from the delivery cart blew into Jinghua's face, stinging her eyes, but the woman delivering the coal continued with her task of unloading, seemingly unaware of the change in the weather. Then Mrs. Jia came out of the building carrying a dustpan full of broken pieces of briquet and said, "That last delivery of coal was full of dust—it just crumbled when I touched it. Could you change some for me?"

The delivery woman just continued to shovel the coal as if she had heard nothing. Mrs. Jia laughed awkwardly, tipped the broken briquets onto the cart and helped herself to four fresh ones. Fast, and as though she had eyes in the back of her head, the delivery woman swung round and retrieved two of the briquets from Mrs. Jia's pan, then continued with her work without saying a word. She stood on tiptoe and strained to reach the last briquets as she emptied the coal cart at the far end. Mrs. Jia went on grumbling to herself, the smile no longer visible on her face. "Such a big pan and you'll only let me have two briquets. . . " She continued to take a briquet here, a briquet there, until she amassed a small pile of her own.

The delivery woman, very tired now, but still aware of Mrs. Jia standing behind her grumbling and watching, chose to ignore her. Jinghua jumped up onto the coal cart and helped her unload the last of the coal. The woman still remained silent, but just as she was about to leave she said to Jinghua, "When you need another delivery of coal, just phone up. My name is Zhou."

The wind became stronger, carrying with it the cool smell of distant rain. Jinghua had to move all the coal in before it rained. Her blouse was puffed up by the wind and as she worked the sweat began to trickle down her back. Mrs. Jia meanwhile kept watch over her small pile of coal and continually glanced at her wristwatch in agitation. "What can I do? The family will never get out of work before it starts raining and I cannot carry it up the stairs." Mrs. Jia had a pair of "liberated feet," or feet which had been unbound, and although walking was no serious problem for her, carrying the coal upstairs would have been difficult. So Jinghua naturally had to help her, knowing full well that at the next meeting of the neighborhood committee she would report to all those other old women, "The other day, you know, they didn't turn their light off until after twelve. Still seeing off visitors in the middle of the night." Or, "The other evening they still hadn't turned their lights on by eight. What do you think they're hiding in there?" The gossiping was like Mrs. Jia's "liberated feet," a legacy of the past. Whether Jinghua helped her move the coal or not, the gossiping would still go on. One had to be realistic: Mrs. Jia needed her help, so Jinghua helped her.

Both of their households were on the third floor and they had five hundred briquets of coal between them. This meant that Jinghua had to make a total of fifty trips and by the time she had finished she felt utterly exhausted, ready to collapse in a heap on the concrete floor. All the while Mrs. Jia prattled on and on, though Jinghua felt so tired that her ears ached and she was unable to take in a word of what she was saying. "Comrade Cao, don't go yet. . . come and wash your hands in here. How about some tea?"

"Don't worry, I've got soap and water in my flat," Jinghua replied, lurching off like a drunkard. But when she got back to the flat she found that the hot water thermos was empty. There was nothing particularly remarkable about this, since it was often empty. However, she regretted it now. She turned on the tap and scrubbed her hands with a piece of soap, but her fingernails remained filthy. She could really do with a nailbrush. . . Then, as she turned around, she suddenly felt as though someone had stabbed her in the back. She fell to the floor in front of the sink. Even the slightest movement was agonizing and she could not move her legs or feet to get up again. When she began groaning, Maotou bounded over and walked round and round her, miaowing anxiously and stretching out her neck as if calling for help.

"Don't make such a noise, Maotou," Jinghua pleaded. "Nobody can understand what you're saying. It's all right, thank you..." As if she understood what Jinghua was saying, Maotou stopped miaowing and with a frightened look on her face pressed herself close against Jinghua's chest, as if she were keeping guard over her.

The thunder followed immediately after flashes of lightning, rolling in through the window and seeming to explode above Jinghua's head. A fierce gale shook the doors, trees and telephone wires, howling and crashing as it went. As if God had at last lost his temper, the storm broke mercilessly over the world, while the earth seemed to shake and groan in protest. The rainwater blowing in through the curtains quickly formed a pool on the floor. Soon Jinghua's legs were soaked and the damp cold of the concrete floor seeped up through her body making her teeth chatter violently. She could not just go on lying here, she must somehow crawl to her bed. She raised herself up with her arms and tried to push herself along, crying out with pain. Maotou started miaowing again and wrapped herself around Jinghua's legs. She couldn't move any further and so she stopped struggling. Who could help her up onto her bed? How she needed someone with a strong pair of arms, but she knew that no such person was likely to appear. As she lay helpless on the floor, she was acutely aware that she would never again know what it was to be loved by a man, but would live the rest of her life alone. Why was it like this? It seemed as if all three of them were separated from men by some unbridgeable chasm. Was it because men were historically more advanced than women—or women more advanced than men—so that they could no longer find any basis for communication? Well, if this was the case, then neither men nor women could really be blamed. No one could help or change the historical circumstances which had gone into creating these distorted positions.

She remembered a foreign film she'd seen the previous year,

A Strange Woman. There was nothing especially strange about her —what she wanted from men seemed perfectly justified, but it was said that the film had met with considerable criticism. The things that woman sought were exactly those things which Jinghua and most other thinking women looked for. No matter what race, nationality or language, these seemed not to matter—the problem was one of universal dimensions. Jinghua thought one day she would write a study of this problem. . .

She tried again to move and couldn't get as far as the bed, but she did just make her way to the sofa. She pulled down a small quilt and put it beneath her back to protect herself from the cold floor. It would still be a long time before Liu Quan got back from work, but when she did Maotou would get up and run over to meet her. The pain was hard to bear but she knew very well that even if she shouted nobody was likely to turn up in a downpour like this.

At last Maotou bounded out of the room. It was not Liu Quan but Liang Qian who came in, looking as if she had just been fished out of a river, her raincoat dripping all over the floor. Jinghua at once felt her pain ease. "What on earth are you doing here in such a downpour?" she asked. "Aren't you staying at the dormitory?"

"Good lord! What on earth is wrong with you?" said Liang Qian, squatting down next to Jinghua without even taking off her coat. Then, realizing that her coat was dripping all over Jinghua, she took it off in a flurry and threw it onto a hook on the door. After the third attempt to lift Jinghua she said, "put your hands round my neck and we'll try it this way," and then she half-carried, half-dragged her up onto the bed. She clasped Jinghua's icy, unwashed hand and said, "We'd better get you to the hospital."

"In this rain? Don't worry, there's not much they can do for me there. I'll be fine again in a few days' time." Now that she was on her bed Jinghua felt a lot better.

"You really should see a doctor. Look, your hand is still shaking. I'd better go and get you something warm to wear." She took a cotton jacket and a pair of clean trousers out of Jinghua's wardrobe, but trying to change her clothes was too painful for her. When she lifted up the quilt Liang Qian noticed that Jinghua's feet were still covered with fragments of coal. "Ah! Now I know what you've been up to." Then she went to get some hot water to wash Jinghua's feet.

"I'm afraid you won't find any hot water there," said Jinghua weakly.

Liang Qian opened up the stove to make a fire and then put a pot of water on to boil. The lid of the pot hadn't had a knob on it for a long time and the hole on top looked like the mouth of a volcano. She found a cauliflower in the corner of the room, cut off a piece and used it to stop up the hole. When it came to household matters she felt clumsy and inept, so once she had set the pot to boil she felt as if she had made a major achievement. "Wait a moment while I go and call a cab," she said. "We should get you to the hospital right away."

"It's raining too hard now. Don't worry." Jinghua did not have the patience to go to the hospital; she was quite content to wash her feet and lie in her warm bed. "They'll only give me pain killers and send me home again. What's the point? Just plug in my diathermy machine for me, won't you, and put it against my back. But she wondered who could look after her at home? Liu Quan was still busy with her American delegation, and with her transfer due any day now, she couldn't very well ask for leave. At the moment Jinghua couldn't even do small things for herself, like going to the bathroom.

So it was decided that Liang Quan would stay home and take care of her. Luckily Liang Quan's work was just about finished—the sound mixing had already been completed and now all that remained was for the film to be approved. She braved the rain today in order to especially invite Jinghua to go and see a preview of her film. Just now, speeding through the storm on her bicycle, she had felt exhilarated, as if she did possess the strength and stamina to press on after all. Few women could enjoy such a feeling of freedom. True liberation was more than gaining improvement of economic and political status; it was also necessary that women develop confidence and strength in order to realize their full value and potential.

"What a pity, Liu Quan and I will miss seeing the film tonight." Jinghua said.

Liang Qian adjusted the diathermy machine beneath Jinghua's back. "Don't worry. . . it will go well and you'll have another chance to see it. Just rest now."

"How can I help worrying? I know that this film is your baby."

Yes, it was Liang Qian's "baby." When she had given birth to Chengcheng she had felt this way too. At that time she still hadn't understood the responsiblities of motherhood and Chengcheng's arrival had caught her quite unprepared. Now she was unable to find any trace of herself in Chengcheng, but her film, in contrast, contained much of what was her. One generation is connected to another merely through blood ties, but a work of art is a direct reflection of the artist and through it the artist may live on. What did it matter that Bai Fushan had cast her off like a piece of old clothing, or that Chengcheng might not grow up to be a person of exceptional value to society? In her work she could find her own kind of security.

Liang Qian's eyes lit up, making her look unusually pretty, as if two lights were glowing in her soul. The rain had stopped and the sky, washed clean by the storm, was filled with a clear soft light. The sound of dripping from the roof became slower and slower, and all around lay the tranquility of the calm following the storm. "Look, a rainbow." Liang Qian pointed to the horizon.

Jinghua strained round to try and look out of the window. "It looks so near, as if you could touch it." She loved rainbows, how they could transport the imagination to the beautiful world of fairy tales.

Liang Qian stared out into the twilight, moved by a feeling of peace. Her mind wandered back through the past, and into the future where further troubles and bitterness might await them, and through it all they would become even more mature. She did not want to give Jinghua any false words of comfort or encouragement; they were no longer children and the truth was that the time would inevitably come when Jinghua would be paralyzed and unable to get out of bed. Jinghua herself knew this better than any of them, though it was never spoken of. But Jinghua's spirit would always stand erect and she would certainly leave her mark in history. If she ever got around to writing that thesis she had been planning she would certainly shake up those people who were still bound up by the rules of conventional wisdom.

"Jinghua, you mustn't go on with your woodworking," she said suddenly. "If you do I'll throw out that plane of yours!" Liang Qian patted Jinghua's back with the diathermy machine.

"Ouch! Don't hit me! What else can I do if people won't allow me to write? Whatever I say, there is always someone ready and waiting to attack me." Jinghua felt her anger rising.

"It's tragic, said Liang Qian, "that those people have completely lost their progressive spirit. They carry around the identity of a Communist Party member, but have long since forgotten the meaning of Marxism. Or perhaps they never really understood it in the first place. Anyway, even if for now they enjoy a momentary status, they are bound to be laughed at by later generations. You really shouldn't degrade yourself by bothering about them."

Liang Qian rarely spoke in such a direct and serious way about her work and Jinghua's interest was aroused. Everybody had their troubles, but if you could get past dwelling too much on them, life might be more rewarding. She remembered seeing a crane in the forests with a bald patch on its head and had been told that once the crane became mature that bald patch would turn red. Sooner or later their heads would grow a patch of red too and then they would be able to soar higher and higher. . .

"How do you want me to be?" she asked Liang Qian.

"I want you to write, write, write. . . I want you to make a contribution towards revolutionary theory, or if you can't do that, I want you to support those who can, and not let them struggle on alone."

"I'm afraid your hopes for me are a bit too high."

"You can do it." Liang Qian looked at the tormented figure of Jinghua lying on the bed, at her sunken eyes, her unwashed, blackened feet and her tattered clothes. How long could she go on like this, in pain, barely able to live her life. The image of a nearly burned down candle passed through her mind. But could she say to Jinghua, "give up the flame?"

"Please go on 'recharging' me," Jinghua said. Whenever one of them had found herself in trouble and was feeling low, the other two would "recharge" her, and this word had become part of their vocabulary over the years since childhood. Endurance was a quality which marked their generation and they were proud of it.

"All right then, I'll try." Jinghua's eyes sparkled as they hadn't for years, in the way they did when she was a child, full of life and mischief and plans for some delightful joke.

* * *

It had started all over again, this life of pleading and begging. Whether you wanted to get a divorce, an apartment to live in or a suitable job, it always involved grovelling at the feet of others in the hope that they would show pity and understanding. What was so extraordinary about such requests? They were not asking for more than their fair share. When would Liu Quan at last know what it felt like to stand up proud and straight? She was not yet old, but she felt as if her back had been bent for a whole long lifetime.

The sound of footsteps coming closer echoed down the corridor. Liu Quan cast her eyes downwards and concentrated on pulling a loose thread from her skirt. She felt hostle, yet apprehensive at the thought of seeing the stern look in his eyes. In an instant he could change and become very polite, although condescending, as if showing forgiveness for some small transgression. But perhaps she was just being oversensitive.

The footsteps went past. No, they were not coming here after all. But Liu Quan continued to strain her ears in anticipation, in case Xie Kunsheng did come. She had been sitting here for two hours already, ever since his office had opened at eight o'clock this morning. It seemed as if Xie Kunsheng had never been so busy before, coming in and out of the office, picking up the telephone and putting it down again. . . and even when Liu Quan had a chance to break in with, "Director Xu. . . ," he would politely cut her short saying, "Wait a moment, won't you? You can see how busy I am." When people used that cool politeness, who would dare interrupt them?

Yes, he was busy. All this time Liu Quan had overheard various discussions about whom they should invite to the banquet that evening. As far as she could make out, these discussions had already been going on for days without any conclusions being reached. The banquet was being held in honor of some representatives of a foreign electronics company, and choosing the guests was a process requiring great care and diplomacy. How many times had a certain engineer been invited? Had some department chief or other been invited often enough? But nobody seemed quite sure of the answers to these questions—the only thing certain was that Xie Kunsheng's presence was indispensible. How then could Liu Quan, with her trifling personal problems, be permitted to disrupt such important work? There was nothing else she could do but wait.

Liu Quan mechanically rubbed the hem of the light brown dress she was wearing, an action which helped to calm her nerves. She felt as if she had been done up in some sort of theatrical costume: Liang Qian had given her the dress, a fashionable style with a loose waist and matching belt; her high heeled shoes had come from Jinghua, who seldom bought any feminine luxuries for herself. The clothes represented a kind of simple hopefulness for the future. It seemed that no matter what hardships they suffered, their approach, their attitudes were a little childish at heart, even though they knew that nothing came easy in this world. Liu Quan remembered that her grandmother used to say these words of enlightenment: "Life is full of hardship and if you don't temper yourself to withstand it, you won't survive." She had lived to the ripe old age of eighty-one, and because of her philosophy she had kept well and had never seemed old or decrepit.

"Lao Xie, Lao Xie!" Zhu Zhenxiang shouted as he went by, and this time he noticed Liu Quan sitting in Xie's office. He was the bureau chief above Xie Kunsheng. Every time he had gone by Liu Quan rose up tentatively and forcd an expectant smile.

"Director Xie was here a moment ago," Zhu said. "If there's anything important you'd like me to say to him, I could pass it on."

Liu Quan's smile made Zhu Zhenxiang feel a little ill at ease; he would have felt better if she hadn't smiled so eagerly. He could feel she was worried and needed help. She seemed quite nervous, like a young girl whose family's ill-fortune had forced her to go out and fend for herself. He knew little about Liu Quan's circumstances, but during his contact with her over the past twenty days, when the American delegation had been making its visit, he had been impressed by her dignity, endurance and efficiency.

When the American delegation had arrived, they had been unable to find enough luggage trolleys and their guests had to wait around for half an hour. With all the foreign visitors to China lately, the airport couldn't keep up with the demands on its services.

Finally Liu Quan had thought of a way out: she told the interpreters to keep an eye on any cart already in use, then grab it as soon as it was free. This plan was all very well, but there were several people who did not like the idea of running around after other people's trolleys. Zhu Zhenxiang had noticed that Qian Xiuying didn't stop preening herself in front of a plate glass window. She always lingered any place where she might catch a glimpse of herself. She had drawn her belt tightly around her, causing the excess flesh of her waist to push upwards, filling out her boldly striped dress so that it looked like a butterfly about to burst out and fly. Zhu Zhenxiang could tell from her expression that Liu Quan's idea had dampened her enjoyment and that she resented Liu Quan's presence, probably wondering what anyone would want with someone who bosses everyone around.

Zhu felt rather uneasy about Xie Kunsheng for several reasons, but he had settled on no way of dealing with him. Although he himself was the bureau chief, he exercised no real authority over the head of the foreign affairs office. Xie could always find ways and means of getting round him. The Foreign Affairs Bureau had quite a number of interpreters, but few were really competent. So when it came to key functions they always had to borrow interpreters from other units. This state of affairs should really have been put right long before, but it was very hard to make adjustments in personnel. Yet what was Zhu Zhenxiang to do when he saw Qian Xiuying displaying her ignorance of Chinese history in front of foreign guests? He could always try to get her moved to another job, but he feared that Xie Kunsheng would never stand for it. As far as appearance, ability and behavior went, Liu Quan seemed superior in every way to Qian Xiuying. She had seemed so full of self-confidence in her work, and yet now she looked so helpless. Women were hard to make out. On the last evening, when some leader had held a farewell party for their guests, all the other interpreters had suddenly disappeared, leaving Liu Quan to cope alone. Zhu Zhenxiang had felt quite anxious on her behalf, though in fact she had managed admirably, successfully putting across the leader's jokes so that the Americans had roared with laughter. At the end, the leader had made a special toast to Liu Quan: "Thanks to the interpreter for doing such a good job."

Liu Quan had smiled just faintly, the smile of an educated woman who recognizes her own intelligence and has gained the respect of a man. But the Liu Quan he saw before him now was quite a different person, like a painting whose surface has been marred by time and neglect. What could be the matter with her? He felt sadness and sympathy towards her. How easily one could be destroyed, even just by carelessness or thoughtlessness. Well, Liu Quan had not come to look for him and he couldn't afford to get involved in her problems, or else he would get nothing else done all day.

"Thank you, I'll talk to him myself," Liu Quan replied.

A completely unexpected and unknown name had appeared on the list of guests for the reception of an English delegation. Zhu Zhenxiang could not make head or tail of it, so he had come to clear up the matter directly with Xie Kunsheng. In the corridor he could hear Xie's voice, "Allright, then, let's leave it at that. If there's any problem, I'll see to it myself."

Xie Kunsheng was always ready to take command of the situation wherever he went. He believed that unless people like himself were around, nothing would get done.

"Were you looking for me, Director Zhu?" Xie Kunsheng always had an expensive cigarette-holder in his hand, one with traditional Chinese landscape designs on it. And there was always a cigarette smoldering at its end. His clothes were made at the best tailors in Beijing and he wore them proudly as a symbol of his status. But Zhu Zhenxiang always had the feeling that these clothes were like a costume rented for a wedding photograph, and that whatever airs he might have had about him, one couldn't help but detect a certain coarseness of character which he couldn't entirely conceal. At the root of his coarseness was an intense preoccupation with the opposite sex.

Liu Quan had stood up once again, a cautious, forced smile on her lips. Her smile at once drew a sharp line between them. On the one hand, there was a jovial, self-important little bureaucrat, on the other the petty clerk, reminiscent of the clerk in Chekhov's story, "The Death of a Petty Official." If one side so much as coughed, then the other would have to ponder over it for three days. Whatever others thought about it, Zhu Zhenxiang for one could not bear this kind of self-deprecating behavior. He much preferred to be on terms of equality with other people.

The scene was being played like a comedy. Xie Kunsheng's face showed a false expression of courtesy and concern, though he continued to fidget with the documents on his desk. Then he opened every drawer of his desk, as if he were looking for something and then closed them again. It was going too far and Zhu Zhenxiang felt impatience and disgust. Could the head of his office really behave like some Yamen chief in old China? "Go on then, Comrade Liu Quan," Zhu Zhenxiang urged her, trying to come to her aid. If she had been more like Qian Xiuying she could have gotten her way with a pretty smile. Qian Xiuying always remembered that she was a woman, whereas Liu Quan often seemed to forget it.

Liu Quan's face began to grow red. No matter whether it was Zhu Zhenxiang's sympathy or Xie Kunsheng's false politeness, she still felt the humiliation of having to plead with others; her self-respect vanished in such situations.

Two days ago, after the American delegation had left, she attempted to buy meal tickets at the catering section and was asked which work unit she came from. She told them the Foreign Affairs Bureau, but the ticket-seller was unable to find her name on his list. When Liu Quan explained that she was working there temporarily, the ticket-seller insisted that temporary staff had to buy their tickets through their own divisions. Liu Quan had no choice but to ask Qian Xiuying for help, but she had replied, "Oh, I don't even know where the catering section is. I've never had to buy tickets myself since other people always get them for me. But of course I'll help you if I can." Obviously thinking of all the men who had happily bought her tickets, Qian shook her long hair to one side.

Liu Quan felt driven to her wits' end by this kind of superficial behavior, this attitude that anyone could treat her as if she hardly existed at all. She felt like a small stone lying by the side of the road, trodden on over and over again by a myriad of feet. Not one person stopped to wonder: does that stone feel pain?

When she had been doing physical labor at cadre school during the Cultural Revolution, Liu Quan had always felt anxious about the little grey donkey they used to pull carts. It strained every muscle in its body to pull the cart uphill on legs so thin they looked like they might snap. Liu Quan would always push the cart from behind to help the poor creature. The donkey seemed to appreciate her kindheartedness and would look at her obediently with its pretty, placid eyes while she patted its neck. This led some people to nickname her "The Donkeyist." Well, she could really do with a bit of "donkeyism" just now.

"I've bought you three yuan's worth for the moment," said Qian Xiuying importantly, handing over the tickets and twelve yuan in change. This was clearly her way of affronting Liu Quan. If she had not wanted to buy her tickets, she could easily have said so in the first place, rather than deciding of her own accord to buy only three yuan's worth. Even she had some power over Liu Quan, or so it seemed.

That same day Liu Quan had asked if she might have her own desk in the office. The head of her group had smiled at her apologetically and said, as if addressing everyone at large, "Don't worry about a desk just now, this office is too crowded already. You'd better come and share my desk—I'll clear out a few drawers for you, O.K.?"

Late that afternoon, after they all had a chance to rest and reorganize their working arrangements, Qian Xiuying was particularly cheerful, sitting at the other end of the office chatting and laughing triumphantly. "Look!" she called out to everyone. "It was no problem for me to squeeze ten yuan out of them!" And she waved a ten yuan note in the air. The virgin-fresh note rustled crisply. Its owner must have hated to part with it, yet was still more than ready to let it go for the sake of the heavenly Qian Xiuying. "What shall we get to eat, then?" she asked, bestowing her favor on all and sundry. "What. . . keep it for the leaders? Well, I'm going to take my share anyhow. You can all do whatever you like with the rest!"

Qian Xiuying, the immortal! She felt pretty sure of herself, compared to such a good-for-nothing as Liu Quan. Everyone willingly came under Qian's command and she gloried in her great power and achievements. Liu Quan felt as if her every movement were under constant scrutiny by Qian Xiuying, as if Qian had eyes in the back of her head and an extra pair of ears specially designed to keep track of her.

At the time, Liu Quan had seen nothing unusual in these events.

But when she had received a formal notice that her work here was now complete, thanking her for her help and telling her to return to her original unit, she began to attach significance to Qian Xiuying's behavior. She was being sent back and there was no mention of her transfer. So that was how it was to be! She felt overwhelmed by the deceit, and humiliated, but she knew that she must not shed a tear in front of Qian Xiuying. Whom could she turn to? She was not like other women, who had their husbands to run to for solace and comfort. All she could do was retreat to the washroom and cry silently behind the lavatory door. The foul-smelling, filthy toilets, with their little baskets full of sodden paper were almost unbearable to the senses. Luckily one of the pipes was leaking, so the sound of water drowned out her sobs. She heard people coming in and out of the washroom, even Qian Xiuying had come in and tried the door of her cubicle. Then another woman who had entered with her said, "Those sandals you're wearing are really pretty. Where did you get them?"

"Pretty?" Qian Xiuying repeated in a deliberately off-hand manner. "My old man got them in Shanghai for me when he went there on business. Over twenty yuan, they were. Really! A waste of money, I say. He always buys all sorts of junk when he goes away on business. Well, it'd be a waste of money not to wear them, though they're pretty awful. I'm always saying to him, 'Don't buy me anything else, I don't need it.' But he just won't listen. He's so annoying!" Liu Quan could just picture Qian Xiuying, sweetly pursing her hippo-like lips as she spoke.

"Good lord! How can you call him annoying?" the other woman asked. "How many men can you find who love their wives so much these days?"

"Who cares!" Qian Xiuying said contemptuously, though every inch of her glowed with the pride and satisfaction she felt from all her husband's pampering.

Liu Quan knew well that attention to this kind of thing was shallow and debasing. But how she yearned for the pleasure of sometimes speaking to another woman in these ways. The shoes she was wearing were pretty, too, but they were not even hers, only borrowed from Jinghua.

Liu Quan thought back about her own husband without any leftover anger or resentment. He was strong and had a broad chest, ample enough, she had thought, to protect her from the ravages of everyday life. During the early days of the Cultural Revolution she had spent her time rushing around, vainly trying to clear her father's name. He had once studied in England and was branded a traitor and a spy. In the evenings, exhausted from the effort, how she longed to come back to her husband and tell him of the humiliations she had suffered, to find shelter with him, as if that broad chest of his had been like a lush grassland on which she could find comfort and renewal. But at that time he had been the head of some minor faction and was very full of himself. He would come home drunk and foul-tempered, and force her to make love. He was rude and loud and treated her as if he had bought her merely for her body and was determined to get his money's worth. Liu Quan hated to see the darkness come. Every night of their married life had been a terrifying, inescapable trial, and as the dusk began to thicken a cold shudder passed through her body, as if she were suffering from a fever. How she had wished she could have grasped the sun and prevented the night from coming on. He grabbed her roughly and asked. "Are you my old woman, eh?" But he did not seem to regard her as his wife at all, only as something he could use for sex.

What had it all come to and what was the point of it all now? Liu Quan felt completely at sea. Her present situation was in some ways even harder to bear than the conditions she had worked under before coming to the Foreign Affairs Bureau. She could almost hear Manager Wei laughing at her plight. His laugh had always filled Liu Quan with loathing, a sensation of being plunged into an icy, bottomless pool on a cold autumn day, and being unable to swim, just floundering about helplessly. And passers-by on the bank not only offered no help, but even thought her struggles rather amusing, wondering why she didn't save herself. She could not imagine why she had gotten into this state of affairs and what she had done to deserve such treatment. And she acted like a maid, unjustly dismissed, who returns over and over again to beg for her master's mercy.

Liu Quan could see clearly that Director Xie Kunsheng was trying to put her off. She wanted to storm out of the room, or pick up the ink bottle and smash it onto the floor, showering him with ink from head to foot. But this would have done no good at all. The effort of trying to control herself made her very nearly forget what she had come here for in the first place.

Though Zhu Zhenxiang had not directly said anything to help Liu Quan out of her predicament, his words had encouraged her and she felt drawn to him. But successful people are easily kind and well-meaning, and any show of support she thought was coming from him might just be her imagination, a symptom of her unbalanced state of mind and inability to judge correctly. She was finding it more and more difficult to string her words together. "It's just something to do with my work. . . ."

"That's all right," Zhu Zhenxiang replied. "You talk about it first. I can come back later."

Zhu Zhenxiang thought it better to leave Liu Quan to discuss the matter privately with Xie Kunsheng. Even if it was only a work matter, he felt that her sense of propriety and her shyness might keep her from discussing it in front of others. But it was actually Xie Kunsheng who felt that there was a breach of decorum in this situation—even though Zhu had done nothing himself to give such an impression. "I can see you in a few moments, Director Zhu," he said, "I'll be finished right away."

Fearing that Xie Kunsheng might now find some other excuse to put Liu Quan off once again, Zhu said quickly, "There's no hurry. I've got other things to do in the meantime." Then he turned to Liu Quan and, as if trying to console her, said, "I'll leave you to chat, then."

Liu Quan really wanted to thank him but her tongue seemed to have frozen to the roof of her mouth. During her brief contact with Zhu over the past few weeks, Liu Quan had felt that he was not only a competent official, but in some ways a kindred spirit whose warm heart was hidden behind a dispassionate exterior.

Xie Kunsheng assumed a stern expression and asked in a most correct manner, "Were you looking for me?"

What nonsense! What did he think Liu Quan had been doing, waiting there for the last two hours? And in any case, he knew perfectly well what Liu Quan wanted to see him for. "Yes," she answered.

"All right, then, tell me what it's about." He yawned, casually picked up a newspaper and glanced over the headlines.

"My section head has told me that my work here has already

come to an end. He thanked me and told me to return to my old unit."

"Oh, I see." Xie Kunsheng turned over his newspaper.

"But you told me yourself, and my unit also said that my transfer notice would come through after I had moved here. You said that you badly needed people here."

"Did I say that?" Xie Kunsheng raised his eyebrows in surprise.

"Yes, you did. If I go back now, what can I tell my leaders? What do you think I should do? Am I not good enough for the job, or have I done something wrong?"

"Oh no, but the situation changes, new things enter in. . ." Then, after thinking for a while, he said, "How about this. I'll telephone your unit and explain the situation to them. All right?" Xie Kunsheng seemed quite moved by his own suggestion, as if he had suddenly become some great and noble benefactor. He always attended to the smallest matter in person.

"No. Thank you, but there's no need. My unit is not the real problem. The real problem is whether or not you can fulfill your promise."

Xie Kunsheng's expression changed from pleasure to great distaste. How could she be so ungrateful? He put his newspaper aside and said, "This kind of decision is not one I can make on my own. It involves collective discussion and investigation." He assumed an expression which said, "You're on your own. . . do as you like," and he resumed his work on the guest lists. But what could she do? "Collective discussion and investigation." Once they brought out these magic weapons there wasn't much one could do. At one time this had been the correct way of going about things, but now it had all too often become merely another way of sidestepping the issue, and when no one bore the responsibility, there was no way you could fight. Xie's words left Liu Quan utterly defeated. There was nothing more she could say.

Liang Qian had told Liu Quan to wait outside the entrance to the theater. It was said that when she and Bai Fushan had first fallen in love she had asked him to wait for her outside the public lavatories on Xidan Street. She was always choosing unusual places to meet people. Already several youths in tight-fitting jeans had come up to Liu Quan by the ticket window, a bundle of ten cent notes in their hands, and asked, "Do you have a spare ticket?" They thought she was there, like they, for diversion, to escape boredom.

Liu Quan shook her head "no," and turned around to face a theater poster which had been disfigured by idle scribblers. The vegetable basket she was carrying grew heavy, making her fingers ache. She shifted it to her other hand, dropping two green beans in the process. As she stooped to pick them up she remembered the young supervisor she had just passed in the free market. He was outrageous, going up to a stall and just grabbing a handful of beans without paying for them. And the old peasant selling the beans had just looked on blankly, not daring to utter a word of protest.

"Why didn't he pay you? Do you know him?" Liu Quan asked the old peasant.

"No," the old man had smiled bitterly. "People are just like that."

"Why didn't you ask him for money?"

"Ah, this is their territory. There's nothing I can do."

Liu Quan had then gone to the hut where the young man, the supervisor of the free market, had his office. She noticed that the table was covered with piles of fresh tomatoes, beans, peppers and eggs. It would all have made a good subject for a still life, but, she wondered, had any of it been paid for? He was sitting by the table eating a tomato, the juice running down from the corners of his mouth. Liu Quan just stood there watching him. He was healthy-looking with a superb muscular frame. It seemed pathetic that this young man, who should have been so noble and disciplined, could not even resist the temptation of pinching a few tomatoes, beans and peppers.

Ignoring Liu Quan, he finished eating his tomato noisily and then threw the stem out of the door, where it landed smartly on the shirt of a neat young girl who happened to be walking by. "Oh!" cried the girl, hastily brushing down her shirt and looking at him with contempt.

"Fuck you!" said the youth, wiping his hand on the doorframe and effectively silencing the girl by his rudeness. The girl walked off in a huff and the youth turned abruptly to Liu Quan and said, "Who're you looking for?"

"For you," Liu Quan replied.

"Me?"

"Why didn't you pay for those beans just now?"

"Who says I didn't pay for them?" He didn't seem in the least bit provoked or irritated. A world-weary expression appeared on his face.

"I do. I saw you." Liu Quan felt her back straighten, as if doing something useful made her very stature rise.

"How do you know I won't pay for them later? I didn't have any money along with me. He patted his pocketless shirt. "I'll be going over to pay in a moment."

There wasn't very much Liu Quan could say to that. Something about him exasperated her, and yet she knew that against him she was absolutely powerless. "You'll pay in a moment, eh? Who'll be able to prove it? You've already given a bad impression by taking those beans—now are you lying to me? If you don't take your job seriously, that's your affair, but you're supposed to represent the State and keep control of illegal practices. If you break the law, what will the peasants think?" After saying all this, Liu Quan still felt she hadn't gotten across to him.

"Who are you, anyhow? What do you do?" asked the youth with a grin, as if he had just been listening to some saleswoman trying to sell her wares.

"I'm a journalist," Liu Quan lied confidently. "I'm doing a special report on the state of the free markets and I often come here. If this sort of thing happens again, I'll report it to your leaders." She really had a stubborn streak in her! Even now, when she had reached the end of her own rope, she still had the guts to try and straighten out the youngster.

As she walked away, through the baking sun, the sweat trickled down her back, giving the sensation of ants crawling over her body. There was not the slightest breeze and the leaves on the trees were motionless. Even the expected coolness from the shade they cast seemed to have been driven away by the intense heat. This year was extremely hot and many people had suffered from sunstroke. Well, Liu Quan may not have had a sunstroke, but the heat had certainly affected her temper. She did not usually have a bad temper, but the way things had gone for her lately had pushed her to her limits. Liang Qian was really lucky, having an official for her father. It meant that she always had some weight behind her and people would never really dare to use her so poorly.

The friendship between the three of them was one area of their lives which was clean and untarnished. They knew how hard such friendships, those that had been cemented through struggle and hardship, were to come by in this vast world. And, indeed, the bond had taken work and, at times, cost each of them dearly. Experience had taught them the risks as well as the value of friendship, and now that they were entering middle age and had lost their youthful vigor, it turned out to be the only solid element in their lives. When Socrates was building himself a house, people had said to him, "It is too small!" But Socrates had replied, "That is of no matter, so long as it can contain true friends."

Liang Qian eventually turned up on her orange, two-seater moped. From far off she seemed to possess all the vitality of youth, in her black skirt, tight-fitting blue embroidered blouse and white leather shoes. It was rare for her to dress up like this. Only the broken straw hat she wore looked out of place, just like the words which at once poured out of her mouth when she saw Liu Quan. "Bloody hell! If I was Zhu Zhenxiang, I'd really have it out with Xie Kunsheng, the bastard!" She had obviously been talking a lot and rushing about under the blazing sun. Her lips were parched. "Let's have something to drink first."

Liu Quan had no idea that they would meet Bai Fushan in the nearby cafe. And to make matters worse, he had with him a less than attractive girl in a wide-collared, short-sleeved shirt, exposing even more than was called for in this hot weather. Liu Quan felt disgusted. She stood in the narrow doorway of the cafe, not knowing whether to march in and ignore him completely, or to beat a hasty retreat. Liang Qian pushed her from behind and said, "What's the matter. Haven't you seen her before?" As they passed the table where Bai Fushan was sitting, Liang Qian looked past the girl and said indifferently, as you would to a casual acquaintance, "Out for a stroll, eh?"

The girl obviously had no idea who Liang Qian was and instinctively looked her up and down, as if trying to assess a new rival. Then, obviously deciding that Liang Qian was no match for her, she lowered her head with the pitying, condescending look of a young woman who meets a woman already past her prime. Poor little fledgling!

"Let me buy you a drink," Bai Fushan said with great gusto, rising to greet her.

"There's no need, thank you," replied Liang Qian, pushing him back down with her outstretched fingers, as if he were some filthy object. Then, aloof, she marched over to another table.

"Two bottles of soda and two chocolate sundaes," Liu Quan ordered at the counter. While she was waiting for the cashier to give her the tickets, she noticed Bai Fushan whispering something in the girl's ear, almost certainly something about Liang Qian. The girl's bright, cat-like face at once turned pale and sullen. Liu Quan sat down and sucked hard at her straw, finishing half her bottle of soda in a single gulp. "They're leaving," she said, turning toward the entrance of the cafe, her glance meeting Bai Fushan's. He waved his hand and Liu Quan nodded in return. No doubt it had been the girl who had wanted to leave, finding the situation too uncomfortable.

Liang Qian had not uttered a word all this time and was just sitting there, tracing incomprehensible Chinese characters on the wet tabletop. She, too, had her sorrows, but she hid them deep in her heart, so that they were as mysterious as the letters she was forming. She would often pour out her anger or her joy, but rarely would she reveal her sorrow—not even to Liu Quan and Jinghua. She felt that sorrow was an emotion which could only destroy the will. In some ways her life had been nothing but a series of failures and setbacks, but she still retained her confidence in life. She possessed neither the unshakeable optimism of previous generations, nor the blind pessimism of the younger generation. Her generation was the most confident, the most clear-minded and the most able to face up to reality. She came up out of her reverie and looked at Liu Quan "What do you plan to do?" she asked.

"What—" Liu Quan was not quite sure what Liang Qian meant. Frequently her train of thought took great leaps, like film clips which have been spliced together in the wrong place. She remembered that Liang Qian had once taken her to her studio to watch a film which had been edited in a hurry, with the strips of film set in back-to-front. The people, cars and airplanes all moved backwards, and this had made everyone laugh till they were in stitches, though if you thought about it carefully it really wasn't very funny. Who can be sure that there will not be one part in everyone's life which will be spliced in the wrong way?

"I think I'll just have to go back to my old company." Liu Quan was no longer able to decide which would cost less to her self-respect, to go forward or to retreat. Either way would mean a battle.

"What, and let all my effort go to waste? Ridiculous!" Liang Qian never gave in, neither did she allow others to give in.

"I've already spoken to Lao Dong. He was furious and said, 'What do you want to go and humiliate yourself like that for? Stop degrading yourself by pleading with the Foreign Affairs Bureau. Come back here and I'll try and make things better for you here.' It seems like it'll make less trouble for me simply to go back."

"I don't agree with your attitude at all. You can't go on allowing yourself to be dragged down like this." Liang Qian picked up her bottle of soda and peered through the yellow liquid, so that all around her seemed to be submerged in it. She really should suggest this to her studio as a method of portraying people's emotions. She continued, "We often ask ourselves if there are more good people in the world than bad. I've thought this over carefully and come to the conclusion that there are still more good people. Then why is life so hard? Well, I believe that although there really are few evil people, their powers are considerable, and this forces good people into defensive positions. But if anything is going to change we must break their backs, stop them from ruining people's lives." Liang Qian's eyes grew bigger and bigger and the veins stood out on her neck. Her complexion was dull and unhealthy and her face resembled a wrinkled old apple.

Liu Quan felt very uncomfortable, as if she had been accused of being a parasite, while Liang Qian had been fighting hard all the way for what she believed. "It's all right," Liu Quan said. "Just forget about it. I don't expect my friends to go on wiping away my tears forever."

"Don't be so stupid!" Liang Qian took the cigarette she had just lit from her mouth and rapped the table with her fingers. "Do you know what's going on—what they've been saying about you? They've been gossiping about what you might have been doing with your foreign guests that lunchtime." Then Liang Qian sat back silently, waiting for Liu Quan's response.

Liu Quan was stunned and horrified. She fiddled involuntarily with her fingers, knocking over her bottle of soda so that it rolled across the table and then smashed to pieces on the floor. The waitress looked over at the clatter.

"Well, that's one way of getting them to pay attention to you when you want to be served. It's worth paying twenty cents for the bottle if it can save you a twenty-minute wait!" Liang Qian was doing her best to try and cheer Liu Quan up.

"Of course they know where we were! Mrs. Brown said that she wanted to go to Wang Fujing Street to try some local food and then Mr. Link said that he wanted to go too. I reported it to my section head and, anyhow, we were only out for about an hour."

Liang Qian quickly estimated that it would take thirty minutes at least to get to and from any of the restaurants in Wangfujing Street from the Beijing Hotel, and that would only leave another thirty minutes. "Hm!" she snorted. "Thirty minutes—that wouldn't even be enough time to take your trousers off! How absurd!" She felt infuriated by Liu Quan's passive, compliant attitude. Why did she have to look for justifications, as if she *had* done something wrong? What had happened to her self-confidence?

"There's no need to exonerate yourself to me and there's no point in trying to escape either, when you still have all this filth following you around. Remember that some people won't believe you no matter what you say or what proof you offer. You've just got to fight it out with them. If you really want this job you'll just have to kick up as big a stink as you can. Meanwhile I'll try and get things moving at a higher level and not leave it in Xie Kunsheng's hands. Anyway, it's just as well you went to see him; now we know what the root of the trouble is. It seems to me that Zhu Zhenxiang is pretty perceptive. So I suggest you go straight to him and tell him what's on your mind. I'm sure he'll help you."

Liu Quan occasionally felt that a good argument would add more color to her life, but her social position was different from Liang Qian's and the methods she suggested were foreign to her. Liang Qian was becoming more and more argumentative, and in this state she became irrepressible and high-spirited. On the surface she appeared forceful and decisive; underneath she was as weak as the rest of them

"What's the matter?" Liang Qian suddenly became calm. This was the real Liang Qian.

"It's nothing. . . ." Liu Quan stretched out her hands and clasped Liang Qian's across the table.

Liang Qian put her cup down, leaned over and, as if she were a man, patted Liu Quan's shoulder. "Have your ice cream. It's already melted."

Ah! Liang Qian had patted her shoulder. . . as if she were a man!

* * *

All the televisions in the courtyard were on. From the array of lighted windows with their various styles of curtains came the same sound of a woman weeping, her voice practiced and well-modulated. Contented after their supper, everyone had settled down comfortably to a few hours of melodrama. But who in real life ever wept so melodically? Liu Quan felt like telling the woman not to cry in such an absurd way, if she wanted to keep the viewers' sympathy.

The empty street below was peaceful. It was not a through-road that carried buses, and in the evening few cars came to break the stillness. It was like a tiny garden in the midst of the city, with trees, grass and bushes. There was even a small orchard surrounded by wire fencing, with hard green apples growing silently, almost idiotically, in that dark, cheerless place, becoming red and sweet for the sake of self perfection alone. The street lamps cast a yellow glow over the youngsters sitting on the grass, murmuring to themselves as they reviewed for their examinations, as well as over the neighbors out strolling in the cool air. It did Liu Quan good to look out and see people relaxing, probably living full, happy lives. She was tempted to go down and lie on the grass for a while and do nothing at all, but count the stars in the sky, or dream like a child fast asleep in a carriage. She could not face going on like this, jumping up and down like a springbound toy. She had once bought Mengmeng a mechanical monkey which could perform somersaults. Even though it had been well-made and of metal, it soon became chipped and dented.

Liu Quan still hadn't had her supper. A little earlier Jinghua had made her some malted milk, but she could not bring herself to swallow even a drop. If she tried to swallow anything more than water, it immediately made her want to vomit. She wanted to take some stomach medicine but could not find any in Jinghua's drawer. They could never find anything they needed. Perhaps she was suffering from the heat. She had spent the whole day on her bicycle under the blazing sun in search of Liang Qian. Liang Qian advised her to hold out a bit longer, even though Manager Wei had sent her an ultimatum telling her to return to work. She continued to be told "The transfer notice will follow shortly." But how long could such promises go on? She had been certain she would hear something definite by today.

She had looked for Liang Qian everywhere, at the dormitory, the cafeteria, the workshops, but could not find her. There had been some problem over the film and she'd heard that the Party Committee at the studio would not approve it. She began to wonder if Liang Qian had gone off and hung herself in a rage. She often made remarks like, "I'm so furious I could hang myself!" But more than likely she was somewhere busily arguing with someone. Liu Quan could picture her storming around, clenching her delicate little teeth, reciting her views.

Eventually, on her second round of the entire film studio, she found Liang Qian in the production department. Since her film had been completed long before, Liu Quan wondered what she was doing there. All the glassed-in booths were in use, the cameras poised like canons, ready to capture the various emotions being acted out. Booth number two was empty, its lights blazing, as if everyone had run out abruptly and left them on. Then she saw Liang Qian sitting in there on the floor, staring vacantly into the distance. With the reflection on the glass of filming props—brightly colored leaves, graceful willows, gentle clouds, wonderfully shaped rocks—she looked like a hibiscus floating freely in the middle of an artificial pond. Her arms were drawn around her legs, her chin held tightly between her knees, and her eyes fixed vacantly ahead. Liu Quan felt rather taken aback by this unfamiliar picture of Liang Qian.

"What are you doing here? I've been looking for you all day." Liu Quan was still standing some way off, hesitant to enter the booth and startle her.

"It's nice in here, isn't it?" Liang Qian said softly.

This wasn't like her in the least. Liang Qian hated all that was artificial—paper backdrops, plastic flowers, jewelry. She always insisted her filmings take place in real settings. Could she really have been pushed to the point of discarding her own values? If she had, she might find it possible to live a less turbulent life. "What are you doing here?" Liu Qian asked her again.

"Sitting." Liang Qian straightened her shoulders and brightened up, though Liu Quan could see that beneath this act she was terribly distraught. "I'm looking for a certain emotion, a specific type of feeling." She spoke with the words and the tone she used when she acted or directed other actors. She made an effort to pull herself together, and smiled at Liu Quan.

What kind of feeling was she after? She wouldn't find much feeling in the midst of this glitter and artificiality. "You're really too much!" Liu Quan scolded her. "There's no need to put on such an act. You are just you. Changing your character isn't as easy as just crossing the street, and you know it." It was true; the time had run out for them to make any great changes. They were all like nameless old windmills standing out in the wilds, relentlessly, unhurriedly turning, turning. . . each following her own direction. Every joint creaked, but if they tried to change direction or install a modern motor they would simply crumble and fall to pieces.

Liang Qian chuckled awkwardly as if she had at last been exposed. "It's just as well you found me here since I can't leave. Someone from some committee is coming here to investigate my film." She could see that Liu Quan was weak and exhausted and she had news for her. "Well, as far as your job is concerned, your transfer has been approved, at least at the top. That cunning little devil Xie Kunsheng keeps repeating that there won't be any problems in his office. But now the personnel department further down the ladder has put up a hurdle. I've heard they agreed to your transfer long ago, but now they say they are waiting to hear 'the opinions of the masses.' What nonsense! Anyway, now that it's been approved at the top, there's no reason why they should mess things up. It seems that the real cause of the trouble is Xie Kunsheng, who has someone else in mind for the job. And as far as the 'opinions of the masses' are concerned, this seems to be some trick of Qian Xiuying's. But Zhu Zhenxiang says that these 'opinions' can be cleared up easily enough. They're not going to ruin everything for you just because of her. He's really a good sort, not like the others who won't even give one a chance to argue. He says he'd like to talk with you."

"When does he want to talk to me, and how long do you think it will take to sort everything out?" This all sounded good, but there was a big difference between words and deeds and, in the final outcome, all Zhu Zhenxiang's promises might mean nothing.

"You can see him this evening—I've already arranged it. Just call him up yourself in case he suddenly has some other last minute engagement. I'll give you his home phone number." She leafed through her address book. "I really can't afford to lose this book. . . 'The ways to the top are many and varied'." Liang Qian laughed; she enjoyed quoting from operas written during the Cultural Revolution. She was always laughing. But Liu Quan could detect the first traces of gray in Liang Qian's hair, like the first yellow leaves of autumn. She was already beginning to fade, a little too early, a little too soon. . .

Liu Quan made the telephone call on the way back from the film studio. A woman with a soft, gentle voice had answered the telephone. "He isn't back yet, I'm afraid," she said, "would you mind phoning again in a while?" None of that suspicion, coldness or arrogance to which Liu Quan had become so accustomed. She had not even asked who Liu Quan was, which unit she came from or what she wanted. Her response was rare indeed, calm, experienced, self-confident. Perhaps she was their housekeeper, though she didn't sound like it. Could she have been Zhu Zhenxiang's wife? With them so obviously well-suited, their married life must be a very happy one.

Now, later, Jinghua was going with her to make another telephone call. All the way to the public telephone, Liu Quan was worrying whether or not this was a suitable time to call. "Won't they be having their supper just now?" She didn't want to spoil Zhu Zhenxiang's appetite. Such things could easily prejudice her chances, even though they had no direct bearing on the matter at hand. She knew that people who succeed in life take every factor, small or large, into consideration.

"It's already after eight. They'll have finished by now." Jinghua felt she should accompany Liu Quan to the telephone, since she had suffered so many setbacks recently. In her confusion she had begun to doubt her right to telephone whoever she chose, not to mention her right to exist.

"Won't he be washing just now?" If he were in the middle of washing, she would have wasted another telephone call and would have to call back yet again. And if she phoned three times in one day, they would begin to get annoyed . . .

"What's the matter with you? You're not asking him for any favors. You have the right to talk to any person you please. And whatever rumors follow you around come from other people, not from who you are. You weren't born with any disgrace and all this gossip can be washed away."

But the fact of the matter was that she did have to plead for help, and for her to think now as Jinghua did would just be obstinacy. She couldn't force herself to change, to not be so concerned about her reputation.

When they reached the public telephone the woman in charge of it was just closing up the wooden shutters. Jinghua smiled and said, "Excuse me, mother, we would like to make a telephone call."

"No." The old woman shook her head, "it's too late."

"But it's urgent."

"That's not my affair. I've got something urgent to do too—my daughter is sick with a high fever and she's just about to go to sleep. How can she ever get better if people are always disturbing her with their telephone calls?" The old woman was stubbornly set to close up, but who could blame her? If her daughter was seriously ill, she would be anxious about being able to find a decent doctor and good medicine for her. Everyone has their own misfortunes. But Liu Quan now felt her troubles were multiplying. "What should we do?" she asked Jinghua.

"There should be a telephone in the reception room of that office block further along the road. Let's try there."

"You go back. I'll try myself." Liu Quan said, her voice sounding thin and disheartened.

"No. I'll come with you," Jinghua answered. Liu Quan needed support, even if only from someone as weak as herself. Jinghua had not yet told Liu Quan about how Lao An's intervention had saved her from severe criticism. But after he spoke up for her some gossip started, about an "improper relationship" between them, and this was hard to bear. Difficult to believe that this sort of gossip came from the mouths of educated people, yet it happened all the time. If they wanted to destroy someone, especially a woman, there was no better way than by trying to ruin her reputation. Liu Quan could never understand the scheming, so she was constantly bewildered and made to suffer. People who set about to disgrace others defile the solemn beauty, the original idea of love.

Nearly half a century has passed since Lu Xun heaped scorn on such people in his satire "The True Story of Ah Q" and yet the logic of these people still remains on the same level as that of Ah Q: love merely means sleeping together. Lu Xun was truly a great writer; in "Ah Q" he managed to personify the corrupt mentality of the old society.

Jinghua had finally finished reading the love letters Lao An had received. They were full of gentle, womanly affection and the language was a little old-fashioned, a mixture of modern and classical Chinese such as Jinghua had not seen for years. She expressed herself with a kind of mocking politeness, reminiscent of women in the thirties. No doubt the love felt by a woman like her would also be, like her writing, a combination of old and new, not as openly expressed as with most women nowadays. Lao An's judgment of her had not been quite fair: she certainly was not too "foreign," even if she did resort to an occasional English quotation in her letters. And what was wrong with being too emotional, so long as these emotions caused no great harm to others? There was nothing wrong with people over sixty falling in love, and Jinghua wanted to encourage Lao An to make up his mind quickly and get married. If Jinghua lived to eighty and then met a man she could truly love and respect, she would certainly not be as hesitant as Lao An was being now. But, unfortunately, such things were unlikely to happen to her.

The office block loomed up ahead of them, solid and stern and dignified in the night, giving both of them a quite groundless sense of hope. They quickened their pace, like moths flying towards a light, and hurried up to the gatehouse. The telephone was standing on the broad, brown windowsill of the reception room. There wasn't a soul about, only the crackling and whining of a worn-out radio echoing off the walls.

"Is there anyone there?" Liu Quan looked around. "Hello!"

The radio answered. Crackle, crackle, w-h-i-n-e . . .

"It doesn't matter. Just make your call," Jinghua told her.

Liu Quan put out her hand to lift up the receiver.

"What's going on, eh?" A stout figure suddenly appeared from out of the darkness of the corridor. He looked just like a Buddhist temple guard, with chest muscles even bigger than Jinghua's bulging beneath his string vest. His waist was a good three feet in circumference. Even when Liu Quan had been pregnant, she hadn't been that fat. Jinghua could tell that they were dealing with no easy character. "We'd like to make a telephone call," she said.

"You want to make a phone call? Go and find a public telephone then."

Well, no beating about the bush with him. Jinghua could imagine that this creature wouldn't feel the slightest qualms at strangling a dog or a cat.

"The public telephone has already closed. We've got an urgent call to make. Please . . ." Liu Quan's face creased in a smile. Her wonderful smile was usually most affecting, with dimples appearing on her cheeks, but now she looked foolish.

"No. Get out of here at once!" he yelled, as though he were scolding a dog caught stealing some food. Liu Quan blushed, but she kept on smiling.

Jinghua no longer saw anything touching about that smile. She had the countenance of a dog who has been driven away, and creeps off, wagging its tail apologetically. "Liu Quan!"

"But it's urgent . . ."

What was the matter with her?

"That makes no difference. What if an important call arrives for one of our leaders while you're using the line?" He brandished the status of his leaders while he himself had not an ounce of prestige. What he said was ridiculous since the offices certainly had their own telephones, and all the leaders would have had phones right in their homes. By mentioning the leaders, he believed he became as powerful as they. In fact, he was nothing—his whole huge bulk was a complete sham.

"Come on then, Liu Quan, let's go to the telegraph building."

"I really should get myself a husband who's got a bit of clout," Liu Quan said agitatedly. "And a telephone. Then I wouldn't have to go on suffering this sort of humiliation." Oh well, she thought, inadequate people always will think of impossible solutions. She felt like bursting into tears again. But this wasn't the time to cry.

"Let's go." Jinghua was already on her bicycle.

At the telegraph building there were three telephones, but all of them were being used. Which one was likely to be free first?

". . . Is there some left over? How much? Oh! Well, darling, you could always steam it for lunch tomorrow. Or you could just fry it . . ."

They certainly couldn't wait for this conversation to finish. As the famous comedian Hou Baolin had once said, by the time this kind of intimate conversation was over a whole evening's performance could have been acted out. Jinghua suddenly grabbed Liu Quan's arm. So *he* was here!

Bai Fushan was totally engrossed in what he was saying. His head was bent low over the telephone, his back was arched and his hands grasped the receiver tightly. "Yes . . . yes, yes. Those leaders have seen it and say that the film has serious faults. What? Certainly not. Just don't worry. I'm thinking only of you. Otherwise why would I be calling? . . ."

Jinghua shuddered in disgust. "Can you understand what he's saying?" Liu Quan held her arm more tightly. His voice carried easily over to them.

"Did my old woman tell you that? Surely you didn't believe that sort of thing! She's just jealous and wants revenge, I tell you. She deliberately tries to cheat people and now she's lying. You can't imagine everything that's been going on the last few days. Well, just so long as you know. That's all right . . . O.K., then? Goodbye."

Bai Fushan finally put the receiver down and turned around. That calm, cultivated appearance of his was disappearing: his trousers and jacket were not as neatly pressed as before, and his shirt hung loosely on him, crumpled like a sack. The top two buttons were open so that his collar flapped around freely. His shirt was soaked in sour, sticky sweat.

He spotted them. Dammit! Now what? Those old bags were really tiresome, like half-dead dogs who keep on trying to bite you. Bai Fushan would have loved to have been able to kick them out of his path—and he wouldn't have minded doing the same to Liang Qian if he had not been so dependent on her. He walked out as if he hadn't seen them.

Liu Quan felt her anger rise. "Well, I doubt whether he's capable of any shame, but this should at least have made him a bit uncomfortable." She would have felt a good deal better if she had detected a trace of discomfort in Bai Fushan's eyes, but there had been nothing, only a muddy mass of red veins like a stagnant pond covered with slime. Could he even begin to see the world clearly through those eyes?

"Now there's a husband for you!" Jinghua said beneath her breath. Then she raised her voice, "Well, let's just forget it and get on with our phone call."

They got through right away and were told to come right out to Zhu Zhenxiang's home. Liu Quan said nothing, but rode along steadily. The chain of her bicycle rattled louder all the time; her bicycle really needed a complete overhaul. It was already 8:40 and they still had to go way out to the eastern suburbs. They should really have left their bicycles at Xidan and taken a taxi, but both of them were quite used to hardship, so much so that they often failed to notice if there was an easier way.

Red light, green light . . . Green light, red light. How they wished for a whole stretch of green lights. Jinghua already felt tired and her back ached, but she never complained. She scanned both sides of the road. There were fewer cars about by now and the many cyclists wheeled along casually, as if they were idling away an evening in the park. None of the others rode ahead as furiously as they. The miles added up and Jinghua was beginning to feel as though they would never reach their destination. When at last she dismounted from her bicycle her legs felt quite numb. All the apartment blocks around them looked identical. They wandered around for a while, as if in a labyrinth, but finally managed to find the right number on the building where Zhu Zhenxiang lived.

Quan was acting quite rattled and the smallest thing could have distracted her away from following through. Jinghua felt drained of all her energy and needed to sit down. "You go up. I'll wait for you here," she said. "Don't worry, just talk to them as we planned. You won't forget."

She turned around, avoiding Liu Quan's pale, frightened face so that Liu Quan would keep going and not collapse. Then, as Liu Quan walked away she sank down onto the ground and lit herself a cigarette. She puffed at it furiously and then groaned, only realizing that she had uttered a sound when a passer-by cast a suspicious glance at her.

Liu Quan had absolutely no idea what she was going to say; her mind felt utterly blank. She had suddenly forgotten everything, even the name of her division chief. Recently she had many mental blocks like this. She had wanted to tell him that she had taken her American guests to a cafe in Wangfujing street, with the full consent of her division chief, but the cafe had refused to take foreign exchange and she had to pay the bill herself. Then that evening her guests had invited her out for coffee in return, which she had also reported to her division chief. A sense of emptiness overcame her—a person of forty having to report everything, even a bowl of dumplings and a cup of coffee! She felt quite sickened by it all and everything she had meant to say faded away. Just like the rear tire of her bicycle, she was deflated.

Zhu Zhenxiang's wife, Zhonglan, carried in two cups of plum juice with ice and put them on the small table between the armchairs in which Liu Quan and Zhu Zhenxiang were sitting. Even the china in this house carried the mood of compassion, understanding and serenity.

"Please have a drink," her hostess said.

"Thank you." Liu Quan started to stand up.

She did not say a word, but just smiled and gestured to Liu Quan to remain seated. Then she took the tray and went out, gently closing the door behind her to cut out the soft sound of music which wafted in from another room. She had barely turned around to look at Liu Quan and had cast no suspicious or disapproving glances in her direction. All this should have made Liu Quan feel more comfortable, but she still felt stunned. She had been doing too much thinking and had grown wary and over-cautious, like a small injured animal. What she imagined or perceived was often very different from what she knew to be true, so that she constantly found herself in situations which threw her off balance. If she had lived in Zhu Zhenxiang's kind of environment, she would have been a lot more confident.

Zhu Zhenxiang really wanted to assist her in some way. She really seemed pitiable now as he looked at her. He knew that Liu Quan's work had been very satisfactory and she was a good deal more competent than Qian Xiuying, who always had to have an English-Chinese dictionary handy. And whenever Qian Xiuying was chatting idly with the guests or fixing herself up in the washroom, Liu Quan would be busy working out her time schedule or making arrangements to satisfy their guests' wishes. She never, as Qian Xiuying often did, got one of the guests to take an instant photo of her. Then why was she so helpless when it came to looking after herself?

"Where do you live?" Zhu Zhenxiang asked for the sake of something to say. Once they started talking she would relax.

"West City District. Lotus Lane."

"Is there really a lotus pond there?"

"No, but there probably was one there long ago." She started sweating. Her hands were icy and her whole body felt limp. The room started to fade and she had to rest her head on the back of the sofa. What was the matter with her? She hadn't yet said the things she must say.

"Most of Beijing's alleyways have some interesting story behind them. . . ." Zhu Zhenxiang glanced at Liu Quan and was startled by her pallid face. He quickly went over to open the door and called, "Zonglan, come quickly. Comrade Liu Quan isn't feeling too well."

Zhu Zhenxiang's wife came in, lifted Liu Quan's eyelids and felt her pulse.

"Shall I call a cab?" he asked.

"No, just go and get a glass of milk, and add some sugar." She spoke quickly, but her voice remained clear and calm.

"I'm sorry," Liu Quan said weakly.

"It doesn't matter. Everyone feels like this once in a while." Then she whispered, "Don't worry, there's no problem which can't be overcome." She took the cup of milk from Zhu Zhenxiang and handed it to her, asking, "Can you manage it on your own?"

Liu Quan smiled in embarrassment.

"Drink this and you'll feel a lot better. I'll get you something to eat. It's not serious—just a spell of low blood sugar. I have this problem myself. You should be fine once you've had something to eat."

The round, moist face looking down at her made Liu Quan think of the moon gently shining on her, giving her calm and peace. Suddenly she did feel hungry. She took the cup and obediently sipped the steaming milk.

Zhu Zhenxiang turned around and looked at her, worried that she might feel embarrassed by what had just happened. Something about the sight of Liu Quan, sitting there drinking her milk, almost brought tears to his eyes. His intuition told him that she was not one of those unprincipled types, so why were they acting so unjustly toward her? People should not be subjected to this sort of humiliation.

"Don't worry, Comrade Liu Quan. I can help you." Zhu Zhenxiang said comfortingly. Yes, tomorrow he would call all the people from the Foreign Affairs Bureau together for a meeting, including Xie Kunsheng. If they had anything against Liu Quan they could bring it out into the open and provide proof, though he suspected that no one would be able to come up with anything. She was a single woman working hard to support herself and should not be treated so mercilessly.

He looked out the window into the evening. The view from the tenth floor gave one the feeling of watching the world from a great distance. The lights of the city spread as far as the eye could see. The world was so beautiful—could it offer Liu Quan no foothold? Was it because the world was changing so rapidly? In twenty years time, it was said, it will be possible to move icebergs to drought areas, or to mine minerals on other planets, or to process polluted water for fuel. . . . But little advancement had been made in elevating man beyond his more bestial characteristics, his self-ishness and cruelty, his hypocrisy. So had there really been much progress over the last few thousand years? In another ten thou sand years historians will look back at us and see little to distinguish us from primitive man.

His wife came in, carrying a bowl of noodle soup in one hand and a dish of cold chicken and a pair of chopsticks in the other. Zhu Zhenxiang went over to asist her, but she said, "No, it's all right. I can manage." She placed the food down in front of Liu Quan. "I put some mustard with the chicken. I'm afraid I forgot to ask you whether you liked it or not."

Liu Quan began to feel rather ill at ease, as if she had, for no reason at all, demanded the hospitality of a complete stranger. But seeing the sincerity behind their generosity, she could not bring herself to refuse.

"It doesn't matter. I can eat anything. But really, this is too kind of you."

"Just try it. It might be a little bland. I'll go and find some salt."

Zhu Zhenxiang felt a little embarrassed by his outburst a few moments before. Zonglan had a wonderful way of saving people from embarrassment, which said a great deal about her considerate and kindhearted nature. Every day he was able to find something beautiful about his wife. She was more tolerant than he was and would never display the impatience he did. She found it easy to maintain her emotional equilibrium, no matter what went on around her. She simply carried on in her own quiet way, doing whatever she felt was right. Perhaps women were superior to men in their ways of loyalty and steadfastness.

Liu Quan felt another wave of exhaustion, and she wanted to cry. She quickly took up the bowl and chopsticks, but her hand had no strength and shook so much that she almost upset the bowl. She put it back on the table and let the chopsticks slip from her hand, one of them falling at the feet of her hostess.

"Never mind. I'll go and bring you another pair." She turned around and went out.

Liu Quan watched her, marvelling at her gentleness. "Your wife is so good," she said to Zhu Zhenxiang with deep appreciation. At last she could speak. She suddenly felt more relaxed, as if a great weight had been lifted from her shoulders.

A strong wind had started up, whistling and moaning through the thick leaves, and frightening Jinghua and Liu Quan. Crash! They heard a loud smashing noise as a tree came down in a large gust. They were waiting under the overhead gateway of the building and were not sure what to do. Liu Quan could not go back up again, certainly not with Jinghua. But Jinghua doubted whether they would have the strength to cycle all the way home. But they couldn't just go on waiting here much longer.

"We'd better go then. If we can't ride our bikes we'll just have to push them. Or perhaps we'll be able to get a lift on a truck." Jinghua went out, her short hair blowing in the wind. It was impossible to speak, so she just beckoned to Liu Quan to start out. As they pushed their bicycles unsteadily onto the road, Jinghua suddenly shouted, "Hey! The wind's with us!"

Liu Quan got onto her bicycle. There was no need to pedal—all she had to do was hold onto the handlebars. She felt an almost unreal sense of exhilaration, as if she were floating through the air.

"The wind's with us!" Jinghua shouted again, her voice filled with surprise and elation.

"Even *we* have the wind with us sometimes, eh?"

* * *

Liu Quan had sliced up the beans and there was nothing left to do but wait for Liang Qian to return before she put them on to cook. Tonight Liu Quan wanted to please her with her favorite: plain bean slices with a little ginger added. Liang Qiang was still at the film studio waiting for the final decision on her film. Over the last few days she had been making the rounds of all the people concerned, and from the rumors she heard, it most probably would be passed this time. But her patience was exhausted and she was cursing all the time: "Hell! No wonder our efficiency is so poor. You've got to spend seventy per cent of your time buttering up the leaders and that only leaves you thirty per cent to get on with your job. . . ."

But Liu Quan thought about how she had forgotten to include all the time and effort she had spent in trying to free herself from the destructive relationship with Bai Fushan, and with raising Chengcheng. Chengcheng had now become more distant. Liang Qian got up early every morning and came home late at night after Chengcheng had already gone to sleep. From time to time she would remember her maternal responsiblities and buy Cheng-cheng a present, but she could never think of anything suitable to buy him or would get him something quite unsuitable and then feel guilty about it. He was already sixteen and no longer wanted to play with the childish toys she brought him. When she managed to arrange a free day to spend with him, she found they had nothing to say to one another. She felt restless and confused and her mind kept reverting back to her film. She talked with Liu Quan and Jinghua about the painful contradiction between her mater-nal feelings and her own ambitions. But as she had said herself, there was no longer anything she could do to save the situation and she could only grit her teeth and plough on. No question about it: A successful woman must be a good deal stronger than a man, since she must always contend with two worlds at once.

Mengmeng came to the stove to see what they would eat. "I'm hungry, Mom. Why hasn't Auntie Liang come yet?"

"Just wait a bit longer. There's some cake in the cupboard—have some of that first."

"You're always telling me to wait. You told me to wait for a bike. Are you ever going to buy me one?"

"Mengmeng, I don't have the money. . . ."

"Why haven't you got any money? You get fifty-six yuan a month, plus extra for sundries and travelling expenses. . . ."

"Mengmeng!" Liu Quan was shocked to hear him speak this way. "Who taught you to speak like that?"

"Dad told me!"

What could he be teaching the child? My god, what a father!

Jinghua, who was washing turnips in the sink, could not control her anger. "Mengmeng! What do you mean by talking to your mother in that way? If it was your father who told you that, let me tell you that even though you live mostly with your father, your mother has to contribute ten yuan a month to him towards your maintenance. And she buys most of your books, shoes and clothes. Don't forget she also has to pay for food and rent. . . ." Jinghua didn't add that over the past few years they had had to scrape together every penny they had, to buy the right connections, first to get Jinghua transferred back to Beijing and now to try to get Liu Quan's job transfer. This had taken all the money they had, though their shabby offerings had been of questionable influence on those complacent well-endowed officials.

Jinghua was sorry—she should not have talked to Mengmeng in that way. Such matters were not for the ears of children. The less they learned of all the ugly things in life, the better. If someone had never been exposed to evil before, was it really necessary to rub their nose in it? "Mengmeng, I shouldn't really be talking to you about such things, I know, but you're growing up and should be old enough to understand.

"For your mother to buy extra things like books, clothes, toys and bikes, on top of the amount stipulated by the divorce law, is just a sign of how much she loves you. You must understand your mother's difficulties, and that she gives you everything she can."

At first Mengmeng's little round eyes showed surprise at this outburst, then indignation. He had always heard an altogether different story. "I didn't know! When my shirt is torn Dad says, go and get your mom to mend it. If I need a new exercise book he says, ask your mom to buy you one. If I ask him again he hits me until my neck hurts so much that I can't even turn my head. It's been awful over the last few years, but I haven't said anything. What was Dad thinking about; why did he refuse to get divorced unless he could keep me if he doesn't want me? Can't that divorce paper be changed now so that I can go back to my mom?" Mengmeng started crying.

Who could explain why he had insisted on having Mengmeng? He was simply a stubborn person and would make Mengmeng into someone as emotionally inadequate as himself. Couldn't he see the crime he was committing, demoralizing an innocent, defenseless soul?

"Don't cry, Mengmeng. Your mother and I will put our money together to buy you a bike."

"No! I don't want one now!"

Liu Quan was grateful that Mengmeng could grasp things well once they had been explained to him clearly. She saw now that she shouldn't have married in the first place, and certainly she shouldn't have had a child without knowing he would have everything in life he would need.

Liang Qian arrived. "What on earth is going on here? All of you in tears. Come along, don't look so sorry for yourselves, O.K.? Mengmeng, what sort of a man do you think you are, crying your eyes out like that? *Aiya!* Stop that! Who's going to help me?" Her arms were laden with packages of all different sizes and on her back she was carrying a heavy canvas knapsack, stuffed full with more.

"What are you thinking of, buying so many things? They'll all go bad," Liu Quan asked her skeptically.

"They're all to be eaten. Look at us all, as thin as scarecrows."

"How about your film?" Jinghua asked.

Liang Qian looked at them, not knowing whether she should break the bad news. "Forget it. I don't want to talk about it." She started unpacking the things from her knapsack. Bang! She put a bottle of beer down on the table.

Bang, crash! Another bottle of beer, and another . . . four bottles altogether. "Put them in some cold water to cool. After all our struggles we still haven't got ourselves a fridge!" Liang Qian busily emptied out all the parcels, stuffing a piece of cold chicken into her mouth as she worked.

Jinghua could see at once what was the matter.

"What on earth is it?" Liu Quan asked, staring at Liang Qian. She was always a bit slow on the uptake.

"It's over!" Liang Qian took another piece of chicken.

"Stop eating," said Liu Quan, grabbing the chicken from Liang Qian's hand—you won't be able to eat your supper!"

"Why?" asked Jinghua.

"Who can know why?" Liang Qian kicked at a chair. "Some leader called Wu said, 'that, er, worker . . . why did you make him snore so loudly while he slept? Is this supposed to be some sort of insult to the working class?' Then Xiao Nie from the processing workshop commented, 'Well, I snore a lot louder than that!' The bastards! Then they asked, 'Why does the lead actress have such a high bust? Is it real or artificial? To be frank, we see this as a serious ideological error which must be carefully discussed. This kind of pornography could easily lead our young people astray. We mustn't start turning out pornographic films now, must we?' I said, 'Well, if you want to know whether it's real or not, all you have to do is have a feel!' Good Lord! Is it a crime to have a big bust? She's just like that, do they want her to chop some away? What's all this false righteousness about, anyway? As Lu Xun said in his story, 'Soap,' 'If they catch a glimpse of a bit of arm, they immediately begin imagining something else'. "And she laughed bitterly.

"Wu looked at me sternly and said, 'Comrade Liang Qian, will you please behave more seriously?' Then I said, 'What do you mean, behave more seriously? I am being perfectly serious with you. Nothing is more important than my work and our rights as women. I've had to sacrifice a great deal to gain these rights, and there are still plenty of women who are struggling for them. Women's liberation is not only a matter of economic and political rights, but includes the recognition, by women themselves as well as by all of society, that we have our own value and significance. Women are people, not merely objects of sex, wives and mothers. But there are many people, women among them, who think that their sole purpose in life is to satisfy the desires of men. This is a form of slavery, an attitude of self-depreciation left over from the ideas of the past.' I told him that it seemed quite clear from all they had said that they regarded me and all women as nothing more than a tiresome problem, while men were always the kind bene-factors. Why must they always pour their blame and scorn onto us women?

"Well, I knew after what I said that my film was done for. But for some reason I just couldn't control myself and when I finally finished, my film was already written off. On top of everything else, Bai Fushan had spread the rumor around that certain leaders were 'very dissatisfied' with the film. Well, we all know plenty of people like Wu, people who don't have any ethical sense toward their work or their comrades; they simply react according to whatever false rumors they pick up. Isn't art supposed to be rich and varied? Isn't socialism supposed to be progressive?"

Splendid! Jinghua was filled with admiration bordering on ecstasy. Everything Liang Qian did was brilliant, even if it did end ultimately in defeat. But she had been a fool to be so carried away by her emotions, by her ideals, and jeopardize the film. Jinghua felt like scolding her but there was no point since it was already a "fait accompli". You cannot undo what has been done. All they had was the future.

"Surely that's not the final decision. Doesn't it still have to be considered by the leaders higher up?" Jinghua asked.

"Of course a problem like this will have to be referred to the higher levels. At the grass-roots level they are never willing to take decisions on their own. They can't even solve simple housing problems without getting approval from above. What good do any of these lower cadres ever do, sitting around stuffing themselves and pushing every decision up to the next level? And if there's ever any real work to be done, they get those beneath them to do it."

Liu Quan felt overwhelmed by a sudden sense of dreariness. Taking off her apron, she flopped limply onto the sofa, right on top of Maotou who had been purring quietly to herself, as if reciting the Buddhist scriptures. Maotou startled Liu Quan when she screeched and pulled herself free. "Won't things be alright, if you talk to them?" she asked Liang Qian hesitantly.

"Huh! I'm afraid I'm not that optimistic," Liang Qian replied. "You can't be sure of anything until it's happened. Who knows what could happen now. Look at your own situation. Did you ever manage to get your transfer notice?"

"I've got it!"

Liu Quan's expression showed so little pleasure at having finally got what she had wanted that Liang Qian couldn't help asking, "Where is it? Let's have a look. Getting that notice was like trying to get a favor out of the Jade Emperor himself!"

The transfer notice from the Foreign Affairs Bureau, that precious 20 x 27 cm. piece of paper, was now lying on the table, soaking in a pool of water, like some flower offering to the Buddha.

Where had that water come from?

"Mengmeng, did you do this?" Liu Quan asked furiously, desperately trying to dry the paper on a corner of her blouse.

"I . . . I don't know!"

Jinghua could see that Mengmeng really didn't know anything about it. Why should he have poured water all over this slip of paper?

"You don't know? So where did all this water come from?"

Jinghua tried to calm Liu Quan down. "Forget it . . . It'll be alright once you've dried it off."

But in Liu Quan's present state of mind, this little incident seemed to take on major proportions. Mengmeng cautiously began to explain, "Just now I poured myself some water and. . . ."

"Well, why weren't you more careful?" Liu Quan would not give in. She was on the verge of letting go of all the layers of anger hidden deep within her.

"I don't know . . ." Mengmeng looked more and more terrified.

"You don't know? Why don't you know?" Liu Quan raised her hand, then abruptly stopped, holding her hand in mid-air. Looking into Mengmeng's eyes, she saw for the first time the bewilderment, suspicion and fear he was beginning to feel toward the adult world, impressions which could quickly lead to total disillusionment.

Liang Qian picked up the crumpled transfer notice and went out onto the balcony. "It's all right, it'll be dry in a moment."

"Careful, don't let it get blown away," Liu Quan cried frantically. "Find a stone to hold it down. No, get that paperweight from your table . . ."

Liu Quan was really overdoing things now, building things up into a melodrama, though Liang Qian knew that usually she never made a fuss about anything. The long wait, the tensions of obtaining this slip of paper had cost her just about all the patience she had.

"Come on, let's make supper. We're all starving." Jinghua handed Liu Quan her apron, scolding her quietly, "Don't make the child into a scapegoat."

Liu Quan sat down quietly and had to ask herself, was she any better, any more enlightened than those people who took advantage of her weakness to push her around? She had only cared to vent her anger on Mengmeng because he was even weaker than herself. She decided she must add some sugar to the situation—to make peace with her son, to give him the opportunity to forgive her in a formal way. The feelings of sweetness would follow. And it was a way, through her child, that she might regain her dignity. This was one of the first ways in which parents instilled within their children the concept of strong character. She opened one of the small packages Liang Qian had brought home. Now she should add some vinegar to this. But what had happened to the vinegar? Liu Quan could not think clearly, though her hand moved mechanically to the second shelf of the cabinet where the vinegar was kept. She was sorry the situation had gotten out of hand. She felt anxious and looked around, convinced that someone was watching her, reading her thoughts, but they were all in Jinghua's room. Liang Qian was telling some joke, trying to cheer Mengmeng up. But even if he temporarily forgot the incident with his mother, the memory would linger on and could grow into a quite different emotion in later life, perhaps into scorn and contempt, like the small, gnarled apples behind the chicken wire in the street below which had grown from neglected buds.

"Mengmeng!" she called.

"What is it?" Mengmeng asked glumly. The cheerful laughter suddenly ceased.

"Here's some fish roe for you." Liu Quan had fried the roe into a delicious, yellow crispness. Mengmeng was especially fond of this delicacy and although Liu Quan knew that she should not really make anything special for him, since this would only heighten his sense of the injustice she had just committed, her motherly love had won out. She rarely knew how to act in such situations so she fell back on her instinct to serve him.

Mengmeng made no response, allowing a momentary look of disdain to pass across his face, wondering whether or not he should accept this offering. He felt that his self-respect had been injured by the sudden, unjustified scolding he had just received, but seeing his mother waiting there with an apologetic, hopeful expression softened his heart. Still frowning, he accepted the roe and took a half-hearted bite out of it, though with no pleasure and only to stop Liu Quan from losing face.

Mengmeng was a kind, generous child. If only he could still be

like this when he grew up! "Mengmeng, don't be cross with me."
Liu Quan felt a peculiar sense of shame and sadness at the generosity shown by her child. She turned around in embarrassment
and began stirring the vegetables in the pot.

"Auntie Liang has been telling us about the trip to the Great Wall
tomorrow." Faced with an awkward situation like this, Mengmeng
was already able to display a remarkable maturity and calmness.

Thank you, my child, Liu Quan thought.

"Carry this dish over, will you please, Mengmeng?" Jinghua
asked.

I think we should just make the most of our lives," Liang Qian
said, opening the leaves of the table. "We've been waiting and
waiting, and if we go on like this until all our problems are solved,
we'll never be able to enjoy ourselves. As soon as one problem is
solved, another one pops up. Why do we always allow ourselves to
be pushed down like this? We simply have to go on living our lives
and then we'll feel a lot better. I've decided not to wait any longer.
I've already made plans for us all to go to the Great Wall tomorrow.
I've even arranged for a car, and I've bought plenty of food for a
picnic. Do you approve of my plan, Mengmeng?"

"Yes, yes! I approve!" Mengmeng shouted enthusiastically. No
one had ever taken him to the Great Wall, the Ming Tombs or the
Fragrant Hills, places almost all people living in Beijing had visited.
His mother never felt like going and his father wasn't interested in
taking him.

"You're right, Liang Qian," Jinghua said mockingly. "It's always
been as you say. It's about time you took charge and got things
straightened out."

"Who needs straightening out?" Liang Qian retorted. "We're
perfect already!"

"Hooray! We're off to the Great Wall! Can you sing the Song of the
Young Pioneers, Auntie Cao?" Mengmeng asked.

Yes, it was the same for Mengmeng as it had been for them. All
their memories of youth—the hikes, the parades, the trips and
excursions—all were filled with the memory of singing, continuous singing . . . How they had loved singing. . . .

Mengmeng sang:

> A little bird leads our way,
> The wind blows us along;

> We are like the spring,
> Coming to the meadows and gardens.
> With our scarlet scarves
> And our pretty clothes. . . .

Like spring! Everything had felt so fresh and full of vitality. Jinghua was not sure what songs Mengmeng liked to sing or even if his generation enjoyed singing as much as they had. "Of course I know it!" Jinghua laid the chopsticks on the table and started singing, her head nodding in time to the song.

> "Little pine tree, little cypress. . . ."

Liu Quan came in carrying the soup and said, "When we were in the Young Pioneers our song went like this. . . ." She started singing shyly, her tone of voice betraying a slight feeling of bitterness:

> "The children of our New China,
> The pioneers of our New Youth. . . ."

Liu Quan's voice was as sweet and gentle as ever and her song brought back the beautiful memories of childhood. But they felt moved less by the beauty of the memory than by the recognition that these were things of the past, lost to them forever. Liang Qian at once started singing too.

> "The forces of darkness,
> Have been swept away. . . ."

"Wait," Jinghua broke in. "That's the second verse. The first verse goes like this. . . ." The three of them sang together:

> "Unite! Continue the task of our forebears!
> We're not afraid of hardship,
> We're not afraid of the burden. . . ."

Liu Quan smiled and glanced at Mengmeng who was watching them curiously, observing these three old friends reliving their youth. He had never heard this song before. Its tune did not seem especially moving and Mengmeng could not understand why it should have made the three of them so excited. None of his friends had ever got so worked up over a song. Could it be that in the past these songs had meant so much to them?

As she went on singing, Liu Quan's face began to quiver and her voice grew fainter and fainter. Jinghua and Liang Qian, on the other hand, carried on singing merrily, not noticing anything strange in Liu Quan's behavior. Only when she suddenly burst into tears did they stop singing.

The moment of joy suddenly vanished. No one spoke and they just sat around dejectedly. The sound of Liu Quan sobbing echoed around the room, filling it with her agony of hopelessness and misery. At this moment the same thought was passing through their minds: How much had happened in their lives since the days of that song. They had never imagined what the future held for them when they first sung it together.

Jinghua was wondering who should take the blame for the events which caused Liu Quan's tears. Was it the fault of their inadequate education? The education they had received had been flat, two-dimensional, like the blackboard on which their lessons had been taught, whereas life itself was like a colorful sphere. Was it the increasing sense of materialism which was taking hold around them? Who could say? It was so many things combined, a collection of grief in a life which held so little refuge.

Liu Quan's eyes had quickly swollen up to the size of two peaches. Liang Qian went into the kitchen to fetch a basin of water for Liu Quan to bathe her eyes. Even with several thermos flasks lined up on the dresser, there still wasn't a single drop of hot water in any of them. Even if they had bought ten more flasks, they still would never have any hot water when they needed it! How typical, these small dislocations, for people whose lives had been disrupted and unsettled as theirs had. Well, she could still boil some. Liang Qian took the kettle from beneath the sink—the knob was still missing!

Such sharp changes of mood left Mengmeng feeling confused and irritated. What was going on? He was hungry and wanted to eat, but he dared not move. He sat there awkwardly watching the steam rising from the plates of food. He had wanted to come to his mother's place to find love and affection, like a young tree stretching out its branches to receive the sunlight; but so much emotion was unbearable, a kind of suffocation. Could his mother really be so feeble, like the little girls in his class, crying because someone had wickedly put a caterpillar into one of their books, or dipped one of their braids into a pot of ink? His mother was a woman. Perhaps there was no real difference between her and those little girls. If it had been him, he would have found a better way to get revenge, and not just sit around crying. That was the way he dealt with his father. Once Mengmeng's father had given him a severe beating. In return Mengmeng had secretly ruined all his father's film by exposing it to the light. Whenever his father beat him, he would always think of some novel way of getting back, like spitting into his father's teacup or setting his alarm clock to the wrong time. Mengmeng was racking his brains to think of some way he might help his mother, but he could not figure out who had been bullying her.

Everyone was sitting there with a stony, expressionless face, as if his mother were not crying her heart out. Only Maotou made any sign, jumping up onto Liu Quan's knees and then licking the tears from her face. Maotou really was a humane beast! Liu Quan went on sobbing more mournfully than ever. A long time seemed to have passed.

"Mother. . . ." Mengmeng could not bear it any longer, but could not think of anything suitable to say.

"Don't cry, Liu Quan," Liang Qian said. "Mengmeng's still waiting for his supper." This was probably the only way she could quiet Liu Quan. Liang Qian believed that the best way to relieve one's misery was not to forget the problems, but to persist, to continue shouldering one's responsibilities.

"You eat first," she replied.

"How can we do that?" Jinghua asked. "That way, none of us would be even as good as Maotou." Maotou let out a "miaow," apparently understanding Jinghua's meaning.

People can never do exactly as they please. Liu Quan had no choice but to swallow her sobs, though her heart was still filled to overflowing. The hot flannel over her eyelids felt very comfortable and her eyes were no longer smarting with pain. But when she got up to look in the mirror, the face she saw was still pale and swollen.

"Hmph!" When the spring rain falls, the pear tree blooms. But once a flower loses its petals it will be ready then to turn gradually into a fruit. Whenever they passed through any period of hardship they grew riper, more mature. Liu Quan should have had plenty of experience behind her by now, but her protective shell was still too soft and life treated her no more kindly because of her weakness. But what should she do? It was like the multiple-choice questions she used to be faced with in her examinations at school: after not having prepared adequately she would hesitate for ages over where to place her mark. She had been asking herself questions for years but never came up with any satisfactory answers. Maybe constant failure was just part of her fate, just as it is some other people's fate to become leaders. She did not find it as easy as Jinghua and Liang Qian to find an emotional equilibrium, because she was too easily upset by things going on around her. Maybe part of the problem was that she did not have a special interest to keep her occupied; her scope seemed narrower and more confined. They certainly had had no easier time of it than she had, yet they rarely expressed their bitterness through tears; if they cried, it was for far more important reasons. Maybe she simply was not able to keep her teeth as firmly clenched as they did.

At least her efforts had not been entirely in vain: she had at last got her transfer notice and this would give her the chance of using some of her talents. She wanted to spend more energy developing herself, and she hoped that in the future her work would pull her ahead and give her a chance to contribute more. She needed for her life to become more meaningful so that she no longer spent her evenings idly reading English magazines, yawning wearily and then slipping into bed where she would lie sleepless for hours. She would at last feel she had some sort of a goal—and once you had a goal, life seemed a lot simpler and easier. She sighed at the mirror one last time, then came back to the table.

"O.K. then? Is the storm over?" Jinghua glanced at Liu Quan, glad that her emotions were at last returning to normal. All of them started handing her food, including Mengmeng.

"Don't worry, I can help myself." Liu Quan covered her bowl with her hand. She felt embarrassed about her behavior.

"You shouldn't get so upset," Jinghua said. "Those who should really feel upset are people like Manager Wei. Morally, you are the real winner, and not only morally either!"

The rumor was that Manager Wei had received a notice from the Disciplinary Commission and had to write a confession. He had been found guilty of various forms of corruption: encouraging factories to sell off their fixed assets and using the profits to pay bonuses to their workers; taking personal possession of gifts presented at trade exhibitions by foreign companies; using public funds to buy "Red Flag" limousines for his own use, though his status did not entitle him to one. He had always been so self-

important and domineering, treating Liu Quan exactly as he pleased, with no consideration of her feelings. So at last she was heart-
ened to see that this society could bring justice to bear.

"Wait a moment, you pair of old teetotalers," Liang Qian called
from the bathroom. "I've got some cool beer here. It's not iced, I'm
afraid, only water-cooled." She came out carrying two bottles of
beer in each hand, as if she were carrying four sodden hand-
grenades.

"Where's the bottle opener?"

"We've never had one." Liu Quan took a bottle, not quite sure
how she was going to open it.

"Give it to me—you're too clumsy!" Liang Qian took the bottle
from her and bit at the top with her delicate teeth.

"You're even more clumsy than Liu Quan," Jinghua laughed.

"You try it, then," Liang Qian challenged her.

Mengmeng sniggered. She wasn't any better at doing these sorts
of things than his mother, though he did not dare say this out loud.
"You should do it like this," he said.

"How do you mean?" Liang Qian asked him earnestly.

The three women stood around Mengmeng, waiting to see how
he would open the bottle. Mengmeng put the bottle top against
the edge of the table and then brought his right hand down on it
hard, so that the top flew off with a loud "pop!" The beer sprayed
out of the bottle, catching Liang Qian full in the face.

"Wow! That beer's got punch!" she said, laughing, as she wiped
her face dry.

"Oh no! My table!" Liu Quan cried, anxiously feeling the edge of
the table, which now had a small white chip in it.

"Well, that shows how useful it is to have a man about," said
Jinghua sarcastically.

"Quick, get some glasses!" Mengmeng shouted, as the beer
bubbled out of the bottle.

They finally managed to gather up four glasses, all different, but
after they settled down they noticed there were plenty of glasses
on the cabinet shelf, all waiting to be used.

Seeing the full glass of beer in front of her, Liang Qian suddenly
became more serious. "I'd like to propose a toast," she said. She
looked at Liu Quan and Jinghua for a long time, before finally
coming out with these words. Every one filled with the accumula-

tion of hardship and torment she had experienced. "I drink a toast to women!" she said.

Jinghua's hand began to tremble and she gripped her glass tightly. That was a good toast, indeed. A toast for the rights women had won, or would later attain, the sacrifices women had made or would make in the future, the untold suffering they had experienced, their hopes and aspirations, already realized, or waiting to be realized. Every woman could unashamedly accept such a toast, and drink to herself.

"If no one else is going to drink to us . . ." Liu Quan said. Her lips began quivering again.

"Someone certainly will," said Jinghua decisively.

"Mother, I will. . . ." Mengmeng raised his glass.

Jinghua put her hand over his glass. "No. Wait until you're grown up."

Yes. If only Mengmeng's generation could grow up to understand: How difficult it is to be a woman!

December, 1981

Translated by Stephen Hallett

Biographical Note—My Boat

Human beings, the most intelligent of all animals, are sometimes foolish. Otherwise, why would they travel long distances to places like Penglai Peninsula just to see constantly changing mirages? Even though people know such things are illusory, they still eulogize them and are reluctant to leave, showing that the yearning for beauty has not been quelled in the bloody struggle of life and death. This is perhaps the most fundamental difference between human beings and animals, although they share the instinct for survival.

I had more or less this kind of feeling when I first started reading literary works. It seems to me that literature actually gives more to people than real life does. It expresses what it is that people love and what they hate in a more concentrated form. Or, at least, the feelings that it evokes are unique. Chernyshevsky once claimed that no work of art was ever as beautiful or as noble as reality. I think his view is too extreme. God created man in his own image and writers create their characters in the image of their own souls. Through the various art forms human beings express the beauty of *creation*.

Artists communicate with society through their music, their sculpture and their painting.

I have always wondered why artists must use such painful and difficult forms, why they must grind their hearts on millstones, pour out their souls. Is it because, like us, they sometimes feel a profound loneliness, because they hope to gain the understanding and forgiveness of humankind?

I believe that many human misfortunes are caused by our inability to understand and to communicate.

Because of this I feel closer to literary characters, feel that they are easier to understand. I wish that I could just live my life in books, and never go out again.

It is literature that has awakened in me hitherto dormant ideas on all manner of social phenomena. Many of these ideas, unscientific and imperfect though they may be, go some way perhaps to explaining why I have been so battered in this world. But I have no regrets; people are never that objective or rational when they are deeply in love with something or someone. You must always pay for what you love and sacrifice—if indeed it can really be considered sacrifice. I rejoice at having been made a human being by it, a living human being with defects, a human being with feelings. Without it, I would not have been able to write a single line. Tolstoy once told one of his brothers that he had all of the virtues of a writer, but none of the essential defects, that he did not go to extremes.

It is rather amusing that in the past, whenever we were asked to summarize our ideological remoulding and I was supposed to try and uncover the class and social origin of my long-standing and unreformable bad habits—no strong sense of class struggle, low political consciousness and slack discipline—I always heard people comment exasperatedly, "The problem with Zhang Jie is that she has been too deeply poisoned by 18th and 19th century western novels."

I secretly congratulate myself and say that if I have an iota of human feeling, if I do not move up in the world by stepping on other people, do not use others to gain advantages—and I am somewhat proud of this—then it is in large part due to the influence of the human feelings and character, the humanism in classical literature.

History unceasingly discards dross and develops what is good. We do not curse food because we have to excrete. Why are we such thorough-going materialists at the dinner table, yet we pretend to be idealists when it comes to spiritual sustenance? We are afraid of everything except our own regression to bestialism. Has a history of 20 million years all been for nothing?

For me literature increasingly represents not just a hobby to drive away monotony and sadness but a longing for all my unrealized ideals.

Nothing apart from literature can interest me and hold my attention over a long period. I once thought I was like a darting dragonfly, with no goals in life and no substantial pursuits. Only through literature did I discover myself. Successful or not, I am still very persevering. I don't know how other people deal with this problem, but I often feel that to be able to find oneself is such a difficult thing. Some people can spend a whole lifetime and still not find or understand themselves. Others, of course, have a much easier time of it. For me, it took all of forty years. A little too late, and so I treasure it all the more. A life still unfinished, ideals demanding to be realized. Beautiful, despondent, joyful, tragic. . . . All manner of social phenomena weave themselves into one story after another in my mind; if this happened, then it would. . . . Like an artless tailor, I cut my cloth unskillfully according to old measurements and turn out garment factory clothes sold in department stores in only five standard sizes and styles.

Because of this, my rather undistinguished works always cause suspicion in some quarters. Was this or that piece copied from a size 3 or size 5 pattern?

Some people say, "That story was about Zhang Jie herself," and take it upon themselves to make investigations—in a certain month of a certain year there was such-and-such a person, such-and-such an event. . . . All so authoritative that it seems true.

It is common knowledge that characters in literary works are perhaps composites of many people in real life, but they are still fictitious, something created by the author through logical reasoning.

The truthfulness of literature and the truthfulness of life are two entirely different matters. But there are people who insist on confusing them. Is this just stupidity, feudalism or backwardness? Not at all; it is a kind of weapon.

Because of writing *Madame Bovary*, Flaubert had ten years of litigation.

Xu Junyin was decapitated by the Qing government for the sentence, "Why turn the pages when the clear* wind cannot

* In Chinese, "clear" and "qing" are homophones.

read?"

Comrade Wu Han was persecuted to death for writing *Hai Rui Dismissed from Office*.

What made me think about all of this very seriously was one persistent question: Why is it that writers, both foreign and Chinese, past and present, get into trouble over their work? I feel keenly the contradiction between the social responsibility and the social conscience of a writer and the treatment he or she receives from society.

When the Guangdong People's Publishing House printed a second edition of my story collection *Love Must Not Be Forgotten*, I designed the cover: Two white medieval boats sailing on a dark green background. But because the selection was part of a series, the publishing house wanted a uniform design and it was not used.

Now can it be that my boat is stranded, that I can only listen at a distance to the pounding waves deep in the night? In the past, I had the courage to struggle against fate.

Do I give up easily? No, I wouldn't be me if I did.

If I did, I would be letting my readers down.

Among the letters from readers I have kept are many which say, "If misfortune should befall you one day then come to me."

What greater reward can a writer expect than a just hearing?

Apart from getting old or falling ill, about which I can do nothing, I don't think I'll necessarily encounter misfortune; life, after all, must go on.

Of course there are those readers who curse us too, I would reckon about one to three percent.

And when I think of that figure I ask, who is it that I am writing for, that I am living for?

So I've come to Beidaihe Beach. I've been laughing away, talking non-stop, swimming to my heart's content. Like a boat drifting about on the waves, I have cast aside my self-control and let myself be buoyed along in a state of happy abandon. I have taken the sea to my bosom, let the waves lap at my feeble heart. My skin gleams like bronze in the sun, and when I look in the mirror, my face is like that of a Red Indian. My teeth gleam when I smile. I seem to have recovered my health and strength. And so I renovate my boat, patch it up and repaint it, so that it will last a little longer. I set sail again. People, houses, trees on shore become smaller and smaller and I am reluctant to leave them. But my boat cannot stay beached for ever. What use is a boat without the sea?

In the distance I see waves rolling toward me. Rolling continuously. I know that one day I will be smashed to bits by those waves, but this is the fate of all boats—what other sort of end could they meet?

Translated by Yu Fanqin

Article written by Zhang Jie about herself and reprinted from *Chinese Literature*, Summer, 1985.

The Translators

Gladys Yang, the first student to have obtained an honors degree in Chinese at Oxford, England, is one of the foremost translators of Chinese classical literature. Together with her husband, Yang Xianyi, she has translated many classical works such as *A Dream of Red Mansions*, *The Scholars*, etc.

W.J.F. Jenner is a lecturer in the Dept. of Chinese Studies, University of Leeds, England. He has translated many Chinese works into English, including *Journey to the West*.

Janet Yang is in film co-production in Los Angeles, and worked for a year as a translator in China.

Stephen Hallett teaches at the International School in Beijing.

Yu Fanqin is a long-standing translator at "Chinese Literature" magazine.